THE C.T. FERGUSON MYSTERY NOVELLA COLLECTION

TOM FOWLER

TOM FOWLER WRITES

Do you like free stories? After the end of this book, look for a special offer to get four C.T. Ferguson short stories absolutely free.

The C.T. Ferguson Mystery Novella Collection is copyright © 2019 by Tom Fowler

Editing by Chase Nottingham

Cover design by Germancreative

 Created with Vellum

For Lisa and Isabel

THE CONFESSIONAL

Novella #1
The Confessional

CHAPTER 1

THERE COMES A POINT IN EVERYONE'S LIFE (WELL, ALMOST everyone's) when the person realizes he or she isn't as smart as once thought. This realization is usually brought on by some cruel event to hammer the point home. The young man sitting on the other side of my desk just experienced this epiphany. And he didn't look happy about it.

"Let me make sure I have this right," I said. "You confessed to a murder."

"Yes," he said with a nod.

"One you're telling me you didn't commit."

"Yes."

I sighed. When one operates a free detective business, one is beset with crackpots. My first two months on the job taught me this. "And you did this—why, exactly?" I said.

"For my blog," he said as if people confessed to murders they didn't commit all the time.

"For your blog."

"A classmate suggested it," he said, digging his hole deeper.

"Your classmate is an imbecile," I said.

"Yanni's good with all the web stuff, even marketing. He does it for his dad's business."

"Someone named Yanni suggested your false admission?"

"Yes."

"You should ignore Yanni in the future. If you have a classmate named Kenny G, ignore him, too." I only knew of those two artists because my parents enjoyed them. My mother, well aware I disliked both, always played them when I visited. For a woman pushing sixty, her troll game was strong.

"Too late for that now," he said.

The young man's youthful, chubby face led me to guess his age as twenty. He was about five-ten, giving me four inches on him, and had a physique suggesting he updated his blog regularly. I looked at his coloration and features and—drawing on my thirty-nine months in China—concluded he was half-Chinese. When I judged his actions, I concluded he was all idiot.

"Sometimes, I wish I believed in regrets," I said. "You're going to have to give me something more than 'my classmate said so' or 'for my blog.'"

"I run the *Murderphiles Blog.*" He paused there, waiting for me to react. I'd never heard of his site, so I shrugged. He sighed and continued. "We've been getting a lot of good hits the past few months."

"I hope the Google Ads revenue can buy you a lawyer, then."

He waved a dismissive hand. "Look, I got inspired by the *Serial* podcast. A lot of murders happen in Baltimore." That was inescapably true. Season one of *Serial* focused on one such murder from almost twenty years ago. A lot more had taken place since. "The police don't tell us everything about them. The papers don't tell us everything. That's where we come in."

"Because victims' families love talking to bloggers?" I said.

"They want the truth," he said. "They want justice."

"Aren't their odds better in the legal system?"

"You're C.T. Ferguson. 'The P.I. who helps the little guy,' according to your ad. You run a free detective service." He frowned. "There's no way you're a big believer in the legal system."

He had me, even though I wished he'd omitted the dreadful tagline my father devised. Since no potential client ever put those pieces together before, I had had to give this blogger his props, at least in this narrow case. "I'd trust it over a guy with a blog," I said. "Especially when the guy with a blog does something colossally stupid."

The young man sighed. "What am I going to do? The police are after me to turn myself in."

"It's exactly what you should do."

"But I didn't kill anyone!"

"Then you shouldn't have made a public confession. The police are going to take an interest when you do."

"I figured the ploy would just get me some publicity and spur the investigation," he said. "I never thought it would get this far."

"But it has. You need to turn yourself in."

"Can I hire you?"

I laughed. Then I drank some water and laughed again. "Seriously?"

"You could find the real killer," he said.

"I don't work for morons," I said, and he frowned anew. "You got yourself into this mess because you wanted publicity for your blog. It was stupid but mission accomplished. Now go deal with it. If you didn't do it, the police will figure it out."

"But I'll get arrested."

"Yes."

"And go to jail."

"What do you think happens when you confess to a crime like murder?" I said.

The young man slumped in his chair. "You won't take this case?"

"Not a chance."

He got up and walked out. I shrugged, refilled my water bottle, and went online to check his precious blog.

* * *

AN HOUR LATER, I had read a bunch of articles on the blog. Other than my profound objection to the fake word "Murderphiles," I thought the site featured good content. I saw details news reports and police officers would exclude. All the information gained came from no special access or privilege. It was a good bit of reporting, especially for a blogger.

He turned out to be Ernest (Ernie) Chin. The blog resided on a paid site running WordPress, and for some reason, Ernie failed to remove himself from any of the Whois records. Every website lists contact information for the people responsible for registering and maintaining it. Those cataloged Ernie, his address, and phone number. I found him in about five seconds. Maybe I could help him by suggesting simple measures like anonymizing his info. Bloggers who go into deep details of grisly crimes shouldn't be broadcasting their personal information for the world to see. Not everyone knew about Whois records, but a killer would only need one friend who did.

Another hour later, I heard the Baltimore Police Department arrested Ernie Chin after he confessed to the murder of Dave Waugh. The media already found perverse delight in the fact that Ernie confessed and then tried to plead his innocence. Their delight must have stemmed from the fact he posted information they didn't. Old media will always hold a grudge against the new like the town crier despised a printed newssheet. I believed Ernie was innocent. More importantly, I believed he was stupid, and this would teach him the limits of driving traffic to his blog.

Later during the night, my cell phone rang. The caller showed as blocked. I try not to answer such calls, but the nature of my job compels me. "Hello?" I said.

An automated voice said, "This call originates from the Central Booking and Intake Facility in Baltimore, Maryland. Would you like to continue?"

Every instinct and scrap of common sense I had screamed to say no. Instead, I assented.

"C.T.?" said a voice I remembered from earlier.

"Why the hell are you calling me?" I said.

"I got arrested."

"Yes, Ernie. The whole city knows."

"You know my name."

"You really should check the box to anonymize your Whois records."

"Anyway," he said, "will you take my case now?"

I hung up on him.

He didn't call back. After another hour of Netflix, I went to bed.

* * *

THE NEXT MORNING, I ran through Fells Point, along the Baltimore Harbor, and back through the streets to my apartment. I liked the city at this hour. The downtown area bustled with cars and starched shirts, but Fells Point, several blocks removed, kept a lighter pace. Businesses were opening. Restaurants and bars started their daily prep. Aromas of coffee, bread, and seafood wafted through the brisk January air, urging me forward.

After a shower, I made breakfast in my smallish kitchen. It boasted enough counter space for me to work, but if I ever had a date serve as my lovely sous chef, the quarters would be tight. I chopped mushrooms and onions and shredded some fresh spinach, throwing it all in a pan to sauté. When everything had cooked nicely, I added the eggs. I put multigrain bread in the toaster while I tended the omelet, giving it a careful flip and adding a sprinkle of pepper jack cheese before I folded it. Somewhere, a French chef would cringe at my cheese choice (and my technique as well). I would console myself with a delicious omelet and the fact I wasn't French.

I was about halfway through my omelet when my phone rang. Another number I didn't recognize flashed across the screen. After a moment of consideration, my stomach emerged the victor, and I declined the call. Not one savory bite later, the same number called again. I answered this time.

"This is Liz Fleming with the Public Defender's office," said the lady on the other end. I liked her voice; it reminded me of a girl I dated for much of my sophomore year of college. My half-full gut told me her tone would be the only thing I liked about this conversation.

"I have a feeling I know why you're calling," I said.

"Let's hear it."

"You have a persistent cretin for a new client."

"I get a lot of cretins," Liz said. "Most of them are guilty. Few of them are persistent."

"Lucky you," I said, "but I can't help you."

"Can you come to my office?" Liz seemed undeterred by my rejection. Her persistence matched Ernie Chin's. I hoped she outstripped him in intelligence and common sense.

"When?"

"As soon as you can."

"I'm eating breakfast," I said. To emphasize the point, I ate a bite of toast with my phone held to my face. Somewhere, I could feel my mother cringing and tsking.

"So I hear," said Liz. "How about after breakfast?"

I finished chewing the toast before I answered. "I'm sure I'll need another cup of coffee," I said. "Then I'll have to digest. And get some work clothes on. Then I'll—"

"Just be here in an hour," she said and hung up.

The exchange made me smile. I didn't much care for Ernie Chin, but at least I liked his lawyer.

* * *

No OTHER POTENTIAL clients queued up outside my door after breakfast. I might as well hear what Liz and Ernie had to say. I got dressed, putting on a pair of gray chinos and a maroon button-down shirt. An hour and eight minutes later, I walked into Baltimore City Office of the Public Defender. Two minutes after, a receptionist talking into a headset mic pointed me to Liz Fleming's door.

"You're late," came the reply when I knocked.

I opened to find a desk chewing up most of the square footage, and the other furnishings made moving and turning around an adventure. Ernie sat in one of two shopworn chairs. I couldn't tell which looked more drab and lifeless. Bags hung under his eyes, his hair begged for a comb, and he didn't even acknowledge me when I walked in. Liz Fleming, on the other hand, sized me up as I entered. She wore a sharp navy suit. Her long brown hair framed a pretty face and got a mild taming from a beret above her left ear. I pegged her around my age and hoped for her sake she hadn't been in this job since college. Liz propped her feet on the desk, forcing her skirt farther up her legs. The legs told me she ran to keep in shape. I liked what I saw.

"Close the door," she said. I did and sat in the other old chair. Liz kept her desk moderately organized. No stacks of papers littered it, but a neat freak would still look upon it and despair. I chalked it up to her caseload, which must border on the Herculean. "You're late," she repeated.

"I'm always late," I said.

"I can't be late," said Liz.

"Did you call me here to compare punctuality?"

"For him." She nodded toward Ernie, who glanced at both of us but said nothing.

"I've already told him no twice."

"Maybe the third time is the charm, then. I'm going to ask again."

"Your office must have investigators," I said.

"We do," Liz said, "and they're stretched even thinner than the lawyers."

"And now you want my help."

"Ernie, can you give us a minute? I'll have the receptionist send you back when we're done."

Roused from his reverie, he grunted, stood, and trudged out of the room.

"Thanks . . . I didn't want to call him an idiot a third time," I said after he left.

"What's your story?" Liz said, narrowing hazel eyes.

"I'm smart, handsome, and good at my job. What else do you want to know?"

"You showed up on the scene a couple months ago. I've read about your cases. You don't charge your clients?" I shook my head. "What's that about?"

"A man needs a little mystery," I said. Bonus: it sounded better than the truth. I worked for my parents' foundation, and they paid me to solve cases for people who lacked any other recourse. Liz might appreciate my forced altruism, but I figured being vague was the better play.

"Humor me," said Liz.

"I humored you when I came down here."

She picked up a coffee mug that had been hiding behind her laptop and took a drink. It made her grimace. "I suppose you did," she said. "Still, I don't know about you. You weren't a cop, you weren't in the military, but now you're a PI."

"I'm sure the articles covered this. I haven't exactly hidden from the press."

"I was just wondering if you had anything to add. You know. . . something that may not have made it into the puff pieces."

"Those puff pieces have allowed me to help several people."

"If you say so."

"If you think I'm some random guy," I said, "why do you want me to help with Ernie's case?"

"I don't have much of a choice," Liz said. "Considering that he confessed, this case isn't getting a lot of resources. My boss didn't give me an investigator, and none of them have the time to pitch in."

"So I'm your last resort."

"Basically."

"Something a guy loves to hear from a girl," I said.

Liz gave a nice smile at my comment. It put dimples in her cheeks and added warmth to her eyes. "Is that a yes?"

I didn't want this case, but I didn't have any other prospects. And Ernie, dumb as he acted, was the kind of person my parents wanted me to help when they wrangled me into this. "Sure."

"Great," Liz said. She smiled again. I couldn't manage a full one in return. Liz would have to settle for the low-wattage version. Unperturbed, she pushed a button on her phone. "Can you send Ernie back in?"

Liz had kept her feet on the desk. I took another look at her legs, couching it in a scan of the room. They were the kind whoever invented the skirt kept in mind when first putting scissors to fabric. When Ernie walked in, I caught Liz looking at me. She glanced away as her client took his seat.

We went over everything again. Ernie's story didn't change. After he told it again, I posed a question. "I read your blog. Lots of good information in there. Where did you get it?"

"I always try to have stuff the press doesn't," Ernie said.

"Not an answer," I said.

Ernie frowned and thought about it. "I have a source."

I expected more, but he said nothing else. "Who?"

"I can't give up my source."

"Ernie, that's not going to help you," said Liz.

"You're not a goddamn journalist," I said. "You're an idiot with a blog. Congratulations on being a well-informed idiot. Now tell us who gave you the information."

He shook his head. "I can't."

Liz sighed. "This isn't going to be easy."

"I've learned it never is," I said.

CHAPTER 2

I SHARED COFFEE WITH MY COUSIN RICH AT HIS DESK IN THE squad room. He somehow chokes down the swill standing in for coffee in the Baltimore Police Department, but today, I spared him by bringing him something fit for human consumption. Rich spent several years in uniform and got his detective's shield around the time I got my license. The fact he earned two commendations on my cases in the same short time was a coincidence to Rich (and a source of amusement to me).

"You're working for the blogger?" said Rich.

"I think so," I said.

"You haven't decided yet?"

"He has a public defender. I guess I'm technically working for her."

Rich smirked. "Liz Fleming?"

"Yes," I said.

He sipped his coffee. "Good-looking woman."

"I noticed." I remembered Liz's legs stretched out with her feet on her desk. It was a pleasant recollection.

"I'm sure you did," Rich said.

"Are you insinuating I agreed to help because she's pretty?"

"I'm not *insinuating* anything."

I grinned. "Okay, let's just say being a good-looking woman helps."

Rich drank some more of his coffee. So did I. A few cops moved about the room. This was a new squad bay with open-concept seating and glass walls for the few offices. Only the inter-rogation rooms could not boast of the transparency loved by consultants and funded by taxpayers. I wondered how many of my tax dollars the BPD sacrificed for this extravagance.

"Your guy did it," Rich said after a few minutes.

"What makes you so sure?"

"His statement. He mentioned a few things we didn't release to the papers."

"Maybe he talked to the reporters," I said.

"And maybe he stabbed the vic a dozen times in the chest."

I shook my head. "Ernie's a moron, but he's an honest one. He's not a killer."

"You're so certain."

"I have a pretty good record of being right."

"How many cases have you worked?" Rich said with a chuckle. "Four?"

"Six."

"You took statistics in college, didn't you?"

"I know," I said, "small sample size. What about my twenty-eight years of brilliance?"

"Not convincing enough. Reporters know when we're leaving something out strategically. Even the younger ones get it. They're not going to blab it to some asshole with a blog."

"Ernie's written some good pieces. Someone has to be telling him something."

"Or he's a killer," said Rich.

"He's written about a bunch of murders."

"So?"

"So do you think a tubby college student is a serial killer?"
I said.

"Of course not."

I smiled and raised my cup toward Rich. "Not a killer."

Rich rolled his eyes. "Find proof he didn't do it, then."

"You realize the legal system works the other way, right?"

"Don't lecture me on the system," Rich said. "You do as much
as you can to not be a part of it."

"And so far," I said, "I've been successful."

We bantered a little more until our cups were empty, and
Rich said he had work to get back to. I returned to my car. Ernie
wasn't a killer. I knew it but couldn't prove it. Could the state's
attorney prove he was? I saw how Ernie knowing intimate details
of murders might trouble the police. He claimed a source but
wouldn't budge on unmasking said source. I knew he wasn't a
killer.

But was I right?

* * *

ERNEST CHIN ENTERED the world twenty years ago in Baltimore, born to a Chinese immigrant father and a Caucasian
mother of US nationality. Nothing about his history jumped out
as a red flag. Ernie breezed through his first dozen years of school
and got a scholarship to Hopkins, where he studied civil engineering. He completed three semesters before steering his life off
the rails. Perhaps he could put his municipal work knowledge to
use and suggest some design improvements for the roads around
Central Booking.

Somewhere along the way, Ernie became fascinated with
murder, and there were certainly enough in Baltimore to gain his
attention. His popular blog cited the Freddie Gray incident as a
"catalyst" for him, and the *Serial* podcast as an "inspiration." I

almost flew home from Hong Kong when the aftermath of Freddie Gray's death exploded onto the national consciousness, as well as onto Chinese news broadcasts. I felt sympathetic toward the protesters, but my sympathy diminished as buildings burned. Seeing my city in flames was difficult. I was angry and sullen for a few days, and only a new spate of work with my hacker friends pulled me out of it. So if Ernie cited Freddie Gray as a catalyst, I could understand.

What I couldn't understand was Ernie's moronic confession. His interest in murder and his blog were mentioned in all the news stories and TV segments. Traffic to his site spiked. Even old posts saw new comments, though many were uncharitable. If Ernie monetized his traffic—and he seemed savvy enough to do so —then he collected even more money in the last few days.

A lot of good it would do him in prison.

Ernie seemed to think the police would not take his confession seriously. The opposite happened. Because Ernie knew a lot about the murder, the BPD detained him after he confessed. I didn't think he was a killer, but how would I prove his innocence? The state's attorney may come to realize the circumstantial nature of the case. Or he may not, and Ernie might get indicted and face a trial. I once heard someone say you could get a ham sandwich indicted for being eaten. I hoped Ernie's odds were better.

All this for publicity and blog traffic.

A large part of me still thought Ernie was an idiot and deserved an idiot's fate. However, I threw my lot in with him and Liz Fleming. I needed to prove Ernie was just a cretin and not a killer. To do it, I would need to look into the murder victim and figure out who gave Ernie all the insider information responsible for his current accommodations.

As I prepared to unearth his source, I was struck by the similarity to Alice's mad tumble into a deep and labyrinthine rabbit hole. As if the murder victim checked a watch from the pocket of a waistcoat, I followed his white ghost.

* * *

THE BPD HAD a nice case file going. I know because I could sit in my office and read it. During my first case two months ago, Rich had left me unsupervised at his PC. People like me don't need much time to profit from such a mistake. Armed with his IP and hardware addresses, I fingerprinted the BPD's network, found the important resources, and mimicked their IP and hardware addressing on one of my virtual machines. The BPD's network accepted the machine as one of its own. I had never seen a sign they noticed the intrusion.

Dave Waugh's violent end involved more than a dozen stab wounds to his upper body. The crime scene photos showed him in a red shirt beginning its sartorial life as a much lighter color. He was found a block from St. Mark's Catholic Church, a venerable building I recalled looking dated in my youth. The church had a website of equally ancient design, and I snagged their member list in under a minute. Dave or David Waugh did not appear on it. Nothing on his social media pages showed any affiliation with a religion.

I probed Waugh's life. He hailed from Phoenix, born there twenty-nine years ago, a year older than I am. I stared at my screen as I pondered mortality at such a young age. Dave had been stabbed over twelve times. His was a normal job, working as an assistant manager at Staples. Mine was far more dangerous. My parents enrolled me in martial arts classes at eleven, after I got my ass handed to me by a bully. I kept up my studies and could take care of myself in a fight. Knives, however, were an equalizer. Maybe Dave possessed similar training. One lucky swing or stab and none of it mattered.

I shook myself out of these morose thoughts. Waugh lived an unremarkable life. I couldn't find much on his youth in Phoenix. He left after his junior year of college and finished his degree at Towson. Since then, he held a handful of jobs with the current one marking the longest time he spent in any of them. Nothing about him stood out as remarkable, and the only thing I found interesting was the spotty history of his youth.

Waugh sustained a large social media presence, and I dove into it. He had been especially active on Twitter, retweeting a lot of articles and linking to some of his own blog posts. Great—another blogger. This guy should serve as a lesson for Ernie. I followed a bunch of Dave's retweets. They referenced the Catholic church in various uncharitable ways. A common theme emerged after a few: sexual abuse by priests. Waugh's blog posts covered the same subject matter, though with less detachment and more invective.

And he had been found murdered a stone's throw from a Catholic church.

I couldn't consider it a coincidence.

* * *

THE NEXT MORNING, I drove to St. Mark's. I timed my arrival when morning service let out. A few people filed out as I walked up the steps. The building's cornerstone proclaimed 1921. I believed it. The church needed an extended collection drive to power wash and spruce up the exterior. I held the door for a woman who looked to be in her eighties. She smiled and said, "God bless you" as she left. I just smiled and refrained from telling her I hadn't sneezed.

The small vestibule led to heavy double doors, which opened into the church proper. The height of church interiors always impressed me. Even if this wasn't the painted heights of the Sistine Chapel, someone had to get up there and hang the lights. Even smaller churches like St. Mark's boasted very high ceilings. Soft organ music played as I walked down the center aisle. Several of the dark brown pews needed refurbishing, too. I guessed the church would seat about two hundred fifty worshipers. Votive candles burned in alcoves, and the small flames danced in nearby stained glass windows. Even with the shopworn exterior, St. Mark's still had a nice interior identifying it as a Catholic church. I saw the priest talking to an elderly man. I waited near the first pew.

After a minute, the old man bid the priest farewell. I recognized Father Lawrence Toohey from the church's website; he turned to me and offered a tentative smile. I placed him at about fifty, with black hair turning to a dignified gray. He was balding on top, stood about five-ten, and stayed slender into his middle years. "Interested in joining the parish?" he said.

"Not right now," I said. "Is there someplace we might talk?"

The priest held his arms wide. "Only God will overhear us in here." He gestured toward the first pew. I moved down a few feet and sat, leaving Father Lawrence room. He seated himself about a foot away. "Is something troubling you?"

I showed him my ID. "You can probably figure out why I'm here."

He nodded. "That poor man."

"What can you tell me about him?"

The priest sighed. "I barely knew him. He'd come around a few times in the last month or so."

"Was he a parishioner?" I said.

"No, but we don't discriminate. This is a house of God, not a club."

"Father Lawrence, it's—"

"Please," he said, "call me Father Larry. Everyone does."

"All right. You said Dave Waugh came around a few times. Did he attend mass?"

"At least once, yes."

"What was he doing the other times?"

"I don't know. Sitting in the pews, mostly. At first, I thought he was homeless."

"He didn't come for confession?" I said.

"I offered to hear it," said Father Larry. "He . . . wouldn't take me up on it."

"Did he say why?"

"He said he didn't have much to confess."

I would have probably said the same. Of course, my litany of sins to confess would monopolize a priest's time. "You didn't find that odd?" I said.

Father Larry shrugged. "Not everyone wants to confess."

"Some have more need of it than others."

"True," Father Larry said with small smile. "All I can do is ask. People need to be willing to receive a sacrament."

"Did you know Dave Waugh was an active blogger?"

"We barely talked. I never asked him what he did."

"He talked a lot about sexual abuse by priests."

"A sad part of our history," Father Larry said, shaking his head. "I'd like to think the Catholic Church has gotten rid of the bad seeds, if you will."

I looked around for a moment. No one else was in the church. The organist had left. No one came out from the sacristy. "Are you the only priest here?" I said.

"For now."

"For now?"

"We're working on some fundraising," Father Larry said. "It will take a while, but we'd like to build a bigger church—the structure and the congregation to fill it. If we can, I'm sure we'd get at least one more priest."

"How would someone writing about priests abusing boys affect your fundraising?"

"I can't imagine it would help," he said, frowning. "But if you're implying—"

"I'm not implying anything, Father. Just asking questions."

"Yes. Well, since I am the only priest here, I have some duties to attend to."

"Of course."

Father Larry stood and walked out of the pew. "Let me know if you need anything else," he said. "Dave seemed . . . troubled, but I think he was a good man."

"I'm sure I'll be in touch," I said.

CHAPTER 3

SOMETHING DIDN'T SIT RIGHT WITH ME AFTER MY CHAT
with Father Larry. He said he knew Dave Waugh but not too
well, and still felt bad he died. I didn't have a problem with the
last part; in fact, it seemed like a priestly thing to say. The other
part bothered me. I looked at Dave Waugh's address. He lived
four miles from St. Mark's church. Presuming he was Catholic,
plenty of churches stood closer to his apartment than St. Mark's.

Nothing in his history suggested an affiliation with any
specific church, but before, I'd only skimmed his blog. Now I
scrutinized it. Its title, *We are the Violets*, sort of made sense,
trying to answer the question posed in the title of the Auberon
Waugh book. It made me wonder if the surname came with his
birth certificate or got chiseled onto something later. Unlike
Ernie's made-up *murderphiles* word, Dave's title choice didn't
shake my faith in the English language. Waugh updated his blog
a couple times a week, often with stories of priests abusing someone. After a period of decline, reports of abuse trended upward
recently in nearby dioceses. Dave's entries contained a little
investigating, and some of his posts featured interviews with
victims or their families.

I wondered—and suspected—why Dave was such a crusader in this area, but his blog never delved into his own details. He reported on other people's stories, with one curious omission from the most current updates: names. In older cases, where the events and parties were known, the blogs called out the priests. Newer posts didn't name names, however. Maybe a lawyer told him not to identify someone who hadn't been charged or convicted of a crime. Dave's site looked like he'd put some effort into assembling it. Posts were indexed by subject, the layout and theme made sense for the grim subject matter, and comments were lively.

With nothing else on the blog, I dug deeper. Again, I ran into the issue that Dave Waugh didn't have much of a life history before he turned eighteen. Several things could cause this. He could have been home-schooled, thus avoiding traditional school records. He could have lived a boring life. He could have grown up overseas. Or he could have changed his name or identity. Spurred by the literary last name, I latched onto the last one and ran with it.

Public records searches yield only so much information. The good stuff isn't available from a common web search, at least not for free. I never let such concerns deter me, however. Computers are simple machines, and the things protecting them are often equally simple. I learned the science of computers in college. I developed the art of compromising them on my own, refined by my time in Hong Kong.

Dave Waugh's social security number got issued when he was eighteen. He was not an immigrant receiving a number upon completing the citizenship class. It took some more digging to find out the SSN replaced an older one, issued at birth to Donald Watson. Now I had a better starting point. Dave Waugh's past started where Donald Watson's ended.

Donald was a good student and grew up in a Catholic family in Phoenix. They belonged to St. Isaac's. Young Donald served as an altar boy for about six years. He stopped his service, and his family stopped going to St. Isaac's when a priest there was accused of molesting the altar boys. It only took me a minute to find the priest's name.

Lawrence Toohey.

* * *

I WENT BACK TO ST. Mark's. The church itself was empty, so I wandered into the attached rectory. The attendant there, a high school boy, directed me to Father Larry's office. The door was open a crack. I knocked and entered when directed.

"Mr. Ferguson," Father Larry said, a small frown pulling his eyebrows down. "What brings you back so soon?"

"May I sit?" I pointed to one of the two wooden chairs in front of his desk.

"Please."

I took the left chair. Father Larry's office was about the size of mine, which was really my second bedroom. For a rectory, I expected larger. The bookshelf behind him showed many books on religion and theology and an almost equal number about sports. Father Larry's degrees, including a master's in theology, hung on the wall to his right.

"Did something urgent come up?" the priest said.

"I don't know if I'd call it urgent," I said, "but it's interesting and troubling."

"What do you mean?"

"What did you call it, Father Larry? 'A sad part of our history,' I think it was."

"You mean the priests who . . . harmed those boys."

"I mean you," I said.

"Me?" Father Larry must have practiced the taken aback look. He delivered a decent one.

"You said Dave Waugh came around a few times."

"Yes," said Father Larry.

"Did he look familiar to you at all?"

"I don't know." The priest shrugged. Furrows affixed themselves to his brow and threatened never to leave. "I guess. Maybe he just had one of those faces."

"Maybe. Or maybe Dave Waugh was really Donald Watson." I watched Father Larry for a reaction. None came.

"I don't know the name."

"Sure you do. You knew him back in Phoenix. From what I've read, you knew him biblically."

Father Larry's frown deepened, but he didn't give any other reaction. If I didn't find him so slimy, I might have been impressed. "I still don't know what you're talking about," he said.

"Let me guess," I said, "records were sealed?" Father Larry didn't say anything, so I continued. "And you were never charged with a crime while church officials moved you into a teaching role for ten years. Maybe they figured seminary students were too old for you."

"Now you're simply being crass."

"True. However, after a decade of teaching, your record got scrubbed clean, and you were back in front of congregations."

"I don't know what you're after here," said Father Larry. "Maybe you have something against priests. Whatever you think of me, though, I'm not a murderer." He stared at me the entire time he said it. While he looked annoyed, he sat still and didn't yell.

"I think you might be telling the truth," I said.

"I am."

"But what if your parishioners found out about the past?"

"You do know priests aren't wealthy, Mr. Ferguson? I don't think your extortion will get you very far."

"Extortion implies I want something from you, Father."

"Why ask the question, then?" he said.

"Did it make you angry?"

"I am a fallible man."

"Angry enough to want to, say, stab me twelve times in the chest?"

Father Larry did a double-take and sat back in his chair. "You think I killed Dave?"

"He blogged about what happened," I said. "There are two good things in this for you and your parish: he hadn't named any names yet, and no one picked up the story. I don't know how long the second one will last, especially with this whole mess back in the news."

I waited while Father Larry took a couple of deep breaths. "I told you, Mr. Ferguson. I am a fallible man. I'm sure I have let God down in the past, but I meant it when I said I'm not a killer."

"You didn't recognize Dave Waugh as Donald Watson?"

"Not at all . . . and he never said anything about it."

I believed him. Father Larry made an excellent suspect. He had motive; just because no one picked up Dave Waugh's story now didn't mean someone couldn't carry it forward later. Maybe Dave kept notes and retained a list of names to reveal in future blogs. While the abuse he chronicled was in the past, I didn't think St. Mark's parishioners--or any, for that matter--would be forgiving once the truth got thrust into the spotlight. Motive alone was never enough. If I wanted to prove Ernie Chin's innocence, I would need a better suspect.

"I think you're being honest, Father," I said. "But the police would tell you you're a person of interest here. I may need to talk to you again."

"I'll tell you the truth," said Father Larry, "I hope you don't. But I want to see the killer found. It sounds like Dave has been through enough in this life. I hope he has found peace in the next one."

I didn't have much to say in reply, so I left.

* * *

I DROVE BACK to my apartment in Fells Point. It was enough in the old part so getting there required a brief drive on cobblestone streets. However, like most places in Fells Point, a trip down the block revealed a pleasant mix of retro and modern. My building looked newer than it was thanks to careful renovations inside and out. As I approached the front, I saw two large men who were not part of the renovation committee. They stood near the front door with their arms crossed. Both were taller and wider than me. One's blond spiky hair made him look ridiculous; the other sported a shaved head. I felt my pulse jump a bit at the impending fight. Even though I had years of training, a situation like this always drove the beats per minute a little higher. When the reaction stopped, I would be worried.

"Guys, I gave at the office," I said.

"Maybe we're here to ask you to give blood," the blond said.

"Pretty clever," I said, and it was. I didn't think either of them had a good quip in them.

"Enough chit-chat," the other one said. "You know why we're here?"

"You're collecting for TDA."

"The fuck is TDA?"

"Two Dumb Assholes," I said.

Blondie snickered, which earned him a scowl from his clean-pated compatriot. "Listen up, prick," Shaved Head said, "you been asking a lot of questions."

Of a priest, I thought. Would Father Larry call a couple of goons on me? How many priests kept assholes like these two in their contacts lists? "Nature of my job," I said.

"Maybe you should consider a career change."

"You first."

"I don't think he's gonna play ball," the blond one said.

"Let's find out. You gonna keep asking questions?"

"Who wants to know?" I said.

"You ain't playing ball," Baldy said, and he threw a right hook. It came in faster than I would have given him credit for, but I still had plenty of time to block it. While he wound up his left hand, Blondie strode closer. I didn't want to tangle with both of them at once. Their combined size and muscle could give them the edge. I blocked Baldy's left, took a step forward, and kicked his partner square in the balls. His eyes threatened to bulge out of his head as he folded in half and pitched forward.

The other tried to grab me in a headlock, but I slid away. He hit me with a jab in the side as I did. Even though he couldn't get a lot of power behind the punch, it still hurt. He gave me a wolfish grin.

I needed to end this before the goon on the sidewalk recovered. He coughed and raised himself to all fours. When the clean-shaven goon tried another right hook, I hit him with a quick right jab, then a series of rapid body blows. It staggered him enough to give me the chance to punt the spiky blond head and put it on the concrete again. Baldy recovered, and I launched a right kick at his midsection, but he blocked it and grabbed my ankle. There were a lot of ways this could end poorly. I pushed off with my left foot, leaned back, and put what I could into another kick. It took him in the thigh. The impact got him to let go, and I fell to the pavement.

As my bald adversary came forward again, I rose to a crouch. He launched a few punches, trying to end the fight in one swing. I turned them all aside. He kept the blows coming. Blocking them wasn't a challenge. I held a good base and balance. After a few more, punches slowed, and I heard my foe breathing hard. Turning aside a haymaker, I landed a solid right cross to the goon's midsection. He doubled over as I stood up. I grabbed the collar of his shirt, elbowed him twice in the head, then drove my knee into his face. His bald head snapped back, and he fell not far from his unconscious blond friend.

"You were right," I said. "Tell whoever sent you I'm not playing ball."

The would-be bully tried to say something, but it got lost in a sea of coughs and mumbles.

"I'm calling the cops. They have a precinct not far from here. You've probably got about three minutes to collect your buddy and fuck off."

He muttered something uncharitable, so I kicked him in the face. Then I went inside and called the police.

CHAPTER 4

THE NEXT MORNING, I WALKED INTO RICH'S PRECINCT. HE sat at his desk, staring at his monitor. "Maybe this will help," I said, setting a fresh coffee on the desk before him.

Rich sniffed and smiled. "Smells good."

"And it saves you from drinking the sewage they call coffee here."

"Tastes good, too," he said after taking a drink.

"Light roast," I said. "The way you were mesmerized by your screen, it looks like you could use the boost."

Rich took a big swig. He wore a gray suit with a white shirt and a red tie. Knowing Rich, he probably owned ten sets of coats with pants in five pairs—one to wear while its twin spent quality time with the dry cleaner. Wearing the Friday outfit on a Thursday was not calculus Rich could do. His suit looked off the rack, but it was one I would have owned. Rich didn't spend as much time or money on clothes as I did, but he dressed well. Like any consumer with a whit of fashion sense, he never shopped those horrific buy-three-for-$200 sales.

"What brings you by?" Rich said. "I presume you didn't come in merely to give me coffee."

"The Dave Waugh case," I said.

"Still trying to get your boy off the hook?"

"Did you talk to the priest?"

"You think a priest killed him?"

I sipped my vanilla latte. "Did you know the priest was accused of abusing Dave years ago?"

Rich frowned. "No, I didn't."

"Did you talk to him?"

"A couple of uniforms did," Rich said. "He didn't say anything we felt needed following up."

"Good thing you have me here to lead you down the right path," I said.

"Even if the priest did abuse this guy years ago, it doesn't mean he killed him now." Rich went back to his screen. The BPD had Ernie in custody after his stupid phony confession. Rich needed more convincing.

"I talked to the priest twice," I said. "After the second time, a couple goons ambushed me outside my building."

Rich looked at his screen another few seconds, then shifted back to me. "So not only did the priest kill the vic, he also keeps goons in his Rolodex?"

"You *would* call it a Rolodex."

"Do you know what a Rolodex is?" Rich said with an amused smile.

"Sure," I said. "I've watched *Antiques Roadshow*."

"Touché." Rich gave a chuckle.

"You don't find it odd? I talk to the priest a second time, and then a couple of assholes are trying to get me to back off?"

Rich consulted his screen again. "I thought I saw something about two guys getting picked up near your building."

"If you mean on the front steps, yes."

"You went to church when you were a kid," Rich said. I nodded. "So did I. I still go for Christmas and Easter. It's just . . ."

". . . hard for you to think a priest is a killer?" I said.

"Yeah."

"Maybe he's not. Maybe the strong-arm types he called on me are the ones who killed Dave Waugh."

"Not much difference legally," Rich said.

"I don't know a ton about the priest yet," I said, "but I know this much . . . he was in Phoenix years ago. If you looked into Dave Waugh, you noticed he doesn't have much of a history. It's because he was born Donald Watson, who was 'allegedly' the victim of sexual abuse at the hands of Father Lawrence Toohey. I'm sure you recall the Catholic Church had some problems in this area, and now they do again. Father Larry was one of them. He was never charged with a crime, but he got moved from a parish to teaching at the seminary for ten years. Then he gets the tabula rasa treatment and ends up here in Baltimore."

Rich said, "Where Dave Waugh moved years ago."

"Yes."

"I don't know." Rich frowned. "There's a lot of circumstantial and coincidental in there."

"Seems like enough to cast reasonable doubt on Ernie Chin stabbing Waugh."

"Have you been to the public defender yet?"

"She's my next stop," I said.

"All right," Rich said with a nod. "I'll look into it."

"You shouldn't have to look too hard to see Ernie is no killer."

Rich sipped his coffee. "Be careful how hard you look. If you piss someone off again, they might send more than two goons."

"I'll be ready," I said.

* * *

LIKE I SAID I WOULD, I went to see Liz Fleming after I talked to Rich. I didn't have a coffee for her, so I finished my latte before I walked into her office. She sat behind her desk, wearing an unfortunately conservative white shirt and blue blazer. "Got something for me?" she said.

"Good morning to you, too," I eased into one of her lousy guest chairs.

Liz flashed the kind of patient smile I became used to seeing in school. "Good morning. Got something for me?"

"I do." I told her about my visits to Father Larry, the history between him and Dave Waugh, and the welcoming committee outside my building.

"Are you all right?" Liz said. She kicked her feet up onto the desk. Her blazer was part of a pantsuit. I tried to hide my disappointment, but her smirk told me I hadn't.

"Neither rain, nor sleet, nor amateur legbreakers will keep me from my appointed rounds," I said.

Liz smiled. Her eyes brightened and dimples appeared in her cheeks. It was the kind of face a man could get used to seeing. "That's good to know."

"So what does this mean for Ernie?"

"It helps," Liz said. "I just don't think it helps immediately. He confessed. That means something. You've given me good information to work with, but there's a process. We need to investigate it."

"It's not reasonable doubt?" I said.

"It helps toward that, but it's an issue for a trial. I'd like to prevent this case from getting to that point."

"You're saying I need to pin something on the priest."

"Or whoever sent those guys after you," said Liz.

"Why does no one think a priest could have done it?" I said.

Liz shrugged. "Why do you seem convinced that he did?"

"The history between him and Dave."

"OK, so he had a motive."

"And means. Everyone has a knife. And opportunity . . . Waugh came by the church a couple of times."

"Then you need to make it stick," Liz said.

"No, making it stick is your job," I said. "I only need to bring you enough to make it happen."

She nodded. "You really think the priest did it?"

"I think it's not a big leap from sexually abusing altar boys to stabbing people," I said.

"The defense would say most sex abusers aren't violent like that," Liz pointed out.

"Then let them say it at his trial."

"Get me to that point."

"I will," I said.

* * *

I GOT HOME and found no more enforcers waiting for me. The elevator and my floor were similarly clear. Once back in my office, I resumed work. I'd gathered the big-picture details about Father Larry. More had to be there. Between church records and whatever the Phoenix police may have discovered, I wanted to unearth enough to spring Ernie. I made a mental note not to take cases from any more idiots. Possible cheating spouses already topped the blacklist. Stupid people creating their own problems now made the second entry.

The Catholic Church's private records were easy to access. They must not have thought themselves big targets for hackers—perhaps damnation proved a powerful deterrent. I gained access to the full personnel records in a matter of minutes. Father Larry's file said he was fifty-two. He got his bachelor's in theology and then entered the seminary. From there, he spent two years as a deacon before becoming ordained twenty-eight years ago. The first decade of his career in the cloth saw him serve at two parishes. No scandals or issues followed him. The ecclesiastical equivalent of performance reviews said he was a good and popular priest, well-liked by young and old.

Fifteen years ago, the first irregularity appeared. Eight months after arriving at Holy Redeemer in Phoenix, Father Larry got sent to St. Joseph's. His file mentioned "irregular behavior" with the youth of the parish, citing two parent complaints. Neither accused him of sexual abuse, however. The move must have been precautionary, an attempt to head off any more bad publicity on the priests-and-young-boys front.

A year later, it happened again.

This time, Father Larry got shipped from St. Joseph's in Phoenix to St. Matthew's in Casa Grande. I never heard of Casa Grande, so I consulted the Oracle of Google Maps. It sat about an hour outside of Phoenix, breaking up a large swath of desert, and would be considered a much less prestigious assignment, if priests cared about such a thing. The Phoenix PD didn't have much better security than the Catholic Church. Maybe they could confess to using shoddy IT contractors. I checked around the date Father Larry got sent to Casa Grande. The PPD investigated an incident at St. Joseph's, involving an unnamed minor and one Father Lawrence Toohey. I read the detective's notes. He thought Father Larry was guilty but couldn't make the case against him. No charges got filed.

After two uneventful years in Casa Grande, Father Larry got called back up to the big leagues in Phoenix, this time back at Holy Redeemer. There, he met Donald Watson and another altar boy. The PPD opened another investigation. This time, a different detective felt the same way about Father Larry's guilt and experienced the same luck building the case. Again, no charges filed. Father Larry got exiled to the seminary, where he spent the next ten years teaching and getting his master's. Diocese records contained a few notes about "inappropriate relationships with altar boys" but never mentioned abuse. Even if someone lawfully accessed the files, nothing stated Father Larry was an abuser in clear, explicit terms. Reaching such a conclusion required simple inferences, but my feeling was defense lawyers could argue against those simple inferences if something ever made it to court.

During Father Larry's ten years at the seminary, no one reported any incidents. His master record still contained all the issues from the past, but the more compact HR record individual churches saw—and which I saw at first—didn't mention anything. *Tabula rasa*, a clean slate. Pastors and monsignors were unlikely to ask about things like sexual abuse, and I didn't know if they could even see the master files. The church maintained a system to protect their own, regardless if those men deserved protection. I wondered if they would ever learn.

Now I knew more about Father Larry. He was definitely a sex offender, even if the Phoenix police couldn't even charge him with it. Like many guilty men, he could point to the lack of charges against him and exclaim his innocence. Rich's comment stuck with me, however: none of this meant Father Larry killed Dave Waugh. And none of it meant he sicced goons on me. I still needed to make those accusations stand up.

* * *

I STILL LIKED Father Larry for the stabbing. Part of my suspicions was the absence of any other credible suspect. Another part was how well he fit into the role of killer. None of the circumstantial evidence meant he did it, of course, but I didn't have anyone else to investigate. So I drove back to St. Mark's.

The church was open. I walked in and sat in the back pew. Father Larry stood about halfway down the aisle, his back to me, talking to a man who wore a suit I would have been proud to own. Most of the lights were off, so I couldn't discern much more, but great suits are easy to spot in any light. To my right, at the other end of the pew, another man sat. He also watched Father Larry and the mystery man talk. A couple minutes later, the two shook hands. The well-dressed man walked toward the back of the church. The fellow at the end of the pew stood and joined him on the way out.

Father Larry hadn't noticed me. He took a wooden wick in his left hand, held it to the flame of a votive candle, and lit another. I glanced around. A handful of other people sat in pews, not paying attention to Father Larry or me. I took out my phone and used a secure remote protocol called SSH to connect to my server at home. I opened the crime scene photos and zoomed in on them. I'm neither a cop nor a medical examiner—and I considered saying a quick prayer of thanks for both—but the angle of the stab wounds suggested a left-handed attacker.

Another mark against Father Larry.

I remained in the pew. After a minute, Father Larry turned. His grimace told me he noticed me even in the dim lighting. He walked toward me, pausing for a moment to exchange pleasantries with an older lady a few rows ahead of me.

"Mister Ferguson, this is getting ridiculous."

"I know," I said. "I haven't spent this much time in church in years."

"You know what I mean."

"Can't a man sit here and be spiritual?"

"Are you a spiritual man, Mister Ferguson?" said Father Larry.

I shrugged. "It doesn't really matter." I looked around again. Even though the exterior needed work, the interior of St. Mark's remained beautiful. I'd always liked stained glass. "There's something relaxing about sitting in a church."

"Perhaps it's the presence of God."

"Perhaps."

Father Larry followed the sweep of my eyes for a moment. "Was there a reason you came?" he said in a lowered tone. "Other than to toss around accusations, maybe?"

"Who was the man you were talking to a few minutes ago?"

"A parishioner."

"You have many parishioners with bodyguards?" I said. Father Larry didn't say anything. "This isn't a bad neighborhood. Even if it were, the church is mostly empty, so he wouldn't have to walk far to his car."

"We're lucky enough to have a few wealthy parishioners," Father Larry said.

"Wealthy enough to send goons after me?"

My thinly-veiled accusation made Father Larry frown. "I'm not sure what you mean."

"It's pretty simple, Father. Either hiring legbreakers is fine with the current pope, or someone else hired them to take a run at me. I know this pope is seen as pretty progressive, but I doubt it extends quite this far."

"Thank God you weren't hurt."

"Yes," I said with a smirk. "Thank God . . . and years of martial arts."

"Well, I don't think you need to keep coming by. I've told you what I know. This is bordering on harassment."

"Said no innocent person ever."

Father Larry took a deep breath. If we were alone in the church, he might have yelled at me. "I don't know what you're doing here, Mister Ferguson."

"Then you might want to pray for wisdom, Father," I said. "Maybe take a turn in confession."

"Good afternoon." Father Larry walked away.

The man in the suit employed a bodyguard. I wondered who he was and if he sent the legbreakers after me. But why? I didn't see him well in the church lighting, but he didn't look familiar. Did Father Larry ask him to take care of me?

"Maybe I ought to pray for wisdom, too," I said to the mostly-empty church.

* * *

LATER IN THE DAY, Gloria Reading called and inquired as to my plans for the evening. None for me and neither for her. She suggested she come to my place around seven and get dinner; I concurred. Gloria and I enjoyed a relationship of fun and convenience. She came from a similar background but was lucky enough not to work for a living. Gloria played tennis and went to interesting events. If Baltimore had a large enough profile to boast of socialites, she could count herself among them.

With nothing to do for a few hours, I went to the gym. I abused the heavy bag for about a half-hour, lifted some weights, and cycled like I trained for an upcoming race. At home, I showered and ate a small meal to tide me over until dinner. Gloria showed up promptly at seven. I heard her Mercedes rocket-like coupe when it was about a block away. For anyone whose ears didn't split from the sound, the car was helpfully painted bright red to accentuate its rocket-ness.

A few minutes later, Gloria knocked on my apartment door. I opened it and took in the scene. Gloria always looked great, even when she wasn't dressed to the nines. Even her fours and fives were worth an extra glance. She wore light blue jeans appearing painted on and a sweater managing to be loose but still cling to her in all the right places. Her chestnut hair spilled over her shoulders. She smiled as she came in and planted a kiss on me.

We sat on the loveseat and chatted for a few minutes. The conversation inevitably turned to my case. Gloria didn't work, and I thought she found it quaint how I did, but she also listened when I talked about my cases and asked good questions. She never rolled her eyes or blew off my stories. Maybe there was hope for her yet.

"You think the priest did it?" Gloria said after I laid out the details.

"I'm not sure," I said. "At first, I did. He had a good motive."

"But now you don't?"

"He has to be involved somehow."

"It must be weird to go after a priest," said Gloria.

"A little." I gave a slight nod. "No one else thinks he could have anything to do with it. They're all wrapped up in the man-of-the-cloth stuff."

"And you're not."

"There are bad people in every profession. Even if the percentage is lower in the priesthood, they can't all be saints."

Gloria grinned. "Saints?"

"No pun intended," I said.

"It sounds like you've been spending a lot of time in church."

"I have." I looked at Gloria and how her sweater managed to be tight around her breasts and nowhere else. "More than I have in years. I think I need to make up for it."

"Is that so?" Gloria's brown eyes sparkled as she leaned in to kiss me.

"Definitely." I kissed Gloria's neck, and she grabbed my head and wrapped her fingers in my hair.

"What did you have in mind?" Gloria wriggled onto my lap.

"Lots of fornication," I said, recalling the Biblical term.

"I like the way you think," Gloria said as she took her sweater off.

CHAPTER 5

AFTER A NIGHT FILLED WITH THE PROMISED AMOUNTS OF fornication, I left a sleeping Gloria and hit the streets of Fells Point for a morning run. I made a left on Thames and ran past a lot of shops and eateries, some of which had yet to open. Passing Broadway and the Admiral Fell Inn, I took in the smells of the restaurants open for breakfast and doing their mise en place for lunch. A few cars drove past me. Downtown Baltimore would be playing its soundtrack of car horns and curse words by now, but Fells Point remained quieter. I got near the end of Thames, sprinted up Caroline, and then went to the right on Aliceanna. The aromas from the Blue Moon Cafe almost pulled me in for coffee and a pastry, but I kept going.

When I approached the intersection of Aliceanna and Ann Streets, I noticed two musclemen standing with their arms crossed and blocking the sidewalk. Anyone nearby gave them a wide berth.

Neither looked familiar. How many of these assholes did Father Larry know? I wondered about the man in the nice suit who left with his bodyguard. These two were burlier, but they could all work for the same man. It would make more sense than a priest having a bunch of legbreakers on speed dial. Both men glared at me as I approached since I hadn't slowed.

As I got near them, I feinted toward the one on the right. Then I sprang off my left foot, leaped between them, and drove my left elbow down into the face of the no-neck on the left. He grunted, staggered, and fell. The other threw a punch as I came down. I ducked under it and hit him in the stomach. It only made made him glower more.

He swung again, quicker than I expected. I was unbalanced and while I blocked it, it knocked me on my butt. The first one I put on the sidewalk still covered his face and moaned. I avoided tripping over him as I scooted back to the curb and regained my feet. The second man drifted to my left. Behind me, the prone goon stirred. If he recovered, I would lose whatever advantage I gained by knocking him down.

I ducked under a left from the one on his feet, blocked a right, and gave him a solid jab to the nose. It didn't break the bone, but it did send him stumbling back a couple steps. The guy behind me must have recovered while I did that; the next thing I knew, he wrapped his arms around me from behind. His pal shook off the blow to the face, saw me in the grip of his friend, and smiled.

This could end poorly. I lifted my leg and drove my heel down onto the toes of the man holding me. He yelled in pain and his grip loosened. I slipped out just in time and wormed away from a hard right taking my sore-footed captor flush in the face. Both men cursed as I started away. We already drew a few onlookers, and of course one of them held his phone out, no doubt recording everything while wondering why no one called the authorities. I didn't want any bystander hurt, even the moron who fancied himself a cameraman.

I ran down Ann and checked behind me. Both goons gave

chase, but they weren't running full out. I slowed my pace, looked back again, and saw they did the same. They weren't trying to catch me; they were trying to drive me. Probably back to the one place they knew I would go: my apartment building. Where Gloria lay sleeping in my bed.

Using voice commands, I called Gloria's cell. She answered in a sleepy voice. "This is important," I said. "I need you to go downstairs."

"What?" She sounded more alert. "Why, what's wrong?"

"A couple of assholes just tried to assault me."

"Oh, my goodness! Are you all right?"

"I'm fine. Listen. Go downstairs. Act like you're getting the mail or something. Tell me if there are any guys lingering outside."

"OK," Gloria said. "I'm going to throw one of your hoodies on." She paused. I heard clothes rustle. I turned left from Ann onto Lancaster. My building wasn't far. "I'm heading downstairs," Gloria said a moment later. Another pause. Then she said, "Yes, I see two guys. They're really big."

I said, "Did they see you?"

"No, they're looking out at the street."

"Good." I slowed my pace a little more. My pursuers just turned onto Lancaster. They jogged toward me. "Here's what I need you to do: Go back to my apartment. Go into my office, open the desk drawer, and grab a gun."

"A gun?"

"Yes."

"Are they loaded?" said Gloria.

"Of course. Keep your fingers out of the trigger guards, and they can't go off. I don't care which one you get. Just grab one and bring it downstairs."

"C.T., I'm worried about you."

"You won't need to worry so much if you get me a gun," I said.

"I'm working on it." I heard Gloria open a drawer. She worried about me. On the one hand, I liked it. On the other, I wondered how it jibed with our relationship of convenience. Right now, I had more pressing concerns. I turned down Wolfe Street. There was one block to Thames, and just beyond that, my building loomed. I could see two figures standing in front of it. By now, they surely saw me.

"I have a gun," Gloria said. "I'm headed back downstairs."

"Good," I said. "Hide it under the hoodie and wait in the lobby. If I need it, I'll let you know."

In my ear, I heard Gloria run down the stairs. A minute later, she said, "I'm in the lobby."

I picked up my pace again as I crossed Thames. Now I could see the two waiting for me were the same pair I dealt with yesterday. If they pulled guns, I would have to keep running and take my chances. I wouldn't involve Gloria in a shootout. As I ran closer, they both took knives out of their coats. While I've always hated fighting people with knives, I preferred them to guns.

"I'm getting close to the building," I said.

"I see you."

"Good. When I approach the stairs, I want you to open the door and throw me the gun. Throw it high so these shitheads can't get it."

"C.T., I'm not sure—"

"Gloria, I need you to do this."

"All right," she said. "I can do it." Waves of apprehension dotted her voice.

I slowed as I approached the stairs. The goons with knives flashed me predatory grins. "Wanna try that shit from yesterday?" one of them said.

"Now," I said.

Behind them, the door opened. The hood of my sweatshirt covering most of her face, Gloria took one step out. Both men turned to look at her. She tossed the gun over their heads. They followed it as it arced over them. I caught it and pointed it at them. Gloria grabbed the .38 revolver. Not my first choice, but it beat a pair of knives.

"How's the saying go about knives and gunfights?" I said. Gloria disappeared back into the lobby.

Both of them frowned and looked at their knives. The one on the right glared, brandished his, and edged forward.

"One more step, and I'll shoot you," I said. He was three paces away. I wouldn't miss. I'd never shot anyone before and didn't relish the possibility, but I also wouldn't let this asshole stab me. Or Gloria.

I considered the possibility they would both rush me. At their current distance, I couldn't shoot both of them in time. One would definitely drop. I stared at the pair as the same math ran through their small brains. It came down to a coinflip. Heads, I live; tails, I get shot isn't appealing calculus.

The wiser goon put a hand on his partner's chest and held him back. I took a few steps to the side, keeping these two on my left. The pair once chasing me now walked down Wolfe. They had to see what happened, so they wouldn't be sticking around. I called the police.

* * *

AFTER I GAVE my statement to the police and they led the two goons away—the first two were long gone by then—I walked back upstairs. During my chat with the police, my hands shook as adrenaline still flowed through my system. I paused outside my apartment door. No more shaking, so I walked in. Gloria sat at the kitchen table, nursing a glass of orange juice. "What the hell was that?"

"Some days, my job is more dangerous than others," I said.

"There were two guys out there with knives." Gloria's eyes widened as she talked. I sympathized. A few months ago, I wouldn't have imagined dealing with threats like theirs. I thought this career would be easy and allow me to work from behind my desk. Each case hammered home how wrong I'd been. Even helping people in China had been simpler—until the Chinese police kicked the door in.

"And two more in the streets," I said. "They seem to have gotten away."

Gloria looked up at me. She held the glass of orange juice. I noticed the liquid trembling. "Were you scared?"

I nodded. "Yes. The day a situation like this doesn't spike my adrenaline, I'm done."

"You're going to keep working?" said Gloria.

"Of course. I've obviously pissed off the right person. Now I need to figure out who it is and how he or she is involved."

"You should give this case up. You could get hurt."

"You can get hurt crossing the street," I said.

"Not the same," Gloria said, shaking her head.

"Fine." I searched for an analogy. "If you lost the first set of a tennis tournament and tweaked your knee in the process, would you forfeit?"

"No. I'd keep playing as long as my knee held up."

"There you go."

"But no one stabbed me in the knee," Gloria said.

I needed a better analogy, and one of my earliest sports memories sprang to mind. "You've heard of Monica Seles, right?" I said.

"You're using that because she got stabbed on the court. Clever."

"I was three or four when it happened . . . one of of the first things I remember from any sport."

"I was too young." Gloria grinned. "I've only heard about it and seen the video. You're older than I am."

"My point is she didn't quit," I said. "An asshole with a knife didn't end her career."

It gave Gloria pause, and she nodded after a moment. "I think I understand. I'd probably understand more if you were competing for millions in prize money."

"If I do this long enough and well enough, there should come a point when I can give it all up."

Gloria smiled. The orange juice stilled in her glass. "That would be nice."

"I chose this career because it seemed like the best of a bad lot. I've come to like it more than I thought, yet I'd still like to walk away after I earn a lot of money."

"As long as you can walk away," Gloria said.

"It's my plan."

"I'm not waiting for you while you hobble along," she said with a grin.

Her joke gave me pause. How did Gloria see our relationship, such as it was, in light of her remark? I chose to ignore it. She could have gotten caught up in the moment. I moved behind Gloria and rubbed her shoulders. "How about you and I walk down the hallway?" I said.

Gloria's chin dropped to her chest, and I swore I heard her purr. "I'm not sure we'll make it there."

We did, but it was close.

* * *

THE WEALTHY PARISHIONER BOTHERED ME. Who brings a

bodyguard to church? Why was Father Larry so evasive when I asked a simple question about the mystery man?

As I thought more about the case, I found myself losing certainty in Father Larry as the killer. Even if he did the stabbing, I doubted the goons who twice visited me were deacons doing a priest a solid. Someone with money or influence (or both) must have sent them. My parents might have known who the guy in the church was from my limited description. Then I thought of someone else who was more likely to know.

One of the perks of living in Fells Point is the closeness of Little Italy. On a nice day like today, I could walk there easily. Up Fell Street to Ann, left on Eastern Avenue, and then right on High Street. A mile (and sixteen minutes) later, I walked in the front door of *Il Buon Cibo*, one of the better restaurants in Little Italy.

In addition to being a fine place to catch a meal, *Il Buon Cibo* was a great place to talk to the man who ran organized crime in Baltimore. Tony Rizzo and my parents had been friends for ages, and the fact they were still friendly meant my mother remained ignorant of his occupation. When I walked in, Tony occupied his usual table near the fireplace. The lunch crowd started to file in. The only tables within ten feet were manned by a pair of enforcers who sized me up as I approached.

"It's OK, boys," Tony said with a smile. "You remember C.T."

Their grunts neither confirmed nor denied their memories of me. "How are you, Tony?" I said. During my three-plus years abroad, Tony lost a good eighty pounds. His face looked a little too thin, though his waistline now inhabited the average range. For a man pushing seventy, he looked to be in good shape. As always, Tony wore a suit, and I knew the tie would be Italian. Probably Versace.

"No complaints," he said, gesturing to the seat across from him. I sat. "What brings you by? You need a free meal?"

"I don't know I need one, but it seems silly to refuse."

Tony chuckled. "You always were practical." He snapped his fingers, and a young waitress appeared. "Take my friend's order."

She spoke to me but also cast an occasional glance at Tony. "Sir, do you need a menu?"

"No, thanks. I'll just have the chicken parm with a side Caesar and an unsweetened tea."

She scribbled on her pad and vanished into the kitchen. After a moment, Tony said, "What really brings you by?"

"I need to know about a mover and shaker."

"Someone I like?"

"I don't know yet," I said. "I didn't see this guy in good lighting." I relayed my imperfect description to Tony. "He was at St. Mark's, and the trip required a bodyguard."

Tony frowned when I mentioned the church. "St. Mark's?"

"You know it?"

"Old Catholic building. They got a priest there now . . . something of a maverick."

I didn't know if Tony referred to Father Larry's dodgy history, so I let it pass. "I'm more interested in a guy wearing a three-thousand-dollar suit and bringing a bodyguard to a church."

"Could be a few people," said Tony.

"Anyone you know well?"

Tony shrugged. "A man like me knows everyone a little." The waitress returned and set my salad and tea on the table. The bowl could have held an entree salad, and the small bowl of dressing would fill half a bottle. The perks of sitting at The Man's table. After she walked away again, Tony continued. "I've heard someone wants to build a new church."

"A new St. Mark's?"

"Yeah. It's old. A new one would be bigger and nicer."

I ruminated on the information over a bite of salad. "And

require quite a bit of construction. Which you just might have a piece of."

Tony smiled. "I just might."

"Where's this great new church supposed to be?"

"Right near the old one, I think. I know there's a lot of fundraising going on. The priest is into it, too."

Something else I could look into regarding Father Larry. Before I could say anything else, my main course arrived. The large plate could barely contain it. A family of chickens must have given their lives for the meal, and the sauce came from a half-gallon carton. "I hope this isn't the lunch portion," I said.

"Guests at my table are taken care of," Tony said.

"I appreciate it." So as not to be rude, I ate some chicken parm before continuing the conversation. It was quite good--the bird was cooked well, and the breading was both tasty and light. *Il Buon Cibo* had always made a mean sauce. "You said this guy is fundraising?" Tony nodded. "For the church?" He nodded again. "You get invited to these?"

"I get invited to every fundraiser in the city. Almost never go, though."

"You know when the next St. Mark's one is?"

Tony asked the nearest watchdog for the calendar. He produced some small-bindered monstrosity stuffed with papers and note cards. Tony opened the binder and flipped through it while I ate. Despite the setup looking like a mess, he found the answer after a minute of searching. "You're in luck," he said. "It's tonight."

I smiled around a mouthful of chicken parm. "I have a feeling my parents' foundation will be buying two tickets."

"You're gonna help build a church?"

"I'm trying to find whoever stabbed the guy near the old one."

Tony shook his head. "I don't think the guy I was thinking of is your man."

"Could have been one of his goons," I said, which earned me a glower from Tony's two. "A few of them have come after me."

"And you think they work for him."

"So far, it's him or the priest."

"Probably not the priest."

"Why?"

"All the guys I'm thinking of are real assholes."

I nodded. "Always a good reason."

CHAPTER 6

GLORIA LET ME DRIVE HER MERCEDES COUPE TO THE
fundraiser. Other than the automatic transmission—Gloria never
learned to drive a stick—I relished my turn behind the wheel.
The engine made going fast very easy. Without even trying, I let
the car ease over eighty on the highway, and I knew I could
double our speed and the coupe would still have more to give. On
top of it all, I felt pretty awesome zooming around in a car shaped
and colored like a rocket and wondered if having my mere Lexus
parked in her driveway would make Gloria the neighborhood
pariah.

We valeted the car and went inside. Years passed since I last
visited La Fontaine Bleue. In that time, the place had undergone
a total renovation in all but its strange spelling. Marble, granite,
and dark wood covered every available surface. Gold trim lent the
appearance of opulence even when the material didn't need it. A
good crowd gathered in the dining hall. I handed someone our
tickets, picked up a couple complimentary glasses of wine, and
headed inside.

The VIP tables were predictably close to the stage. I didn't
want to sit near them. No point in tipping off Father Larry or his

mysterious benefactor to my lurking. Most ringside tables were filled with a bunch of people I didn't know, but a couple I recognized from my parents' foundation shindigs, a familiar goon, and Father Larry. The money man hadn't arrived.

Gloria and I found a spot near the back of the room. We could see the stage, and the classical music playing told us the acoustics would let us hear everything. We made small talk with the other folks at the table, all of whom had at least ten years on us. To my surprise, Gloria chatted easily with everyone. She claimed she didn't relate to people well. Maybe I just needed to take her to more swanky fundraisers.

The wait staff, clad in traditional black and white, brought salads to our group and refilled water glasses all around. The starter dishes boasted of vibrant greens, cherry tomatoes, a lone slice of cucumber, and a bit of onion, all topped with some balsamic dressing. It looked better than it tasted.

After the staff took the salads away, someone got up on stage and made a few opening remarks in a monotone ill-suited for public address. He was Steve Lewis of the St. Mark's Rebuilding Committee, who wished us a lovely meal and promised more comments from more important people later. Gloria and I both needed a second glass of wine to deal with such a riveting agenda.

A few minutes later came the main course. Everyone got a petite filet mignon paired with mashed potatoes and green beans. The first thing I did was cut into the meat. A good steak should be cooked medium. Only barbarians eat it less done, and only philistines cook it longer. The inside showed a little pink, darkening a shade near the center, but no red. A nice medium.

Bits of small talk continued over dinner. Gloria and I both dodged the so-what-do-you-do line of questioning, me by saying I worked in finance, she by saying she decided to go back to school. In a crowd like this, I expect both to get believed with no blowback, and I was right. After the staff collected our dinner plates, they poured coffee.

Steve Lewis took the stage again. "You probably don't want to hear a lot more from me," he said, showing he at least possessed self-awareness. "So let me bring up a man who's been instrumental in our fundraising. We all know him as Father Larry. Please welcome Father Lawrence Toohey!"

The St. Mark's pastor took the microphone. He had swapped his usual priestly attire for black pants, a starched white shirt, and a black tie. Overall, not much of an improvement. He looked more like a mortician than a priest. Father Larry tapped the mike a couple times and cleared his throat.

"I'm not used to talking without a pulpit," he said to moderate laughter. One man at our table found that endlessly funny for reasons puzzling me and everyone else seated near him. "If you were hoping to hear from Mister V, I'm afraid he's not going to be able to make it tonight." Father Larry kept talking while I held my phone under the table and looked up Mister V. It was my first clue to the identity of the benefactor.

A few minutes of clever Googling didn't come up with anything. My mother would have chided me for using my phone at the dinner table during a speech. No one at the table seemed to notice my distraction or care. Father Larry would have Mister V in his phone, but I was too far away to make a Bluetooth attack work.

"St. Mark's has a strong community," Father Larry said. "We need a new church to grow the community." He kept talking, interrupted a few times by applause. The regular practice he got every weekend made Father Larry a decent speaker, if not a compelling one. The odds of me writing a check to St. Mark's began the evening at zero and remained there.

Father Larry wrapped up his speech a few minutes later. The wait staff brought out dessert in the form of a mediocre-looking chocolate cake. A few people lined up to shake Father Larry's hands, and some also gave him a check. An idea leapt into my head. "Want to say hello to the good father?" I said to Gloria.

She frowned in surprise. "Not really. He gave a nice speech, but I'm not going to donate."

I handed her my phone. "Can you go talk to him for a minute? Say whatever. He'd recognize me and try to run away, so I'd rather not go."

"What does your phone have to do with anything?" Gloria said. I smiled at her. "Oh." She grinned. "I should have known."

"If this works, I'll start calling you my lovely assistant," I said.

"It'll work." Gloria got up and walked toward the head table. I watched her departure with some interest. A few women in the room opted for gowns, but Gloria was the best dressed of the bunch. I still wanted to rip the dress off her later. She could afford a new one. I bantered with a few people seated nearby as I kept an eye on Gloria. She queued up near Father Larry, exchanged pleasantries, and shook his hand before talking to someone else.

I found out who in a minute when Steve Lewis introduced the fundraising coordinator. Cheryl Olson blushed and waved to the crowd as Lewis sang her praises. She and Gloria talked for a few more minutes before I got my phone back.

"Everything good?" Gloria said as I looked through my Bluetooth jacking app. It connected to other phones with the technology enabled, told me the owner's name, and displayed all contacts, calls, and texts. Bluetooth has an effective range of ten meters, so the app snagged a bunch of other phones. Father Larry's was among them. I deleted the rest without looking at them. Never let it be said I am not a principled hacker.

"I have what I need," I said. "Thanks."

"Sure," Gloria said. "I was talking to the fundraiser. I've seen her at a few things like this before. She does good work."

"You thinking of getting into fundraising?"

"I don't know." Gloria cast her eyes down.

"You'd be good at it," I said.

"Really?" She looked up and smiled.

"Sure. You're smart, you know a lot of people, and you're up on where to go for what events. You'd be a natural."

"Thanks." Gloria grabbed my hand and squeezed. Then, as if she realized she'd overstepped, she pulled her hand back. The smile remained, however.

"Besides," I said, "if you wear the same dress, men will donate like crazy."

"You just want to get me out of it later." I nodded. Gloria grinned anew. "Make sure it gets folded neatly on the floor."

* * *

IT DIDN'T. Clothing ended up on the stairway in Gloria's house. So did we for a while. Gloria's steps are covered in soft carpeting, but her bed proved a lot more comfortable. Despite living alone, Gloria owned a king bed. Our lustful romps took us over every centimeter of it at some point or another. When we had worn ourselves out, we both collapsed near the middle.

In the morning, I padded downstairs while Gloria slept. This made only the second time I'd seen her eat-in kitchen. I wanted one transplanted directly into my apartment. The problem was her kitchen would have consumed most of my place. For all the square footage, Gloria did very little cooking and confessed her efforts rarely ended well. I rummaged around until I found a skillet and some cooking utensils. The paucity of the refrigerator contents would have embarrassed many a bachelor—me included —but I could work with it. I found a half-dozen eggs, some butter, spinach, and a cheese that sounded fancy—and bore an expensive price tag—but smelled exactly like provolone.

Fifteen minutes later, I set two spinach and cheese omelets on the kitchen table, along with toast from a French baguette, and two steaming mugs of coffee. True to form, Gloria came downstairs a minute later. Eggs and coffee got her every time. "Wow," she said as she sat, "thanks for making breakfast."

"Thanks for having a great kitchen," I said.

"You do pretty well in yours." Gloria ate a bite of her omelet and nodded in appreciation.

"I could do a lot better here, especially if you stocked the fridge."

"Stay over more often, then," Gloria said with a smile. I smiled, too. Then, as if we both realized what our words meant, we ate and drank coffee in silence for a few minutes.

After we finished the omelets and toast and I poured us each a second cup, Gloria said, "Did you get what you needed last night?"

"For quite a while, yes," I said, grinning.

Color rose in Gloria's cheeks. "I meant from the fundraiser."

"I'll look in a little while," I said.

"Not in a rush?"

I shrugged. "If Father Larry is involved, waiting until I get home won't change anything. If he's not, he has to know who it is, and I'll still be able to get the info from his phone."

"What if he deletes the contact and texts?"

"Nothing really gets deleted," I said. "Most stuff is easy to recover."

Gloria stood and sashayed a few steps to me. "Since you're not in a hurry . . ." She swung a shapely leg over me and lowered herself onto my lap. "I got what I needed last night, too," she breathed into my ear. I felt the hairs on my arms stand at attention. "But I think I need more." She planted an aggressive kiss on me.

"I think I do, too," I said.

* * *

BACK IN MY OFFICE, I connected my phone to my computer to comb through the results on a larger screen. Father Larry kept a lot of contacts, none with any context. Because he was a priest, I presumed the women were parishioners or donors. maybe even friends, but not paramours. I saw a few names I recognized while skimming the list, but none jumped out at me.

I dumped Father Larry's phone calls into a database, then did the same for his texts. I could read them later; for now, I wanted to know who he called and texted the most. By a healthy margin, Father Larry's most frequent texting partner appeared in his contacts only as "D.V." The only two phone calls with this person both occurred more than a week before Dave Waugh's murder. I also checked Father Larry's voicemails. He deleted one from DV. The timestamp showed it came in shortly after the murder. I couldn't play the audio, but phone carriers transcribe voicemails now—helpful both for customers and the hackers who have jacked their data.

I heard it's done. He won't be a problem anymore.

Whoever D.V. was, he left a careful message. He "heard" whatever it is, so he didn't directly implicate himself. The "he" was never mentioned, and I imagined a good defense attorney crafting many flights of fancy wherein "he won't be a problem anymore" turned out as a benefit for the subject. The timing was convenient, easily spun as coincidental, and thus fell far short of being a smoking gun. Still, it gave me something to work with, a thread I could try to unravel.

To do so, I needed to find out who D.V. was. Father Larry wouldn't tell me. My gut said he would be as rude to me as a priest could be without feeling the soles of his shoes getting hot. A few clever Google searches later, associating D.V. with fundraising and St. Mark's, I uncovered Demetrius Vasilios.

Another search told me he was the owner and proprietor of Vasilios Construction. An article in The Catholic Review mentioned his philanthropy and his formation of a committee to determine the company best suited to build the new St. Mark's. After exhaustive digging, Vasilios reached the shocking conclusion his company would be best. Several articles mentioned him as a generous donor to various Catholic charities and to St. Mark's in particular. None of them mentioned why.

With Google failing me, I went to conduct an offline search.

* * *

"What do you want to know about that greaser for?" Tony Rizzo said from across his table.

While much of Little Italy had gone upscale, Tony remained the same. He didn't alter his menu to accommodate changing tastes and desires for healthier food, and he could always be counted on for an ethnic slur. "Not a fan?" I said.

Tony waved his hand and scowled. "He's OK, I guess. Don't know why he likes the Catholics, though. Fucking Greeks have their own church."

"Maybe he's a fan of the First Amendment," I suggested.

My remark drew a snort from Tony. "My guess is he prefers the second."

Now we were getting somewhere. "So he's the type who might employ a goon or two." One of Tony's bruisers looked at me. "No offense." He did not look offended; in fact, his neutral expression made me wonder if he were alive.

"Definitely," Tony said.

I sipped my iced tea. When I came in, Tony offered me a meal as usual. I didn't want to make this a long visit, however. While I liked Tony, I knew my career choice didn't enthuse him, and I didn't want to lean on him for dirt on other people. "How legit is the construction business?" I said.

"Totally legit," said Tony. "It's a good company. They know how to get things done and how shit works."

His favorable review meant Tony had a piece of the company. Even the things he did as an organized crime boss were old school. He refused to dip his toe into the ransomware waters, for instance. If I mentioned it, I'm sure he would have a crack about the Russians at the ready. "He headed up some committee to find the best company to build the new St. Mark's," I said. "Guess which company he picked."

"His own. I know."

"You do?"

"You think a big construction project happens in Baltimore without me knowing about it?"

"I suppose not." I waited. Tony hadn't been this specific during our recent conversation.

"I didn't tell you everything I know before," he said. "No point dragging the wrong guy through the mud."

"Now we know he's dirty."

"Vasilios had the paperwork filed weeks ago. Had his permits lined up and everything."

"All before before the story hit," I said, "and before Dave Waugh was killed."

Tony frowned. "He the kid got stabbed near the church?"

"Yes."

"You think Vasilios did it?" I told Tony—without revealing my methods—what I learned about Vasilios' voicemail and texts with Father Larry. "Shitty court case," he said, "but you and I both know what happened."

I needed to ask this question. "Tony, would it hurt you if Vasilios went down for this?"

Tony smiled. I've known him most of my life, and I've seen

him smile a lot. This one was sincere. "I appreciate you asking me," he said. "Vasilios has a younger brother, helps him with the company. Let's just say the kid brother knows how the game is played, too."

"All right," I said with a nod. "I don't know where this is going to go, but Vasilios looks dirty."

"He does." Tony looked at me for a moment. It started to get uncomfortable. "This is an interesting job for you, C.T. I feel your parents' influence in some of it. You're a smart kid. You know a lot of things. I think you can do good work for people."

"Thanks, Tony," I said.

"Don't mention it. Be sure to have a meal next time you're here. You're my friend. I enjoy it when my friends eat here."

"I will." I'd try to stay on Tony's good side along the way. He stabled more muscle than Vasilios, and he hired from a better talent pool. I didn't need to end up on the wrong side of his ledger.

CHAPTER 7

BACK AT HOME, I RESEARCHED VASILIOS' COMPANY. Everything looked on the up-and-up. The company worked projects all across the state, turned a profit, paid bonuses to employees, and volunteered time and labor to charities. I found plenty of pictures of Vasilios smiling or shaking hands with someone else, usually a city or state luminary. More digging on local forums, blogs, Facebook posts, tweets, and subreddits revealed a few people displeased with Vasilios' success. They came armed with uncharitable theories. I figured those naysayers worked for construction companies which declined to pay Tony Rizzo. Vasilios paid his share, and one of the perks appeared to be a wealth of contracts in the city.

I thought about what Tony said. Dave Waugh going public, or the press turning his blog posts into a big story, would expose Father Larry's past and scuttle the new St. Mark's. Such an event would cost Vasilios in both money and reputation. I couldn't help but wonder if he greased any palms inside city hall. It would be more money down the drain or one or more angry city employees who wouldn't be getting the usual graft and could threaten future projects. Either way, bad for Vasilios.

The information was good, but I wanted more. I wanted dirt from inside the company. Their website looked like a professional designed it: it featured sharp pictures, a defined menu structure, and well-edited text. Like many sites, it ran on WordPress. WP is quite good, but as with any popular software or platform, people less ethical than I will discover and post its vulnerabilities. Then the company releases a patch, the hackers poke and prod the new version to discover the weaknesses, and so on. Such is the cycle of life for large software companies.

I soon discovered I didn't need a WordPress vulnerability, though. Vasilios' site had one far older. Database admins use a language called SQL to query and maintain their information stores. Users interact with them, on a basic level, via things like online forms. The databases are supposed to be protected from user malfeasance. However, some sites are vulnerable to people like me entering specific commands into a form and thus swiping the keys to the kingdom. SQL injection attacks have been known for years, and there are several methods to mitigate their effectiveness. Vasilios didn't use any of them. I got full access with a few dozen keystrokes.

It gave me a wealth of information: detailed employee records, accounts payable, accounts received, construction equipment, insurance policies, and a full listing of IT assets and accounts. Never one to refuse so obvious an invitation, I set my sights on a conference room PC. For some reason, it still ran Windows XP years after Microsoft ended support for the operating system. Once I got past the firewall, knocking over the XP box would be easy. I took my time and setup a connection to the conference room PC. One malicious payload later, and I took control of it.

Firewalls are good at keeping people out. Once you get in, however, most firewalls can do little to stop you. It's like a huge stone fence topped with razor wire. Getting past it is a challenge, but anyone who does no longer has to deal with the wall. I was on the inside now. Using the list of IT accounts, I made myself an administrator, migrated to a random server, and then pivoted to the email server. I didn't want to lose time reading the emails. The longer I lingered in the network, the higher the chance someone or something would take note of me. I downloaded email records from the important people in the company, erased my footprints, and logged off.

Something nagged at me, so I went back to the website. On the "Contact Us" page, I saw a link to email the administrator with any problems. I held my mouse over the link. It read *yanni@vasiliosconstr.biz*. Son of a bitch. Vasilios' son planted the confession idea in Ernie's head. I wondered how much he knew about the sins of his father. The old man needed to go down for this.

Light reading lay ahead to make it happen.

* * *

AFTER DOING some of the work onscreen, I needed a break for lunch. I also formulated an angle for what to do with my treasure trove of Vasilios' insider information. My plan required a little help, so I made a phone call and arranged to meet a friend for lunch.

Isabella's Brick Oven sat nestled among a bunch of other Italian *ristoranti* in Little Italy. It boasted of the best pizza of all of them, however, so when Joey Trovato suggested it, I jumped at the prospect. The beige brickwork and classic green awning hearkened back to a different era of restaurants, before things like tasting menus and gluten-free crusts. Perhaps feeling a bit regal, I ordered the King Richard with four different kinds of meat, then sat at a booth across from Joey.

Joey was a black Sicilian who'd struggled with his weight

since we were kids. Despite being six feet tall and three hundred pounds, Joey possessed a surprising amount of athleticism. I knew a bunch of skinny people who couldn't outrun him in a distance race. None of them could keep up with him at a dinner table, either. When I saw Joey nursing a soda and a small eggplant parmesan sub, I was surprised. He most likely expected a pizza and something else still coming out.

"Hi, C.T. Been a couple weeks."

"I can't afford to take you to lunch every week," I said.

Joey grinned. "Sure you can."

"We could meet at your house. I know you can cook."

"I ain't providing the expertise *and* the meal," said Joey.

"Who said this wasn't a social call?"

"You did."

"Right," I said. "Fair enough." The waitress dropped off my pizza. It looked like a meal baked for royalty. The meat generously added, the cheese perfectly golden brown, and the crust managed to look both light and substantial at the same time. There are few substitutes for a good brick-oven pie. I let it cool for a minute before separating a piece and taking a bite. Delicious.

"Where's your pizza?" I said before taking another bite.

"Eh. I'm not very hungry."

I'm rarely struck speechless, but Joey admitting to not being hungry did it. All I could manage between my surprise and mouthfuls was a confused, "Mmm?"

"I had an early lunch," Joey said. "It followed an early breakfast and a mid-morning brunch."

"Makes sense to have a small fourth meal, then," I said. "Gotta save room for the fifth and sixth."

"You're hilarious."

I ate more pizza while Joey finished his sub. After a few minutes, he said, "So what can I do for you today?"

"You've heard of Vasilios Construction?"

"Most people have."

"Most people don't know the owner might be a killer," I whispered.

"Seriously?" he said. I nodded. "Damn. What can I do?"

Joey, like me, worked to help people. He set them up with new identities. He'd been doing it for at least five years. Anytime I needed information about someone who might have disappeared, I talked to Joey. He's seen a lot of people, heard their bad beat stories, and helped them vanish. I could have asked him about Dave Waugh, but I had something else in mind. "Can you make me a press ID?" I said.

Joey frowned. "Being a crusading detective ain't enough?"

"It's more than enough." I paused. "I just . . . have an angle on this one. I think a press ID would allow me to play it up."

"I'm sure you could make one yourself."

"But not a good one. Not one to stand up to scrutiny." A little flattery never hurt. Besides, Joey did excellent work.

"OK," Joey said. "Text me a good picture of yourself."

"Could take a while," I said. "There are so many to choose from."

"I know the feeling," Joey said with a smile.

"Can you drop it off later?"

"You trying to rush greatness?"

I put my hand over my chest and feigned offense. "Me? Never. I am, however, trying to keep greatness on a reasonable schedule."

"Fine," Joey said. "I'll drop it by later."

"Thanks," I said. "It'll give me time to do some more light reading."

"Do I want to know?"

"Probably not."

"Will it help you bust Vasilios?"

"It's my hope."

Joey raised his mostly-empty glass. "To freedom of the press," he said.

* * *

JOEY DELIVERED my press ID a couple hours later. The handsome face looking at me through the plastic belonged to Trent Reasoner of The Investigative Voice. "Is this paper still a thing?" I said.

"Last I checked," said Joey.

I thought about objecting to the name, realized I had no ground to stand on, and scuttled the idea. Joey left, and I finished my research. I read a bunch of internal emails where Vasilios made reference to St. Marks, plus a few veiled mentions of Tony Rizzo. Any references to Dave Waugh were framed by the problems a murder would present to the new St. Mark's project. One email written the morning after Dave Waugh's murder celebrated the fact an unnamed individual got what was coming to him. No further context. It didn't constitute a smoking gun, a cooling gun, or a gun of any sort. I was trying to hit a bull's eye twenty-five yards down range with a hammer.

Getting back into Vasilios' network could give me more ammo. People have gotten more careful in email over the years as accounts get compromised and legitimate records get subpoenaed. Maybe Vasilios harbored something incriminating on his personal shared drive. It wasn't likely, though. Any administrator could have accessed it, and I doubted Vasilios wanted the IT staff to know he took delight in someone's murder. Those things caused people to ask questions.

I looked at my watch. If Vasilios was as hard-working as his website wanted me to believe, he would still be at the office.

Armed with my press credential—and a pistol in the car—I drove to Vasilios Construction.

* * *

THE CLOCK STRUCK four o'clock as I pulled into the parking lot. Vasilios Construction sat in an industrial area of Baltimore on Holabird Avenue. Some of the industry here left when GM shuttered their nearby plant on Broening Highway in 2005. Then a few years ago, Amazon took over the space and used it as a distribution center. It was another sign of the old economy changing in Baltimore. Once-thriving buildings were either razed or remained as decaying ghosts of the bygone era. Soon, only the port would be left. I had no idea if the Amazon facility counted as industry, but I enjoyed getting my packages four hours after I ordered them.

A one-story building about the size of a large rancher looked like the company's office. Past it were a bunch of garages and other spots to keep heavy equipment. I watched someone park a backhoe as easily as I parked my Lexus before I walked into the office. The secretary managed to give me a look merging friendly and wary. She might broadcast a good smile if she cared to. Maybe they weren't used to handsome men walking through the door here. "Can I help you?" I guessed the woman for late thirties. Curly blonde hair framed glasses, and she wore a blue company polo. The friendliness faded from her expression.

I showed her my press credential. "I'd like to ask Mr. Vasilios some questions."

She studied the ID through chic narrow lenses. "Mr. Reasoner?" I nodded. "Did you make an appointment?"

"I'm afraid not," I said, giving her a high-wattage smile. I didn't offer my best smile, merely a good one. Vasilios didn't need his secretary fawning over me, after all.

"What's the nature of your visit?" she said.

"Someone showed me some . . . documents which don't paint the company in a good light. I haven't released them. I was hoping to talk to Mr. Vasilios about them."

"I'll see if he can fit you in." She stood and walked away. Two doors were behind her desk, making her a semi-literal gatekeeper. She opened the one on the left and disappeared down a hallway. I sat on a padded blue task chair of moderate comfort. The secretary's desk held two computers and three monitors, plus a bunch of notebooks, calendars, and schedules. Vasilios needed some apps. Other calendars hung on the walls nearby, each marked up in different colors. Blue dominated the office from the chairs to the window trim to the mood.

A minute later, the lady returned with two men who were not Vasilios. One was the spiky-haired blond goon I met before. The other one was of similar size and build and probably employed for the same reason. "Mr. Vasilios can't see you right now," she said, struggling to contain a grin. "These gentlemen will talk to you instead. Outside." I took this to mean Vasilios' secretary knew he was dirty. She reveled in it. I expected her to watch from the window while Tweedleblond and Tweedledumb tried to convince me to stay away.

"Yeah, outside," the blond one aped her sarcastic tone. His partner wore his brown hair in a short buzz and smiled like a fool.

"I guess we can do the interview outside," I said, playing along. I exited first, careful to keep an eye out for the legbreakers following me.

"You ain't no reporter," the other one said.

"And you're not an English teacher," I said as I walked toward my car parked about halfway down the lot. I watched my escorts in the reflections of every side window and windshield I passed.

"Keep walking, jerk," said the blond one.

About twenty paces later, I stopped at a vehicle not my own. My Lexus sat three spaces away. If we were going to fight, I didn't want my car to be collateral damage. I've owned it since my sophomore year of college, and Lexus doesn't make sports sedans with manual transmissions anymore. "Sure your boss doesn't want to talk to me?" I said.

The brown-haired one glared. "He told us to get rid of you." I didn't doubt it. I also didn't want to wait for his enforcers to make their moves. In the confines of a parking lot, I didn't want to have them dictate the situation to me. When Brown Buzz reached for me from my right, I gave him a quick, sharp jab to the solar plexus. It wouldn't put him down, but it would leave him sucking wind for a few seconds.

I immediately turned to my left. Spiky Hair processed what happened. Before the hamster spun the wheel fast enough for him to make a decision, I stomped on his foot. Pain made him bend down a little, where I elbowed him twice in the face, then shoved him headfirst into the closest car door. Brown Hair had recovered enough to glower and walk toward me by this point. I blocked his punch, slugged him in the stomach, and pulled his jacket over his head. While he flailed about, I boxed his ears, gave him two more good body shots, and put him down with a knee to the face.

I looked at the office. Sure enough, the secretary watched from the window. She didn't look happy. I waved to her as I walked to my car.

CHAPTER 8

After I left Vasilios Construction, I drove to St. Mark's. Father Larry sat in his office reading a book. He frowned at me when he looked up. "'Hot tempers cause arguments, but patience brings peace,'" I said.

The glower softened. "Proverbs."

"It seemed appropriate."

"Did you Google it on the way over?" said Father Larry.

"Where's your faith in other people, Father?" I pointed at a guest chair. Father Larry sighed and nodded. "Considering the company you keep," I said, "I guess I shouldn't be surprised."

"What's that supposed to mean?" Father Larry closed his book, leaving the back facing up. I couldn't tell what it was.

"Your buddy Vasilios."

My comment made the priest frown anew, and he paired it with a vigorous shake of his head. "No," he said. "Not Mr. Vasilios."

"He's in bed with the mob," I said. "He has professional goons on his payroll. And he has motive for wanting Dave Waugh dead."

"That's ridiculous."

"Father, the only two people a preponderance of evidence shows would have wanted to kill Dave are you and Vasilios." I paused while Father Larry continued to wag his head. "I'm pretty sure you didn't do it. Process of elimination leaves your benefactor."

"Perhaps it was a robbery." Father Larry said.

"Not many robbers stab their victims a dozen times in the chest. It's barbarism and suggests hatred."

"What about—"

"He did it, or he ordered one of his men to do it." I watched Father Larry for a reaction. "I think you know it . . . or at least suspect."

Father Larry bowed his head and rubbed the bridge of his nose. "What do you want, Mr. Ferguson?"

"What I've always wanted: the truth."

"I'm tempted to tell you you couldn't handle it," he said with a small smile.

I grinned. "I appreciate the movie reference, Father, but I can take it."

"Fine." Father Larry looked around the room. I followed his gaze as he looked at two Bibles and a crucifix. Maybe they gave him the inspiration he sought. "I'd suspected for a while that Mr. Vasilios knew more than he told me."

"You two talked about Dave Waugh's murder?" I said.

"He was our major benefactor. It's hard to avoid telling someone like him that a man was murdered almost on our doorstep."

"Fair enough."

"Anyway, Mr. Vasilios didn't seem very surprised, even though he said he hadn't heard. He told me all the right things."

"Why not go to the police?"

"With what?" the priest said. "I had a suspicion. That's all."

"And he's building you a new church," I said.

Father Larry paused, then nodded. "Yes. I admit that shouldn't have been a consideration, but I wanted the best for our congregation."

"So you never clued in the cops?"

"Only the basics," he said.

I started to say something, then stopped. Father Larry had come upon the murder scene. He would have seen it all. He hadn't told the police anything special. "You're Ernie Chin's source," I said. "The one he wouldn't give up."

"Yes," Father Larry said with a nod. "I've known Ernie for a couple years. I admit his blog is ghoulish, but he does good work."

"But the things you told him, the level of detail?"

"I have two brothers in law enforcement. Heard a lot of shop talk."

"What were you hoping to accomplish?" I said.

"I meant what I said about wanting the best for our congregation. There was another part of me, though, that wanted to see justice done. I didn't know if Mr. Vasilios had done anything, but I felt he knew more than he should have. I hoped the police would look into it."

"Why not simply tell them?"

Father Larry smiled. It didn't reach his eyes. "Mr. Vasilios usually talks to me in the confessional."

"Clever," I said. "He figures you won't break the sacrament."

"I haven't. I can't."

"What about the conversation we're having right now?"

"You know a lot already." Father Larry shrugged. "I haven't mentioned anything he told me in confidence."

An organ played in the background as I pondered how to get Father Larry to dime out his money man. Even in the rectory, the speakers carried the sound well enough for me to recognize the song. "Ave Maria," I said.

"Our organist practices on Friday evenings," Father Larry said, "not that she needs it."

An idea wormed its way into my brain. If I couldn't get Father Larry to give up Vasilios, maybe I could induce Vasilios to give himself up unwittingly.

"Father, does Vasilios take confession regularly?"

"He does, every Saturday before the five o'clock service. He comes in around four-fifteen."

"So you expect to see him tomorrow?" I said.

"Yes."

"Do you think you could get him to confess?"

Father Larry recoiled. "It's a sacrament, not an interrogation."

"You obviously get along with him," I said. "He trusts you. He wants to build a new church with you at the center. Do you think you could steer the conversation toward a real confession?"

"Even if I could," Father Larry said, "I don't see how that would help you. I won't break the sanctity of the confessional."

"I don't think I need you to, Father."

"I'm not sure I like the sound of that."

"The less you know, the better. But I have an idea. If you want to see justice done, it might work."

The priest sighed and sagged back in his chair. "And what do I have to do?"

"Nothing," I said.

"Nothing?"

"I'll take care of everything."

"I'm not sure I like this," Father Larry said.

"You won't be breaking any of your vows to the church," I said. "The Vatican isn't going to send someone to excommunicate you."

Father Larry considered it for a moment. "Very well," he said. "I will say this, Mr. Ferguson—if whatever you're planning goes south on you, I'm not going to give you any cover."

"Of course not, Father," I said. "Lying is a sin."

* * *

I CALLED Rich from my car. "What are you doing tonight?" I said when he answered.

"I just left the precinct," he said. "Haven't thought much about it. Why?"

"Would you still describe yourself as an audiophile?"

"Have you seen my stereo?"

"No one has stereos anymore."

"My point." Rich paused. "Wait, what plan are you thinking up involving my system?"

"Nothing," I said. "Your stereo will not be harmed in the execution of my scheme."

"Good thing," said Rich.

"I do, however, need your knowledge of wiring and sound."

"For what? Is this about the blogger?"

"I'll be by your house in an hour," I said.

"Can't wait," Rich said and hung up.

He needed to wait about an hour and five minutes. Rich lived in Hamilton in a large Victorian he bought when his parents, my aunt and uncle, died. I loved the large yard and detached garage. Rich's house could have fit my apartment inside it at least three times over. The structure must have been a century old, and it showed its age in a few areas. Rich, however, modernized it with his own two hands—new windows, new paint, a better porch, and wood flooring. Plus other fixes I hadn't seen. If he hadn't chosen the Army and police route, my cousin could have been a hell of a carpenter.

Rich offered me a beer when I walked in. It was an IPA, so I accepted. For his part, Rich drank some pale wheat beer. "What's this about?" he said when we had each lubricated our throats.

"I think I know who killed Dave Waugh," I said.

"You think?"

We sat on opposite ends of the large sofa in Rich's living room. I laid it all on the table for him. He nodded a few times during my monologue but never interrupted. "The priest won't break the confessional. I had an idea to make his stubbornness irrelevant."

"And it involves wiring something for audio?" Rich said.

"Yes."

"What?"

"The confessional," I said.

"Are you crazy?" said Rich. "You can't wire a confessional for sound."

"Why not?"

"Because it's . . . it's wrong."

"It's a small, enclosed room," I said. "It's not far from two large speakers. Hypothetically, if the priest got Vasilios to confess and everyone heard it, we'd have him."

"I wish I were a lawyer," Rich said. "This doesn't sound like it will hold up."

"Why not? He's not confessing under duress."

Rich took a long swig of his beer. As weak as it looked, he would need a couple more bottles to come around. "There's a reasonable expectation of privacy in a confessional," he said.

"Now you sound like a lawyer," I said.

"Someone like Vasilios is going to have good lawyers."

"Then use his public confession to go after him," I said. "Even things like his company emails."

"Why his company emails?" Rich narrowed his eyes at me. "What did you do?"

"Nothing. I happen to think someone like Vasilios might drop hints in an email."

"Incredible," Rich said, shaking his head. "If you've read the guy's emails, why go to all this trouble?"

"If I did something like you're hinting, the police would still need to do it legally as part of the investigation."

Rich finished his beer in one pull and rolled his eyes. He left the room and came back a moment later with a second bottle. I looked at the stereo dominating the massive entertainment center. Rich accrued the pieces over the years and wired everything together himself, including the seven speakers. The size of the system made it the focus of Rich's spartan living room, not the more modest TV. "What about sound in the confessional?" Rich said.

"What do you mean?"

"If we wire it for audio, they'll be able to hear everything in there, too. Vasilios will know he's being broadcast."

"Shit," I said. "Is there a way to silence it?"

"Short of fully soundproofing it, no." Rich paused. "But we might be able to mitigate it."

"Good."

"What's our time frame?"

"We have to start tonight and finish by morning."

"Jesus Christ," Rich said, shaking his head. "You really think this could work?"

"You think you can do the wiring?" I said.

"Yes."

"Then I'll say yes, too. I think it could work."

"I need to get a few things together," Rich said. He looked at his beer. "And I might need another of these. Give me about fifteen minutes."

"Take your time," I said.

At the specified time, Rich came back into the room carrying a box and a duffel bag. "Let's go before I change my mind," he said.

So we went.

* * *

FIVE HOURS LATER, we finished. Getting into the church had been easy. Places designed to welcome people rarely invest in good locks. Rich and I called an audible after we got there. The confessional is near the back of the church, so we wired it into the speakers only at the front of the church. I brought two small microphones and a speaker I previously bought from the local spy store. We set up the mikes to broadcast to the front and spliced off a speaker wire into the well-hidden small one. The organ music it would pipe into the confessional should eliminate the odds of Vasilios overhearing himself telling everything to Father Larry. The combination of a small speaker and a low volume setting would prevent the rerouted music from being too loud.

If the priest upheld his part of the deal.

I couldn't worry about those details at two-thirty in the morning, however. The good father knew his role in this. He said he could do it, and on some level, I think he wanted justice for Dave Waugh. Now I needed him to come through. If he didn't, I would need to dig deeper into the network at Vasilios Construction and hope for the best.

I settled into a fitful sleep.

* * *

BY FOUR O'CLOCK, I was in St. Mark's and told Father Larry of our plan. Without acknowledgement, he helped by having the sacristan rope off the first three pews. Rich was already there along with two officers I recognized only after picturing them in uniform. I sat in the second pew, right in front of Rich. When

Vasilios came in, I hoped Rich's body would screen me from his view. While I sat there, I tried to look devout. It was a struggle.

"I didn't expect the pews to be roped off," Rich whispered.

"Good move," I said, keeping my voice low.

"I'm not so sure. People are going to wonder why we're sitting here."

"Wonder, sure. They're not going to come up and ask us about it. No one wants to make a scene like that in church."

"I hope you're right," said Rich.

"I am."

To keep myself from turning to look for Vasilios, I tried to focus on the organ. Even with the speaker rewiring Rich and I had done, the music came through at what sounded like normal volume. I wondered if we would strain to hear Vasilios' confession.

About ten minutes crawled by, and Rich said, "He's here." I half-turned and saw Vasilios walk in, accompanied by one of the goons who had chased me back to my apartment. Neither appeared to notice me, but I turned around and slouched in the pew in case.

"I hope they didn't see me," I said.

"Doesn't look like it," Rich said, shaking his head. "He's chatting with the priest now. The other guy is sitting in the last row." Rich paused. I waited. "It looks like Toohey waved to the organist. Now they went in."

The organ music grew softer and featured more high notes. Voices came through the speakers. "Good to see you again," Father Larry said.

"Always good to be here," said Vasilios.

"Shall we begin?" If Father Larry were nervous, I couldn't hear it in his voice.

"Bless me, Father, for I have sinned. It's been a week since my last confession."

"Anything you'd like to talk about?" Father Larry sounded like a shrink. I hoped he stopped before asking Vasilios how killing Dave Waugh made him feel.

"The usual," Vasilios said. "It's hard to run a successful business without being a sinner."

Chatter went up in the church, meaning others noticed the voices coming through the speakers. We didn't need them to interfere. Rich and I added some soundproofing to the confessional, but it wasn't complete or foolproof. Some idiot yelling at or banging on the door would spoil everything.

"It's under control," Rich said.

"What do you mean?" I said.

"We have officers over there. No one will interrupt them."

"We'd better hope the bodyguard isn't given to shouting, then."

". . . angered Jesus," we heard Father Larry say.

"Wasn't that about gambling?" Vasilios said. "I don't gamble. Well, not in the traditional sense." Sure. He just murdered people or ordered someone in his stable of hired muscle to do it.

Father Larry's sigh came through the speakers as a soft hiss. "Mr. Vasilios, I think there's something else. Something . . . below the surface."

"What are you, my shrink now?" Valid question. The priest would need to walk a tightrope here.

"Not at all," Father Larry said. "But I can see it in your face. I hear it in your voice. God sees it in your heart."

"You mean that kid?" Vasilios said.

"What kid?"

"You know, the prick with the blog."

"This is a church," Father Larry said.

"Sorry, Father. The guy who was writing all the sh . . . all the stuff. He kicked up a lot of dirt. We couldn't have it."

""Should we seek forgiveness through prayers to cleanse your soul?"

I never told you this. Good thing we're in the confessional." Vasilios paused, took a deep breath, and kept going. " The blog guy guy was a problem. If his story got picked up, it could have ruined everything."

"A new St. Mark's could have another priest," said Father Larry.

"Not the same church, then," Vasilios said. "We don't want someone else. We need you, Father. You're flawed like we are. When you preach about mistakes and regret, I can feel it. It's real. Other priests don't know anything about that."

"I'm flattered, Demetrius, but what are you saying?"

"The guy needed to die. So I had Johnny do it."

Rich nodded, and a smile spread across his face. "We got him," he said. "It worked."

I looked around the church. We were not the only ones interested in the conversation coming from the confessional. The rest of the congregation surged to one side of the church. If they rushed the door, three cops wouldn't keep them at bay. Even the goon in the back row moved up. When he started toward the confessional, one of the cops interceded and kept him back.

"Let's go," Rich said. He and the two other officers stood, and I went with them to the other side of the church. Rich's badge cleared a path for us. Vasilios' bodyguard spotted me and glowered. I smiled at him and waved, which did not improve his mood. When Rich pounded on the confessional door, the henchman tried to slip away. Two cops stopped him and encouraged him to take a seat.

Father Larry opened the door. Vasilios sat in a small chair. He frowned at everyone. "What's the meaning of this interruption?" Father Larry said.

"Demetrius Vasilios, you're under arrest," Rich said.

The congregation applauded while Rich Mirandized Vasilios, interrupted several times by the latter's crowing about his attorneys. The two cops who came with Rich led Vasilios away, and the other three escorted his sidekick.

"I hope we can make this stick," I said.

"Me, too," said Rich. "Hey, at least now you can give Liz Fleming some good news."

Maybe she'd even be wearing a short skirt this time.

CHAPTER 9

THE NEXT MORNING, MY CELL PHONE BUZZING ON THE nightstand woke me. I glanced at the clock as I answered: seven forty-five. Ugh.

"We're going to question Vasilios soon," Rich said. "I figured you might want to sit in."

"Wow, thanks," I said. "You sure a mere civilian like me can hang with a detective like you?"

"Try to keep up," Rich said, and then broke the call.

I showered quickly, then grabbed a breakfast sandwich and coffee at Dunkin' Donuts en route to the precinct. I almost indulged in a donut, but that would have made me feel too much like a cop. I didn't need the feeling anytime but especially not before nine AM. Inside the station, I found Rich at his desk and dropped off the extra coffee I bought for him. "A token of appreciation," I said.

"Thanks," said Rich before he took a sip. "You ready?"

"Do I get to ask questions?"

"Probably best if you keep them to a minimum."

"How's Vasilios still here, anyway?" I said. "Wealthy assholes like him should have lawyers who could spring them."

"We're still considering charges," Rich said, and a smile spread over his lips. "His mouthpiece's pissed and self-righteous, but there's nothing he can do about it."

"Sounds like it'll be fun," I said, and we went to the interview room. It was about ten by ten, with a large table and four shabby chairs in the center. A darkened window dominated the left wall. Vasilios sat in a chair on the far side, handcuffed to a bar on the tabletop. His expression resembled someone who sucked a lemon for an hour. His lawyer, a paunchy black man with a full head of gray hair, looked equally cheery.

"My client does not need to be shackled," the attorney said when Rich closed the door.

"He's not," Rich said. "He's just cuffed."

"You know what I meant."

"Sure, but you bastards always twist what other people say." Rich sat, took out a key, and undid Vasilios' cuffs. "How's it feel to be on the other end?"

The lawyer didn't take the bait. Instead, he nodded toward me and said, "Who's this?"

"The private investigator who figured out what happened," said Rich.

"A civilian?"

"You're a civilian," I pointed out.

"I'm an attorney at law," he said as if it were a point of pride.

"I was trying to be nice."

While the lawyer seethed, Rich said, "Mr. Johnstone, your client confessed to his role in the murder of Dave Waugh."

"I was set up," Vasilios said, rubbing his wrist. He pointed at me. "This prick must've had something to do with it."

I stayed quiet rather than give in to the barb. Later, I would need to pat myself on the back for this show of restraint. "A bunch of people at the church heard him," Rich said. " They make a lot of witnesses for the state's attorney."

"And just why was everyone able to hear my client's words?" Johnstone said. "Confession shouldn't be open mike night."

"Faulty wiring," Rich said.

"Faulty wiring?"

"There's little difference between a speaker and a microphone."

"We'll have some questions about that, I'm sure. Now, what are you charging my client with?"

Rich went over the list, which was voluminous, and Johnstone protested, which was pointless. "Take it up at the bail hearing," Rich said.

"We will," Johnstone said.

Rich and I left while Johnstone conferred with his slimy client. We got intercepted by Lieutenant Leon Sharpe emerging from the observation room. Sharpe was black, bald, and built like a defensive end. When he turned to face us, I saw the bars on his collar. He had been upgraded to captain.

"Captain," Rich said with a nod.

"Gentlemen," said Sharpe. He stopped in the middle of the hallway, blocking anyone over eighty pounds from squirting past him. "Good work on this one."

"Thanks," Rich and I said at the same time.

"Was the wiring really faulty?"

"I thought it was quite good," I said.

Sharpe smirked. "I'm gonna keep watching you," he said to me. Then he turned and walked the other direction.

"He just got promoted a couple weeks ago," Rich said when we were back at his desk.

"What does that mean for you?"

He shrugged. "Nothing yet. Sharpe oversees violent crime enforcement. He's in my command chain but not directly above me. Took him a while to get moved up." Rich lowered his voice. "A lot of people associate him with door-kicking and arresting."

" Aren't those good things?" I said.

"Depends who you talk to. Some say it got a little out of hand, went into harassment territory. Then you add in Freddie Gray and the DOJ report. Leon got some blowback there. But he's smart enough to adapt and overcome."

"Should I be concerned he's going to keep an eye on me?"

Rich grinned. "Probably."

* * *

SINCE I WAS ALREADY DOWNTOWN, I doubled down on the fun by stopping by the Public Defender's Office. To my surprise, I found Liz Fleming there on a Sunday. "You are a very dedicated public servant," I said as I poked my head in.

Sunday must have meant a relaxed dress code. I didn't mind. Standing at a shopworn file cabinet, Liz wore jeans hugging all the right places along with a sweater one size too small. She grinned. It didn't measure up to her smile, but I could live with it. "Just catching up on paperwork."

"How's Ernie?" I walked in and sat in one of her guest chairs. Their comfort had not improved.

"Free," Liz said. "He got released early this morning."

"Good. I hope he's learned something from all this."

"Me, too."

"I'll have to check his blog later," I said. "His lessons need to extend past traffic increases and monetization."

"If he does something like this again," Liz said, "he's on his own."

"Did you talk to him?"

Liz nodded. She pulled a large mug of coffee from behind her laptop. Now I wanted another cup. I was far too young to be up so early on a Sunday. "For a minute or so, right before he got out. He was very grateful to us."

"Us?" I said with a smile.

"Hey!" said Liz, "I filed some paperwork like a boss." She grinned again. Even though she co-opted some of the credit, I would work with her any time.

"I suppose you did. Good thing, too—I'm much better at fighting off goons than I am at busywork."

"We made a pretty good team," Liz said, more or less echoing my thoughts.

"Maybe next time, you can do more of the heavy lifting."

The remark got me a full smile. "But you do it so well. Sure you don't want a job?"

"I have a job," I said.

"Yes." Liz scrutinized me. I didn't give her a reaction. Her inspection spilled over into checking-me-out territory. I didn't mind. "That's still a bit of a mystery."

"Maybe one of your investigators can solve it. If they're not too busy or too incompetent."

"We have good investigators," Liz said, frowning.

"And yet you worked with me," I said, "the newcomer with the mysterious background."

"They were busy."

"I'm sure they were."

Liz looked down at a file on her desk. "I need to get back to my work, Mr. Ferguson. Thanks for coming by." So much for any flirting. If I teamed with Liz again, I would have to stop before comparing myself to her investigators.

"Anytime." I stood. "And call me C.T."

"OK, C.T. Maybe I'll see you sometime."

I hoped so. "Maybe you will," I said and left Liz's office.

* * *

LATER IN THE DAY, the news told me Vasilios had been held over for trial. His motion for bail was denied. His lawyer, whose hair looked like it grayed a bit more since I saw him, told the press about Vasilios' strong business record, philanthropy, etc. None of it spared him from being an asshole, of course, and a killer on top of it all. The attorney also mentioned some rogue investigation. I felt a subpoena would be in my future, and I didn't relish the thought.

Around dinnertime, my cell phone rang with the call I expected. "Hi, Mom."

"Coningsby, your father and I saw the news," she said. My mother always called me by my full name, a family name on her side. I lived with it because pointing it out made her ramp up the frequency. "I'm glad you were able to help that poor young man."

"He really landed in the soup," my father said in the background.

"Tell Dad Ernie jumped into the soup," I said. "There may have been a nudge, but no one pushed him, and I needed to be talked into tossing him a life preserver."

"You can't pick and choose like that, Coningsby."

"Of course I can. I only have so much time. If you want me to help the people who really need it, I have to filter out the less needy ones."

My mother sniffed. She did so whenever someone said something to offend her sensibilities. Every time we spoke, she sniffed more than a cocaine addict craving a line and a mirror. It almost made up for her calling me by my full first name. "Yes, well, make sure you're not turning away the people you really ought to help."

"Ernie ended up with the public defender," I said. "They didn't have any investigators to spare, so his lawyer asked me to help out. I'd already told him no."

"She must be a very pretty woman," my mother said in a mirthful tone.

She knew me too well. "I can neither confirm nor deny her pulchritude."

"Of course not, dear. I hope that awful man who did it gets what's coming to him."

"He's rich and has an expensive lawyer," I said. "We'll see."

"You're so cynical, Coningsby."

"Mom, if you missed the correlation between money and justice, I'm not sure I can help you at this point."

"Anyway," she said, tabling a side conversation I knew she didn't want to have, "your father and I will put ten thousand in your account tomorrow." This was the arrangement Liz didn't know about. Technically, I worked for my parents' charitable foundation. In reality, doing my job got me back into their good graces after my hacker friends and I got arrested in Hong Kong. After nineteen days in a Chinese prison, I would have agreed to almost any devil's bargain.

"Thanks, Mom."

"You take care, dear. Come by for dinner one night this week."

"I will."

"Maybe you can ask that lawyer to come with you," said my mother.

"Mom! I'm not bringing her for dinner."

"Very well, dear. Goodbye."

"Bye, Mom." We hung up. Down the hall, the business line in my office rang. It was Sunday. I had closed a case and money would be waiting for me tomorrow. No need to ruin the rest of the weekend by answering my phone. I let it go to voicemail. A new case could wait for the new work week.

END of Novella #1

Novella #2
Land of the Brave

CHAPTER 1

AS WAS OUR TRADITION, MY COUSIN RICH AND I CELEBRATED another closed case by hoisting a couple pints at a local tavern. This time, we chose the James Joyce Irish Pub in the Harbor East area of Baltimore. Rich honored our Irish ancestors by choosing a Guinness, and I honored them fifty percent more by ordering a Guinness Extra Stout. We sat at a table and sipped our festive brews.

"To another arrest," I said, raising my mug.

Rich tapped his to mine. "Hear, hear."

"You'll make lieutenant pretty soon at this rate." After doing the heavy lifting for my cases, I summoned Rich from the bullpen to make the arrests. He's a decorated detective with the Baltimore Police Department, a good bit earned on my cases.

"I'm doing all right on my own," Rich said. As usual, he refused to see the light on how much I'd helped his career in my ten short months as a private investigator. He'd been a plain-clothes detective about the same amount of time and already earned more commendations than many of his longer-tenured colleagues.

"Now you've added a deadbeat dad to your ledger." I sipped again. Guinness Extra Stout—the beer that drinks like a meal.

"I was surprised you took the case at first." Rich smirked. "Then I saw the mom."

"Are you insinuating I only took the case because the client is attractive?"

"Attractive? She looks like a young Jennifer Connelly."

"I'm not old enough to remember a young Jennifer Connelly," I said. The ripe old age of twenty-nine stared at me from a couple months down the road. Rich had almost seven years on me. An occasional gray strand intruded on his otherwise brown crew cut. His hair was a couple shades lighter than mine, and I could boast of no gray. Rich maintained the hairstyle and clean shave as artifacts from his time in the Army.

"Watch *The Rocketeer* sometime," he said.

"I'll see if I can add it to my Netflix queue." Rich focused on his beer. I looked around the pub. It was a decent crowd for a weeknight with more diners than bar patrons. When I glanced back at Rich, he continued studying his beer as if something profound lay at the bottom of the glass. "You're quiet." Rich didn't answer. "Everything all right?" Nothing. I paused. "I just booked a trip to Mars."

"Mm-hmm."

"Rich." He frowned and looked up. "Something must be on your mind. You're silent and surly, even for you."

"I'm not surly."

"When you grumble, it kind of confirms it," I pointed out. Rich started to protest, but I broke in. "And don't tell me you weren't grumbling just now."

"Maybe a little," said Rich. Normally, he would have smiled or at least smirked. This evening, his expression remained neutral.

"What's up?"

Rich gazed at me for a second, then shook his head. "Nothing. Don't worry about it."

"Troubles with the ladies?" I said. Rich's expression didn't change. "You know, if you need advice from a younger, more handsome man, I'm willing to help."

"I do *not* need advice from you," Rich said.

"Rich, if this were still an era of little black books, you'd be stuck on page two." Now he scowled at me. "I, on the other hand, would be authoring a multi-volume epic."

"No one likes a braggart."

"Many of the names in my little black book would disagree," I pointed out.

"Whatever," he said. "Forget it."

I shrugged. "OK." After a few more swigs of my beer, Rich was just as chatty as before. I decided to give him some space this time. If he wanted to tell me, he would.

Rich looked at his beer some more, downed the rest in a giant swig, sighed, and looked at me. "Can we go to your office?" he said.

"Sure," I said. I paid the tab, and we left.

* * *

My office was an extra room in my house. I lived in an end-unit rowhouse in the Federal Hill section of Baltimore. Whoever owned it before me built an addition for the kitchen and turned part of the first floor into an office. It pinched the square footage of the dining room, but I usually ate in front of the TV, and I couldn't complain about the size of the living room.

I sat behind my desk. Three large computer monitors looked back at me. Rich took one of my guest chairs and busied himself looking around. This was not his first time in my office, and nothing in the room changed since his last trip. Still, I let him take his time and figure out whatever he wanted to tell me. The next time Rich confided in me may not be the first, but I could count them on one hand.

"You ever know my buddy Jim?" he said after a few minutes. "Jim Shelton?"

I shook my head. "Doesn't sound familiar."

Rich nodded and lapsed back into silence. A bad feeling welled in my stomach. I knew very few of Rich's friends, and chief among the reasons was Rich chose his friends carefully. Getting on the exclusive list amounted to a lifetime appointment. Whether I knew the man or not, if Rich mentioned one of his friends to me, I doubted the circumstances were good.

"He's dead," Rich said, confirming my suspicion.

"I'm sorry."

A nod again. "I'm sorrier for his widow and kids."

"Of course," I said.

I didn't say anything else. Rich needed time to unpack this and tell me about it. "Water?" I asked after a moment, reaching for the mini fridge.

"Sure."

I handed Rich a bottle, opened mine, and took a sip. Rich looked at his as if staring at it would compel the cap to open.

"Coroner says it's a suicide," he said.

A coroner involved meant it didn't happen around here. Baltimore, like most cities, had a medical examiner's office staffed with competent doctors. "I take it you don't agree."

"No way." Rich shook his head. "He wouldn't kill himself."

"You're certain?"

"Damn certain."

"Why?"

"We served together," Rich said. I presumed this; most of Rich's friends overlapped his years in the Army, especially the time spent in the Middle East. "When he got out, he . . . had some problems."

"PTSD?" I said.

"Yeah. I don't know if he ever got diagnosed or treated, but he had it."

Rich fell silent again. This time, I pushed on. "I don't mean to sound indelicate, but . . .

"It sounds like a suicide?" I gave the silent affirmative this time. "It does," Rich acknowledged. "But I know there's no way Jim would do it."

"How do you know?" I said.

"We talked about it some." Rich opened his water and took a long pull before continuing. "He admitted he thought about it. Even with a family, he still thought about it."

"What kept him from doing it, then?"

"An organization out there. Land of the Brave."

"Out there?"

"Garrett County," said Rich. The westernmost county in Maryland. Much of it was in the mountains in the panhandle of Maryland, and it offered short drives to both West Virginia and Pittsburgh. I hadn't been there in years and only for a weekend at Deep Creek Lake.

"How's the county doing?" I said.

"Not well. They've lost a lot of jobs. Jim had trouble finding work, and when he did, it usually didn't last long. He felt like he couldn't provide for his family after leaving them for years."

"I'm sure it was tough on him."

"It was." Rich drank more water and paused. I gave him the time he needed. "Land of the Brave got him a job, sort of."

"Sort of?"

"He worked with bees."

"Like a beekeeper?" I said.

"Yeah. He was responsible for several hives. They were set up on farms out there. The farmers leased out some land they weren't planting on anymore. Worked out for everyone."

"And this organization filled the land with bee hives?"

"I guess. Jim enjoyed the work. Said the buzzing didn't bother him. It let him focus. I think it was almost quiet for him." Rich frowned. "He told me working with the bees took a shotgun out of his mouth."

"Wow." I didn't have anything else to say, so I sat in my chair and stayed quiet.

"Yeah. I'm sure he didn't kill himself."

One of these days, I would need to get better at asking questions. I probably should have asked this one earlier. "How did he die?"

"Gunshot to the head," Rich said.

"It appears self-inflicted?" I said.

"Coroner's men found GSR on his hand."

"You think someone else shot him."

"Yes."

"So why would someone shoot an ex-Army guy with PTSD who's a beekeeper?"

"I don't know," Rich said, "but I want to find out."

"You want me to come along?" I said.

It took him a few seconds, and it was as small a movement a human could make to count as a nod, but I saw it. "I don't know if I can do everything myself," said Rich. "Besides, I'm too close to it."

"You're not going to gripe when I break into a database or thumb my nose at the law?"

"I'm off the clock."

"All right; I'll help you." I smiled. "Wow, you're hiring me. I should highlight this day on the calendar."

Rich smirked. It was good to see a positive reaction. "I think I regret it already," he said.

"No refunds."

"Good thing you work for free, then." Rich guzzled the rest of his water. "We'll leave in the morning. Can you be ready at eight?"

"Doubt it," I said. Rich glared at me. "It takes time to look this good. Not all of us have buzz cuts."

"Fine. You think you can finish primping and pampering by nine?"

"I'll manage."

"Good," Rich stood. "See you then. Anything you can find out in the meantime would be great."

"I'll see what I can put together," I said.

* * *

James Alan Shelton died five days ago, three weeks shy of his thirty-eighth birthday. He left behind his wife Connie, ten-year-old James Junior, nine-year-old Carly, and two-year-old Patrick. Before Carly was born, the Army sent Jim to the Middle East, where he stayed a total of six years. Eighteen months later, he left the Army and like so many veterans, struggled to adjust back to everyday life. Calling his post-service work history "spotty" would have asked the word to do work for which it was unqualified.

I pondered how far to dig. Normally, I threw caution to the wind and probed as deep as my considerable skill allowed. This case was more delicate. Not only was the victim a friend of Rich, he was also a veteran. I had no compunction using the Baltimore Police's resources for my own purposes or knocking over random databases. I didn't want to hack the Army. Even with good intentions, it felt wrong. I surprise myself with an attack of conscience from time to time.

During my first case, Rich left me alone at his desk for a few minutes, during which I snagged his IP and hardware addresses, then went home and used them to fingerprint the BPD's network. Ever since, their network has accepted one of my machines as its own. I could have used the BPD's resources to poke and prod the Army's network for more info on Jim Shelton. Doing so would have been lousy, though, and while my conscience rarely intruded, my feeling was Rich's I'm-off-the-clock proviso wouldn't extend so far.

Did I even need military records? Whatever Jim did in his tours of duty, he was several years removed. What were the odds someone tracked him to Garrett County and shot him? Rich and I were going up there to investigate. If we uncovered a tie-in to something related to Jim's service, I could go after the Army files then. Rich would probably approve at such a point, after the requisite moment of frowning and scowling.

Rich mentioned PTSD and the possibility Jim never had it diagnosed or treated. His comments were practically an invitation to snoop around the Department of Veterans Affairs and their databases. Never one to decline such an offer, I went about it. For an agency protecting gobs of sensitive information about the country's veterans, their network didn't present much of a challenge. A few minutes after discovering the VA's servers, I found one running an older version of Linux. One new exploit later, I was logged into it. From there, I moved laterally to some other servers, discovered a database administrator credential in a text file—this is unfortunately common—and looked for records on James A. Shelton. When I found them, I transferred them off the network, erased my tracks, and disconnected.

Since he got out, Jim had seen VA personnel on an irregular basis. I discovered a lot of rescheduled appointments, a few missed ones, and notes with a surprising lack of depth. It seemed Jim wasn't much of a talker, and the shrink he saw wasn't much of a speculator. Thus, no one ever made a formal diagnosis of post-traumatic stress disorder. The only treatment Jim received consisted of aperiodic appointments with a mediocre shrink and no medicine. I felt bad for Jim and his family, and at the same time, I hoped other veterans fared better.

Without much else to go on, I packed a bag for the next few days and went to bed.

CHAPTER 2

RICH ARRIVED PROMPTLY AT NINE THE NEXT MORNING. I don't think he'd ever been late for anything in his life. He was probably born right on schedule. I loaded my bag into the back of his blue Camaro, and we were off. Before we got on the highway, we stopped for coffee. I wanted to hit up the local java shop; Rich eschewed my choice for a Royal Farms because of its proximity to the on-ramp and (admittedly) better parking. Armed with extra caffeine, we got back into the car and headed west.

Oakland would be a three-hour drive. Rich got on I-83, which would take us to the Baltimore Beltway. From there, we would follow I-70 to I-68, and then Route 219 into Garrett County. Rich's navigation system directed him, but I knew he spent at least fifteen minutes last night studying a map—and a physical one to boot. If the Rand McNally corporation were to survive in this century of smartphones and GPSes, it would be on the backs of old folks and people like Rich. On the highway, we passed a few slower drivers and set a good pace. Like any sensible Camaro owner, Rich opted for the powerful V-8 engine. Unfortunately, he paired it with the automatic transmission, for which I mocked him thoroughly after he bought the car. Rich tore up his left knee in the Army, though, so I understood his transmission choice. Despite this, I would still take some occasional jabs at him for it. What are cousins for? "How do you want to play this?" I said when we were on the Beltway.

"What do you mean?"

"Meaning, I know this guy was your friend, and you're the more experienced investigator."

"Nice of you to acknowledge it," Rich said.

"I didn't say you were the better one," I pointed out.

Rich chuckled. It was good to see his sense of humor make a comeback. "No need to say something so obviously true."

I let his comment go. It *was* true, even though I would only admit it under duress. "You want to talk to the family first?"

"No," said Rich. "Too much emotion there. I want facts first."

"Where do you want to start?"

"I've been reading the papers up there."

"They have newspapers in Oakland?" I said.

"The Garrett County *Republican*," Rich said.

"Well, it *is* a red county."

"They've picked up the story. It's become high-profile because of Jim's service."

"So you want to talk to the reporter?" I said. Rich nodded. "What about the cops?"

"Sheriff's Office, too," he said.

"You think they'll mind us snooping around?"

"They probably won't mind me too much. A hotshot big-city PI like you, though, may not be too popular."

"I'll try to be fifteen percent extra charming," I said. "Good thing we're having more coffee."

"Just let me do most of the talking," Rich said.

We lapsed into silence for a few minutes. Rich guided the Camaro onto I-70 East. A short while later, the coffee was ready for post-processing by the ecosystem. We got off the highway and found a donut shop. After availing ourselves of the facilities, we each grabbed a couple donuts for the rest of the ride. I got a pair of French crullers. Rich, of course, opted for plain cake. Chocolate frosting was too much, and a honey glaze was right out.

"You bring a computer?" Rich said.

"Have we met?"

"I figured you would."

"I brought a good laptop and a router," I said. "You can't trust hotel and coffee shop wi-fi."

"Especially not for the kinds of things you might do," said Rich.

"You're the one who asked if I brought it. You're implicitly endorsing my methods."

"I'll have less of a problem with them on this case."

"I'm so glad you approve," I said.

Rich didn't say anything for a couple minutes. I was happy to listen to the classic rock playing on satellite radio. Then he said, "You're right. This is off the books. We need all hands on deck, and I'm glad you're coming along."

"Thanks," I said. "Was admitting it so hard?"

"Yes."

"Fair enough." I took a cruller out of the bag and bit off a chunk of it. Two hours to go. I hoped most of them could pass in silence.

* * *

WITHIN THE CITY OF OAKLAND, Maryland Route 219 became Third Street. Despite its number, it served as the main drag. Oakland is not large, so its downtown is missing both the square footage and the bustle compared to a city like Baltimore. Only past the hospital did businesses and restaurants appear in volume with a Walgreens, McDonald's, Sheetz, and Pizza Hut in the span of a couple blocks. The *Republican* sat a block over on Second Street in a green building I would not have guessed housed a publisher. We parked out back and walked in through the front door.

Any newspaper still being operational in this day and age surprised me. The volume of people I saw when we walked in doubled my surprise. I expected a disenchanted skeleton crew trudging around amid dusty shelves and ancient computers. Instead, a receptionist smiled at Rich and me as we walked in, the people moving around behind her seemed happy to be at work, and the open floor plan looked modern. I couldn't see any computers—I still guessed them to be antiques—but everything else screamed modernity. The receptionist directed us to the second floor after Rich mentioned who we'd come to see.

On the upper level, the building showed its age. The open-concept seating of the first level didn't make it up here. Instead, people sat in a drab cubicle farm, the faded green fabric walls a poor callback to the building's exterior paint job. Offices were situated on the outsides of the cube area, and half of them empty, not even nameplates gracing their doors. The *Republican* put on a good show with the first floor, but the second story drove home the reality of the modern newspaper business.

We found our quarry on the left side. Luke Thompson was lucky enough to have a window seat, but unlucky to have a view of the parking lot. He was young, probably only a few years out of college, though his black hair was already thinning on top. He looked short and compact, built more like a fire hydrant than a news reporter. Maybe getting the scoop in Garrett County often involved fisticuffs. Rich and I each showed the reporter our IDs.

"Long way from Baltimore," he said with a hint of a southern accent.

"Just running down some leads," Rich said.

"You usually bring a private investigator with you?"

I liked this reporter. "I'm here to lend my unique expertise," I said before Rich could respond with something less impressive.

"What are you looking into?" he said. When Rich told him, Luke leaned back in his chair and let out a long, slow sigh. "That's not an easy one. You guys want some coffee?"

"Yes," I said.

"No," said Rich.

"I'll have the intern get us some from Sheetz."

"You have an intern?" I said.

"Surprised?"

"I'm surprised you have a newspaper. Everything else compounds it."

Luke smiled. "People still like getting a paper out here. We're not all office drones glued to our phones and tablets."

The intern appeared when summoned, putting away his phone and appearing eager for work. He was tall and thin with red hair and a young face. He was probably in college but looked like he started shaving only yesterday. I could see the disappointment at fetching coffee darken his features, even when Luke offered to let him keep the change. After he left, Rich and I sat in extra chairs Luke found.

"Speaking of office drones glued to their phones," I said.

"Quincy is studying journalism at Frostburg," said Luke.

A name like Quincy would not help anyone, but I kept my thoughts to myself. There was a reason I went by my initials, after all. Rich filled in the brief conversational gap by saying, "Jim Shelton."

"Like I said, it's not an easy one."

"Meaning what?" I said.

"A decorated soldier kills himself. Always hard."

"You're convinced it was a suicide?" said Rich.

"Haven't seen anything to tell me otherwise," Luke said.

"Gunshot wound looked self-inflicted, and he tested positive for residue on his hand."

"Doesn't mean it was a suicide."

"You know him?"

Rich nodded. "We served together."

"I'm sure it's tough to think he could kill himself."

"It's not tough," Rich said. "It's impossible. He wouldn't do it."

"Lot of guys in his place do," Luke said. "It's sad. This county isn't overflowing with jobs."

"He's not a statistic." I heard anger creeping into Rich's voice. "Even without employment, he found a purpose. He found a reason to keep going."

To try and defuse any mounting tension, I broke in. "Land of the Brave."

"I've heard good things about them," Luke said. "They've made a difference."

"They made a difference for Jim Shelton, too," Rich said.

Quincy the intern returned with three cups of coffee. He set the tray on Luke's desk. A small bag held sugar and fake sweetener packets, a few plastic stirrers, and a pint of half-and-half. I took a cup and added a packet of sugar and enough creamer to turn the coffee a pleasing medium brown. Rich surprised me by using a packet of the yellow stuff. Under normal circumstances, I would have given him grief for it. Today, though, I didn't want to add to his tension. If anything, I wished he'd ordered a cup of decaf.

"You going to talk to them?"

"At some point, yes."

"If you need some notes on them, I could pass them along."

I sensed an ulterior motive here. "In exchange for what?" I said.

Luke grinned. "I can't just be a good guy?"

"You can. Maybe you are. All the same, you're a reporter, and

I don't think you're volunteering a pile of information out of the goodness of your heart."

"Fine," he said. "I want the exclusive on whatever you discover."

"What if we discover it was definitely suicide?" I said. Rich glanced sidelong at me.

"Then I guess I'll have the scoop on the confirmation."

"Fine," said Rich.

We sipped coffee and chatted about a few local things with Luke. He recommended some places to eat—and others to avoid —and said he would send his notes along within a day. Rich and I walked out and got back in his car. "What's the plan now?" I said.

"Let's find a hotel," Rich said. "Then I want to talk to the sheriff."

I noticed his singular pronoun usage. "It sounds like you don't want me to come along."

"Probably best if you don't."

"What if I promise to simply sit there and look handsome?"

Rich smirked. "Can't have the sheriff threatened by your good looks," he said.

"Always a risk," I said.

HOTEL OPTIONS in Oakland were scarce. They were so deficient, in fact, as to be nonexistent. Rich and I chose the Oakland Motel. It was on the convenient side of the road if we needed to leave town in a hurry. The hospital and a few restaurants were short walks away. The motel featured brick exterior walls, dark blue doors, and a fridge and microwave in every room. Rich did not want to share a room with me—a sentiment I cosigned—so we ended with accommodations side-by-side. We paid the weekly rate in case the trip out here took a while.

"No wi-fi," Rich said as I put my bag on the bed.

"Doesn't matter," I said. "I brought a mobile hotspot."

"Couldn't someone figure out it's yours?"

I did my best to look insulted. "Rich. Really? Do you think I would set it up so there's any way to trace it back to me?"

"I suppose not."

"Go talk to the cops. I'll be here."

Rich left and closed the door. As I engaged the lock, I heard his Camaro rumble to life. Within a few minutes, I got the hotspot up and running and a fresh virtual machine on my laptop using it to talk to the outside world. I wondered how easy breaching the cyber defenses of the *Republican* would be. How much could a small-town newspaper put into keeping people like me at bay? It would also mean Rich and I could access Luke's notes even if he changed his mind and decided not to provide them. For now, I would leave them alone. Mostly. I poked and prodded their network, mapping out relevant devices and making my own notes.

From here, I could access the BPD's network. I wondered if they shared any info with the Garrett County Sheriff's Office and vice versa. Such a connection would be easy to exploit. Then I envisioned Rich with steam coming out his ears because I went and messed up the investigation. As amusing as I found the image of my strait-laced cousin as an angry cartoon character, I would respect his wishes. For now.

I passed the time doing research on Land of the Brave. They were a new organization in operation for about five years. The goal was to have veterans do productive work on farmland earmarked for the group to use. The most common work was beekeeping, and the organization sold and delivered the honey across the region and into West Virginia. In other cases, veterans grew other important crops for the area. Land of the Brave claimed to pay the veterans a stipend. They admitted it wasn't a living wage, but they hoped it would get there as more land and access became available. I always take charitable organizations with a grain of salt—my parents' foundation has encountered some charlatans over the years—but Land of the Brave seemed to be doing good, important work. If it saved veterans like Jim Shelton, it was even more important.

Why, then, had Jim killed himself? Or did someone murder him instead? I wondered if Rich learned anything during his chat with the sheriff. Think of the devil, and he shall arrive; the growl of Rich's Camaro announced his return. A minute later, he knocked on my door, and I let him in.

"What'd you learn?" I said.

"Some," said Rich. "Not enough for my tastes."

"You still think someone killed him?"

"We'll see. Put your shoes on."

"Why?"

"The mayor wants to talk to us," Rich said.

"Us?" I said.

"Yes. You, too, this time."

"Clearly my celebrity has spread."

Rich grinned and shook his head. "Yes, sir," he said. "Very good, sir. I have the car ready, sir."

"Well, it's about time," I said.

* * *

WE MET the mayor in an office in the circuit court building. He was tall and slender with blond hair and a goatee, and there was visible gray taking up about half the latter. He wore charcoal pants and a black sportcoat over a white button-down open at the collar. Small-town mayors could relax the dress code. He introduced himself as Ken Dennehy. His hands were large and his handshake grip strong. Rich and I sat across the desk from him.

The mayor immediately insisted we call him Ken over anything more formal.

The office was small and sparse, the desk and three chairs occupying most of it. A meager bookshelf sat against the wall opposite the desk. It contained only a few law books, and they were as dusty as the shelves. Ken, as he wanted to be called, looked to be in his late forties. Based on the strength of his grip and the callouses I could feel on his hands, I pegged him as someone new to politics. "Terrible what happened to Jim," he said.

"You knew him?" Rich said.

"Oh, yes. Not close friends, I confess, but this isn't a big city. I know most people."

"How well did you know him?" I said.

"Enough to tell you he was a good guy in a bad spot. I thought he was going to pull through."

"You think he killed himself?" said Rich.

"Sheriff does," Ken said. "I don't see any reason to argue with him."

"Jim wouldn't kill himself."

"You friends?"

Rich nodded. "We served together."

"I had a feeling," the mayor said. "We need to do a better job for veterans coming home."

"Yes, you do," Rich said.

Ken frowned for an instant—as if he took it personally but wanted to hide the fact. "Land of the Brave does good work," he said. "I made sure they got a grant to give them enough funding to keep going."

"And dead veterans look bad for the city?" I said.

"That's an indelicate question."

"But a valid one."

Ken smiled, but I didn't see any humor in it. "I guess this isn't

Baltimore," he said. "Of course it would look bad, but I'm a lot more concerned for Jim's family than I am for the city. The organization does good work. I'd give them the grant again." He paused. "Have you talked to his family yet?"

"No," Rich said. "Probably tomorrow."

"Why did you want to see us, Ken?" I said.

"To let you know I want you to succeed," he said. "Maybe there's a chance Jim didn't kill himself. I don't know. If there is, I hope you're able to work with our sheriff to figure out what happened."

"If we need some wheels greased along the way?"

"Then I'll try to be ready with the oil."

"Sounds good," Rich said. "Thanks."

The mayor shook our hands again. "Please keep me posted," he said, "and good luck."

In the car, Rich said, "You hungry?"

"Definitely."

"Let's find some food, then."

"And talk about what just happened," I said.

"You think something is weird?"

"I'm not sure," I said, "but I think better on a full stomach."

CHAPTER 3

TOMANETTI'S PIZZA WAS AN ODDLY-SHAPED BUILDING. LONG rather than wide, its front door jutted out, and the brown roof didn't really go with the light red stone exterior. Inside, it fostered an old-time pizzeria feel with round brown tables and matching chair molding. Rich and I each ordered a pizza—pepperoni for him, mushroom and onion for me—and sat with our sodas. About half the tables were occupied, and a few people flittered in to pick up carry-out orders.

"You think something's up with the mayor?" Rich said. No one sat immediately around us, but Rich still possessed the good sense to talk in a quieter voice.

"I don't know," I said, shaking my head.

"He seems helpful."

"Yeah."

"However, you think that's weird?"

"It's a small city. He might know a lot of people, but he wasn't too close to Jim. Why talk to us, then?"

"Like you rather crassly said, dead veterans look bad for the city."

A sheriff's office car pulled up. A young deputy came in and looked around the restaurant. He picked up a pizza and went back to his car. "Dennehy's the mayor of Oakland," I said.

Rich shrugged. "And?"

"He's basically committing police resources to us. He's not the sheriff, and he's not the county executive."

"Do you know how many people live in the county?"

"I checked. Around thirty thousand."

"Right," said Rich. "More live in certain areas of Baltimore. You have a sparse population, not a lot of crime, and not a lot of out-of-towners asking questions."

"What's your point?" I said when he stopped talking without elaborating.

"In this kind of scenario, the mayor of the county seat could pull some strings. It's not like the deputies have a huge murder backlog."

"Maybe. I guess I'm just not used to people being helpful. Especially government people."

"Perhaps it's your typical charming approach," Rich said with a smirk.

Before I could fire off a clever retort, our pizzas arrived. They were cooked beautifully—as cooking shows would extol—with golden-brown cheese and the right amount of char on the crust. Tomanetti's didn't skimp on the toppings, either, and the amount of grease was exactly right. Rich and I put the conversation on hold as we each devoured three slices of pizza. We then got refills on our sodas and worked on fourth pieces.

"I think we're OK with the mayor," Rich said. "He most likely wants to help."

"I hope so," I said. "Let's see if we need the hand at some point."

"The sheriff already said his deputies would cooperate."

"You big-city cops and your fancy badges," I said.

"I'm sure cooperation's part of it. Remember, though, thirty thousand people in the whole county. The sheriff wants to help, too."

"Let me guess: he knew Jim."

Rich nodded. "Said he did, but like the mayor, not too well."

"I realize thirty thousand is a small population, but there's no way one man knows so many people. The president doesn't."

"I'm surprised you're so skeptical," Rich said.

"And I'm surprised you're not."

"What do you mean?"

"I'm here helping you out," I said. "Still for you, this is personal. You knew Jim well. He was your friend. People wanting to lend a hand is a good thing, but doesn't it all seem a little too easy?"

"I think you've watched too many movies. Different law enforcement agencies aren't always adversarial."

Rich certainly held the edge on me in experience. Plus, he worked in law enforcement, while I tried my damnedest not to get closer than the fringes. Maybe he was right. Dealing with unhelpful people in a city like Baltimore could have colored my perception. "OK," I said. "I'll follow your lead."

"But?"

"But if the mayor hires some slobbering goon to whack us over the head, I'm going to say I told you so."

"So noted," Rich said.

We both finished our sodas and got boxes to take the other halves of our pizzas back to the motel. Might as well take advantage of the limited amenities. "I want to stop and see Jim's family," Rich said after we were in the car. "At least talk to his wife."

"You want me to come in with you?"

"As long as you can turn off your conspiracy brain."

Rich pulled the Camaro back onto Route 219. He turned left before our motel and ended up on some twisty county road. Houses were infrequent, and the ones I saw were a mix of gracious Victorians and ramshackle ramblers. "Used to be nicer here," Rich said.

"Unemployment?"

"Big part of it. I think the rest is opioids."

"Even up here?" I said.

"You have a lot of people who worked hard jobs. A bunch of them needed painkillers. When they lost their jobs and insurance, they still wanted the pills."

"I guess it's everywhere."

"Yeah," Rich said. "It's even worse in West Virginia. We're not too far away." He paused. "See that house?" Rich pointed to a rundown small two-story building. Its current state of disrepair belied the fact it once served as a home. If a stiff breeze came along, I expected the structure to collapse. The roof had patches missing and beams exposed. What siding remained was worn and discolored. Most of the windows were gone, replaced with plastic sheets. The door was a large piece of ill-fitting plywood with a large X painted on it.

"What's the X mean?"

"It means first responders shouldn't go in. It's too unsafe, too likely to fall down."

"Do people live there?" I said.

"Doubt it," Rich said. "Sometimes, you get squatters. Often, people go there to do their drugs. Sometimes, they burn the house down, and the fire department doesn't run in."

I shook my head. Another house looking just as unsteady and with an identical X on the door appeared on the other side of the road. I wondered how many there were and how much longer they would still be standing. They threatened to slump to the earth any minute.

Rich made a right turn. The residences looked a little better here. No drug dens, at least. A deputy's cruiser drove past us and went down the road we just turned from. "Is this their street?" I said.

"Yeah, why?"

"Just wondering." *I don't have a conspiracy brain,* I told myself.

* * *

THE SHELTON PLACE looked like a log cabin. Two stories of wooden walls stopped at a traditional roof. None of the houses nearby looked like the Sheltons', nor did they look like each other. Absent anything like a homeowners' association, people built whatever dwelling they wanted and could afford. I liked the libertarian aspect, but looking between a white house, a blue one, a log one, and a rambler, I wished for some thematic unity.

Considering Jim's recent death, conditions of the lawn and gardens were understandable. Closer, I spied signs of age and disrepair—cracks in the logs, peeling paint on the door and shutters, and windows whose age exceeded mine. I wondered how many houses in the county met similar fates once jobs dried up.

Rich knocked on the door. A woman answered and invited us inside. In the living room, she and Rich embraced and exchanged words I couldn't hear. He introduced me to Connie Shelton, and we shook hands as I offered my condolences. Connie looked to be about Rich's age, though her eyes and the lines around them suggested she slept little in the last week. I heard children's voices from another room, but they didn't join us. Connie sat in a blue recliner; Rich and I shared a matching sofa.

The hardwood floors were the same color as the walls. They needed a good buffing to regain their luster. In light of Jim's passing, I tried to dial down my usual judgmental nature. Connie and the children faced other priorities. Floors could be maintained later. There would be time for dusting, cleaning, and putting toys away. I was sixteen when my older sister died; I didn't want to do much of anything afterward, and I wouldn't pretend my situation was the same as losing a husband.

"Thanks for coming." Connie mustered a small smile. "Both of you. Can I get you anything?"

"We're good," Rich said. "Tell me what's happened."

Connie let out a slow sigh. " Oh, dear . . . after Jim died, the coroner did an examination. The sheriff and some deputies came around. They talked to me, talked to the kids some. I hear they went out to the farm and questioned the charity people, too."

"Did anything come of it?"

"No." Connie snorted without humor. "Single gunshot wound to the head. No sign of foul play, the coroner says. No motive for someone to kill Jim, the sheriff says. So they tell me he killed himself." She shook her head as a single tear slid down her right cheek. "I don't believe it."

"I don't believe it, either," Rich offered.

"What are you going to do?" Connie said.

"We'll look around, talk to people, and dig into what happened."

"You think you can figure out who killed Jim?"

"Yes," Rich said right away. I thought odds were good of doing it, but I also didn't want to promise results to a recent widow.

Connie looked at me. "You're Rich's cousin?"

"I am."

"You're not a cop?"

"Private investigator," I said. Describing myself this way for almost a year, it got easier to say, yet it still felt weird to hear myself say it.

"You must be good, if Rich brought you here to help."

"I tend to get results." Rich shifted beside me. I couldn't see his face, but I knew he must have been frowning.

Connie picked up on it. "Is something wrong?"

Rich's response was probably best for everyone. "I don't want to sit here and ask you a bunch of questions," he said.

"I think you know the answers."

"I probably do, but I'm a cop, and Jim deserves my thoroughness. Had anything been unusual lately?"

"No," Connie said. "I think working with the bees was helping Jim. It'd probably drive me batty, but it seemed to calm him down. He was in a better place in his head these last couple months."

"He got along with everyone?"

She nodded. "Charity people were great. Farmer was really nice. I think he was glad someone could use the land."

"Did he have any quotas with respect to bees or honey?" I asked.

"You think someone killed him 'cause he didn't make enough honey?" Connie said.

"People have been killed for less."

She paused to think about my question. "If he had any goals to hit, he never mentioned them to me. It didn't seem like that kind of place. Sure, they could sell the honey, but it ain't like honey sells for fifty bucks a jar."

Her point was valid.. Even if Land of the Brave sold their honey at high-end prices—presuming Garrett County and West Virginia shoppers would pay those rates—they'd need millions of bees to bring in a lot of money. Giving a handful of veterans a few hives each wasn't a formula to hoard cash and retire young.

"We'll figure it out," Rich said to reassure Connie.

I refrained from joining in the affirmation. Even though I liked our chances, nothing about this case made me think we would have an easy go of it.

* * *

"Now YOU'RE QUIET," Rich said as he drove us out of the neighborhood.

"Am I surly, too?" I said.

"Surly suits me more than you."

I fell silent for a moment before saying, "This is a small city and a county with a low population."

"So?"

"So everybody knows everybody else. People are aware of their neighbors' lives; they know their business."

"I still don't understand what you're getting at," said Rich.

"I mean, obviously Jim's wife is going to think he didn't kill himself. What if he hid something from her, though? Something we might find out by asking around?"

"You think he killed himself?" Rich's voice took on an edge.

"I'm trying to keep an open mind. If he got killed, though, someone did it for a reason. He may not have told his wife about it."

"But you think he may have told someone else."

"Yes," I said.

"Maybe. The problem is everyone knows everyone here."

"What do you mean?"

"Because they don't know you," Rich said. "They don't know me. We're outsiders. They're going to protect their own."

"I guess." We got back onto Route 219 for the short jaunt to the motel. "It may be worth trying."

"Let's see how tomorrow goes first."

Rich turned into the motel parking lot. One vehicle we hadn't seen before, a gray SUV, sat near our doors. As we pulled closer, four large men got out of the SUV and took up positions near the doors. "The welcoming committee," I said. "Still think everyone we've talked to has been helpful?"

Rich gave me a sidelong glare as he parked his Camaro in a

spot two down from the goonmobile. "We can't be sure who sent these guys."

"Why don't we find out?" I said as I got out.

Rich called, "C.T.!" after me, but I closed the door. He got out, too. The two men standing near my door sized me up. Both crossed their arms under their chests, and those arms and chests were bigger than mine. All of them stood about six-four, giving them two inches on me and four on Rich. They were built like offensive linemen, so I didn't doubt their strength even as I noticed their unnecessary bulk and paunches.

"You from the local Four-H?" I said as I stopped a couple paces from the pair darkening my doorstep.

"What the hell is a four-aych?" the one on the right said. His long black hair was pulled back into a ponytail. The other one wore his blond hair in a super short buzz cut even Rich would have found severe.

"Hell, I don't know." I thought about it for a second as they looked between each other, then scowled at me. "Head, heart, health . . . you know, I forget the fourth one."

"We ain't from the fucking Four-H," the blond one said.

"I believe you," I said. "They'd never approve of your language."

"Who sent you?" Rich said, plopping a wet blanket atop the banter I had going.

"You two assholes are asking too many questions," one of the two by Rich's door said.

"Right now," I said, "I just want to know what the fourth H stands for."

"You need to back off," Black Ponytail said. "Go back to Baltimore."

"Or what?" I said.

"Or we'll send you there in an ambulance."

"Why would it take us back to Baltimore? There's a hospital around the corner."

"Enough of this shit," Blond Crew Cut said as he grabbed for me. I shoved his arm aside and gave him a short jab in the solar plexus. Sucking wind made him take a step back into the wall. Behind me, I heard the telltale grunts and sounds of fighting as Rich's duo failed to persuade him to leave. The goon with the black ponytail threw the kind of loopy hook a boxing teacher would expel someone for. I blocked it. He lobbed a few more. They were strong but but slow and gave me time to turn all the blows aside.

My blond assailant recovered and pushed himself off the wall. This could get complicated. When Black Ponytail launched his next haymaker, I grabbed his arm and spun him into the parking lot. His momentum carried him into the front quarter panel of the gray SUV, from which he bounced and fell in a heap. I turned back toward Blond Crew Cut in a defensive stance.

He threw a hard jab at my face. I pushed his punch high with my left arm, ducked a bit, and rammed my fist into his stomach. When he bent forward, I drew back my arm and walloped him in the face with an elbow. His head rebounded off the door and his eyes crossed. I did it again, then a third time, until he slumped down the door.

The long-haired goon got to his feet as I waded out to meet him. Out of the corner of my eye, I saw Rich deliver a knockout blow to one of his attackers. "I just remembered what the fourth H is," I said.

"Huh?" he said.

"Hands." I launched a flurry of punches at his body. He managed to turn a few aside, but the majority connected. He rocked back with the impacts and his breathing grew labored. I gave him one last good shot to the midsection, then grabbed his ponytail and bashed his head into the hood of the car. When the first attempt didn't put him down, I did it again. The second one turned the lights off.

Both of Rich's assailants were flattened, too. His split lip leaked a little blood down his chin. "I think my two were bigger," I said, eying the four men splayed out around the motel doors and parking lot.

"I don't think so," said Rich.

I pointed at the one with the ponytail. "He's got more hair."

Rich chuckled and shook his head. "Not everything is a competition."

"Good thing," I said, touching my lip in the spot where his was busted open.

Sirens screamed from nearby. I saw red and blue flashing lights as three sheriff's cars drove into the lot and skidded to stops near the scene. One deputy stepped out and pointed his gun at us.

"They started it," I said as I raised my hands.

Rich and I rode to the sheriff's office in separate police cars. Once we established he was a police detective and I was a private investigator, the deputies decided not to handcuff us. Ambulances took the four attackers turned victims to the nearby hospital. They never told us who sent them. I wondered if the deputies would have any idea and if they would tell us anything they knew.

The Garrett County Sheriff's Office was in the same building housing the district and circuit courts and where Rich and I met the mayor. I got the feeling Ken Dennehy wouldn't be chatting us up tonight. The deputies herded Rich and me inside. The squad-room looked like it had been lifted straight out of 1990s cop dramas and deposited here. Desks loosely organized into rows butted against one another. The vinyl floor was pockmarked with coffee stains. Whiteboards filled with active cases and other official scribblings covered most of the available wall space. Doors to offices and interrogation rooms ringed the exterior.

A tubby deputy led me to one of those enclosures, pointed at my chair, and left without saying a word. If it came down to running away, I liked my chances against him. I would be back at the motel before the ambulance arrived to tend to his coronary. The interrogation room was just as unspectacular as the rest of the area. Paint peeled from the walls in a few spots. I sat on a plastic chair whose design specifications clearly listed comfort at the bottom. The seating reserved for my inquisitor boasted a thin layer of padding covered by gray cloth—probably not much more comfortable. The required one-way mirror dominated the wall to my right. I waved in case anyone watched from the other side.

Then I waited. And I waited some more. If the Garrett County Sheriff's personnel sought to turn me into a quivering mass of gelatin by waiting me out, they would be disappointed. I used the downtime to ponder recent developments in the case. Rich and I talked to few people, yet we still had a quartet of legbreakers greeting for us. No one called 9-1-1, but deputies came anyway. Someone at the motel could have sounded an alarm, but the parking lot was mostly empty. The office was too far away to have a good view of the scrum, and the units didn't have exterior cameras. Right after the law arrived, an ambulance rolled into the lot. The whole thing smelled like a setup to me. It caused me to wonder who would have sent the four idiots to dissuade us, and would the same person have had first responders on standby?

Of course, someone trying to encourage us to abandon the investigation meant there was something to investigate. No one should care about extra scrutiny on a suicide. A murder, though, could not withstand a glut of questions, especially not when posed by someone as brilliant as me. Rich, too, for that matter. Whatever room Rich sat in, I felt certain the same thoughts came to him. We were onto something, and whoever was responsible didn't want us to stay on it. I also wondered if some deputy would come in and suggest we abandon this and go back to Baltimore.

A few minutes later, a middle-aged deputy entered the room. Unlike the fat one who showed me in here, this man looked like he could still play a mean left field in a softball league. His hair had gone gray, but he looked to be about my height and build—six-two and about 185 pounds. His name tag identified him as White, and he was. So, too, would his hair be in another ten years. He set a manila file folder and a small spiral notebook on the table in front of him as he slid into the chair. "You know why you're here?"

"I'm extremely good at defending myself?" I said.

"You put two men in the hospital."

"There you go." His neutral expression told me he was unconvinced. "They would have done the same to me."

"But they didn't," White said.

"Do you really think my cousin and I picked a fight with four guys their size?" I said.

White shrugged. "Couple of hotshots from Baltimore . . . don't know what kind of trouble you'd start."

"You might look at the quartet we laid out. I doubt they're as pure as the driven snow."

"Now you're going to tell me how to do my job?" said White.

"Only because it appears someone needs to," I said.

My comment made White glare at me. I didn't wilt. He moved the notebook aside and opened the folder. Inside, I saw a few sheets of paper. The picture on the top page looked like one of the goons I tangled with. "We already did that," he said. "I guess someone else told me how to do my job before you. All four of these guys are dirty." White leafed through the pages. The print was small, and I was reading upside-down, but it looked like two of the men hailed from West Virginia.

"Local boys?" I said.

"Mm-hmm. They seem to specialize in the work you saw them doing tonight. We've arrested all of them before."

"Yet I'm the one in this room," I pointed out.

White raised both hands and slapped the tabletop hard. I

didn't flinch, though I wondered if the rickety table would survive. Before I worked my first case, I lived in China for thirty-nine months, culminating with nineteen days in one of their prisons. It was an experience I did not care to repeat, but it made me immune to amateur tactics like the one White used. "What did this poor table ever do to you?" I said.

"You're a smart ass."

I was about to say I preferred it to being a dumbass but refrained. White seemed competent and didn't deserve the barb. When did I go soft? "The key word is 'smart,'" I said instead.

"All right, let's presume you're smart. What are you and your cousin doing up here?"

I figured White knew this already, but I played along. "Looking into the death of Jim Shelton."

"Suicide," said White.

"The four men trying to get us to drop our inquiry would disagree," I said.

"Yeah? Why?"

"Real suicides stand up to scrutiny. Murders dressed up to look self-inflicted can't take the spotlight for long."

"You think someone killed Jim Shelton?"

"I was on the fence until we got the welcoming committee at our motel."

White lapsed into silence. He busied himself looking through the papers again. With another chance to eye the reports, I confirmed seeing West Virginia on two sheets. Perhaps the talent market for legbreakers was at low ebb in Garrett County. "Say you're right," he said, and I resisted the urge to say I was right. "Who killed him?"

"We don't know yet," I said, "but I guess whoever sent four assholes to our rooms is a likely suspect."

"You know who did it?"

I shook my head. "None of them said much except the usual threats."

"Maybe you could have given them more of a chance to talk."

"Sure. I'll just get punched around a bit to help your nonexistent investigation." I pointed at my face. "Can't risk the money maker."

"I did some asking about you," White said. "Talked to a Captain Sharpe in Baltimore."

"Leon is a big fan," I said.

"He told me you're a self-impressed rogue with no regard for process."

"He sometimes couches his fandom in tough talk."

White said, "OK, he did also say you're smart and tenacious."

"I told you. He has a foam finger with my name on it."

"Just make sure you keep us in the loop."

"You're not going to investigate?" I said.

"It's been ruled a suicide," White said. "I get your point about the guys coming to visit you, but that's not enough to reopen the case."

I preferred them staying out of it. Rich and I were more likely to find the truth unencumbered by the deputies' investigation. "I'm sure we'll keep you informed," I said.

"Be sure you do. We can haul you in here again. Having a chat with the mayor won't save you from an obstruction charge."

So the sheriff's office, or at least White, knew about our talk with Ken Dennehy. Interesting.

"Noted," I said.

* * *

RICH and I sat in my motel room after the deputies let us go. I sat on the bed. If lounging on it proved any indication, a mediocre night of sleep awaited me. Rich was parked in an office chair.

The room lacked a desk but still featured a padded chair with arms and wheels straight out of cubicle farms. I wondered if it was more comfortable than the bed.

"They grill you much?" I said.

"Not really," said Rich. "They asked why I was here, why I brought you along, why I thought Jim was murdered." He shrugged. "Pretty basic. You?"

"The deputy I talked to didn't seem impressed to share the interrogation room with a 'Baltimore hotshot,' as he called me."

"Did you set him straight?"

"To whatever degree I could," I said. "I still wonder who called nine-one-one."

"Probably someone here," Rich said.

"Look at the parking lot. Three other cars, and none within a few doors of our rooms."

"You think it was a setup of some kind." It wasn't a question.

"I just wonder."

Rich fell silent. Maybe he ruminated on it, too. After a moment, he said, "I want to visit the charity tomorrow."

"What do you think we'll find?" I said.

"I don't know. Hell, there's a lot of unknowns since we got here. Maybe I'm hoping we'll find some clarity."

"I might settle for a couple shady dudes giving us the side-eye."

Silence again served as the only reply I got. Rich stood and pushed the corner of the drab curtain back. He peered out the window.

"Thinking we might have more visitors?" I said.

"I wish I could put a finger on what to expect," said Rich. He still looked out into the parking lot. "Did the deputy believe you about Jim?"

"I think so."

"Same here. Did he say they'd do anything?"

"I doubt it," I said. "He mentioned it's still officially a suicide, so until that gets overturned, they're not investigating."

Rich let go of the curtain and sat back down. "I heard pretty much the same thing. No one even suggested they would talk to the coroner." He shook his head. "I wish this county employed a medical examiner."

"The coroner could be good at his job."

"Maybe," Rich said. "But he's elected . . . in a county where a lot of people know each other. He stays popular, he can keep getting elected even if he doesn't know a scalpel from a hatchet."

"We could always pay him a visit," I suggested.

"No." Rich shook his head. "I'd rather work around him. Let's figure out what happened. Then we'll drop the evidence on the sheriff's desk and make him act."

I hoped it would be enough. "I'm with you," I said.

CHAPTER 5

LAND OF THE BRAVE SERVED GARRETT COUNTY, ALLEGHENY County, and parts of West Virginia from its office near Deep Creek Lake. It was about fifteen minutes outside of Oakland. The area was home to a ski resort, plenty of camping, and a more upscale feel than anywhere else in the County. It seemed a curious place for a nonprofit to make its home, but here was Land of the Brave. They operated from their own building, a single-story structure whose shape suggested it was a restaurant in a past life.

The parking lot butted against Route 219. A sign in the lot simply read "Land of the Brave." No signage or other information showed on the building itself. It featured beige siding, a couple bay windows, and a large ovular door bisecting the exterior. We walked past one of the windows. Inside, a few people sat at desks. Rich and I entered. The receptionist, a pretty blonde girl who looked like she still had a couple years to go at Frostburg State, smiled and greeted us.

"Are you veterans?" she said.

"I am," said Rich.

"Thank you for your service. Do you need some help?"

"We do." He showed his badge. Not to be outdone in the presence of an attractive girl, I flashed my ID. "I think we need to talk to your boss."

"Is this about the poor man who killed himself?" she said.

"Yes," I said when Rich didn't answer. He shot me a sidelong glance. I frowned in return. What was the benefit of keeping those details on the down-low?

"Sure," the receptionist said. She walked past us to the other side of the building. Everything was laid out with an open floor plan save for one office. It was obviously built after the rest of the place. It looked like someone hurried like mad to hang the drywall and sacrificed professionalism for haste. Whoever painted it displayed the same work ethic. Maybe corners like good construction needed to be cut to afford the square footage near the lake. Rich and I waited. A moment later, the girl returned. "You can go in."

The office looked no better on the inside. The painter did just as shoddy a job there. I could not claim painting expertise—my next time taking up a roller would be the first—but uneven applications and bad corner work are easy to spot. A few pictures dotted the walls, mostly of men in uniforms of the five service branches . The desk the director sat behind looked as hastily assembled as the walls surrounding him. He stood and fixed us with a neutral expression. No nameplate was on his desk, but the degree hung behind him—a bachelor's from West Virginia University—identified him as Peter Russell.

"How y'all doin'?" he said. I heard traces of an accent my amateur ear would place as hailing from Tennessee. Russell looked a shade under six feet and quite a bit over 200 pounds. His shaved head made his age tough to guess, but I went with mid-forties. The office was about the size of an extra bedroom in a townhouse, with just enough room for Russell's desk, a couple shabby guest chairs, and a small round table and shopworn loveseat.

"Detective Ferguson," Rich said, giving a businesslike reply while showing his badge.

"And Detective Ferguson," I said, taking out my ID.

"All the way from Baltimore," Russell said as he looked at Rich's shield. A smirk briefly crossed his face, like he knew Rich enjoyed no jurisdiction so far from the big city.

"Jim was my friend," Rich said. "We served together."

"We were all sorry to hear what happened to him."

Rich and I sat in the guest chairs. Russell showed us a smile, but any warmth it held didn't reach his eyes. "Terrible thing," he said. "It's always a shame when we can't reach someone."

To his credit, Rich didn't take the bait. He stayed focused on his questions. "Can you tell me what your organization does?"

"Glad to. We work with veterans. You said you served?" Rich nodded; Russell continued. "You found a good job for yourself. A lot of the ones who come back aren't so lucky."

"I know."

"I'm sure you do. What we do is work with the ones who have problems adjusting to life once they're home. Usually, that's trouble finding a job."

"You don't offer counseling?" said Rich.

"We make referrals," Russell said, "if we feel someone needs help beyond the VA."

"Did Jim Shelton?"

"He was talking to a psychologist we helped him find, yes."

"Recently?" I said. Russell inclined his head. This shrink must not have interfaced with the VA because Jim's records didn't mention any recent visits. "Do you know how his therapy was going?"

"We don't get involved on that end," Russell said. "It'd be a legal issue for us. The therapists do their work, and we do ours."

"So you never hear from them?"

"Their offices let us know if they pick up a patient we referred. We don't ask for anything else."

"Did Jim talk to you or anyone here about how it was going for him?" Rich asked.

"Here and there," said Russell. "He said he found a good medication. We thought he was doing well."

"What about his job?"

"Yes. He was an excellent worker. We gave him a couple choices of what to do. He tried working with the bees once and really took to it. Lotta guys don't even attempt it." Russell paused. "It's consistent work. You're doing the same things a lot. Very . . . rote, if you will. Jim loved it. I think the buzzing sound was good for him, too. He mentioned that he actually found it soothing."

"What did he do?" I said.

"Honey. He checked on the health of the bees and the hives, of course. But he also processed honey, bottled it, and boxed up cases. We take it to local markets and sell it. Organic raw wild honey."

"Very Whole Foods-y," I acknowledged. I'd bought the identical product before.

"Well, we don't have a lot of stores like that up here," Russell said, giving us a brief grin. "But the markets we do have are happy to sell what we give them. Now, we take it to West Virginia, and you get some different stores down there. Even a Whole Foods or two."

"Anything else besides honey?" Rich said.

"Our company leases land from farmers. Most up here don't use all their fields anymore, so they're glad to take money from us. We're limited in what we can do. Honey is a popular seller, so we're looking to gather more by placing hives for pollinating some crops and orchards and keeping the honey. We also grow some fruits and vegetables, and sell bags of topsoil."

"You pay the veterans?" I said.

"What we can," said Russell. "They get a basic stipend, plus a cut of whatever gets sold out of their lots."

Rich said, "So the more they produce, the more they can make."

Russell spread his hands in a modest gesture. "Exactly. It's not as much as a good full-time job, but we do what we can. Cost of living is pretty low up here."

I figured it was quite a bit cheaper in Oakland or border towns in West Virginia than by Deep Creek Lake but didn't bring it up. I didn't want to antagonize Russell. At least not yet. "What about housing?" Rich said.

"What about it?" Russell said.

"You said cost of living is cheap. I've driven around. It's an interesting mix, but there are definitely some not-so-nice ones out there. Do you help people find better accommodations?"

"We haven't yet, I admit. No one has asked. Obviously, we don't want anyone living in squalor. We're not going to butt in, though. People need to learn to ask for help."

"About Jim," Rich said. "His wife is convinced he didn't kill himself."

Russell said, "I don't mean to sound indelicate, but don't wives normally think so? You're a cop in a city with a lot more crime than we get out here. You see many families who agreed with a determination of suicide?"

He drove home a point. I was on Team Rich here, but Russell's statement was valid. Families rarely believed their loved ones were capable of suicide. Even when signs of depression were copious and obvious, disbelief was common. Denial, after all, was the first stage of grief. "Families never agree," Rich confirmed, echoing my thoughts. "Sometimes, they're deluding themselves. Other times, they're right."

"You think they're right here?"

"I do. Jim wouldn't kill himself."

"I'm sorry, Detective. Deputies investigated. The coroner ruled it a suicide."

"I'm here to make sure they didn't miss anything," Rich said. "It was less than a week ago."

"They know you're here?" Russell said.

"Why?" I said. "You going to call them and narc on us when we drive away?"

Russell put his hands up again, this time in defense. "I don't want to see you get hauled off because you're concerned about your friend."

Rich smiled. In profile, it looked just as sincere as Russell. "We've talked," he said.

"Good. I wish you gentlemen good luck, then."

We didn't have any other questions, so we left. Rich stewed all the way back to the motel. I didn't try to talk to him. He needed space and time to process everything, and I wanted to look into Land of the Brave and Peter Russell.

* * *

FREE WI-FI IS A MINEFIELD. People gleefully connect all manners of devices to unsecured networks. If they knew the information a fellow like me could pilfer in only a few minutes, they would wait to look at their cat pictures and political memes. Even an average hacker—and I am well above average—can get login details, passwords, and personal info in short order. The motel didn't offer wi-fi, but my laptop found other networks nearby. Unsecured, of course. Hard pass.

With no wireless I trusted, I hunted around for a wired connection but never found one. Good thing I brought the mobile hotspot. It was a couple years old, but it offered a reliable 4G connection no one could trace back to me. I interfaced it with the router and joined the network. Stage one, complete. I was too paranoid to have one simple layer of protection, however. After obtaining an IP address, I launched a virtual private network. Companies use VPNs so remote workers can connect to the corporate network securely even over the public Internet. Some free ones are out there, but I used a paid service offered by some acquaintances.

After establishing a session with the VPN, I then used an anonymizer to further hide my traffic. With three layers of security in place, I got to work. Land of the Brave had been around for six years. Three years ago, they moved from the second story of a building in downtown Oakland to their current location. Moreover, the organization didn't have increased revenues corresponding with the move. Money earned from selling their products followed a gradual upward trend, but I saw nothing to indicate they could soak up what I presumed to be twice the rent with no problems. So I dug deeper.

I expected Land of the Brave to use WordPress for their website like so many others. Instead, they had their own web server running Apache. Luckily for me, they missed the last couple Apache updates. Any outdated software is vulnerable. A simple search showed me an exploit. A minute later, I had it loaded and ready, and once sixty more seconds elapsed, I gained unfettered access to the server. Their site wasn't bad. Like most small companies, however, their web server got forced into service in other areas. It also operated as their file server.

I poked around for a few minutes and ended up copying everything. Nothing else looked interesting enough to pilfer. I covered my electronic footprints and disconnected. The files were mostly boring. I downed two cups of coffee at breakfast, and fifteen minutes with this information left me yearning for a third.

Nothing in the personnel records raised a red flag. The organization kept data on all the veterans it helped; I ignored all of them except for Jim Shelton's. If we needed to, Rich and I could go back and pore over them later. For now, I wanted to preserve their privacy. I took a small portable printer out of my bag and put the information to paper. I knew Rich would prefer reading a hard copy.

My phone rang a few minutes later, offering me a reprieve from this tedium. Gloria Reading called. If Baltimore could be said to have socialites, Gloria would be first among them. She and I enjoyed a relationship of fun and convenience. Her parents and mine moved in the same social circles, though Gloria enjoyed those circles more than I did. "You're a hard man to find," she said when I answered. I heard the playful edge in her voice and imagined the lascivious look often on her face.

"I'm out of town with Rich," I told her.

"I didn't think you guys were the type to go away together."

"We're not." Gloria knew me well enough to know Rich and I were a distant sort of close. "Rich wanted my help with something."

"Wow. That's a big step, isn't it?"

"I guess it is," I said. "One of Rich's friends from the Army died. It's been ruled a suicide. We came out here to . . . make sure the investigation was good." Even though we knew it probably wasn't.

"I'm sorry for Rich," Gloria said. "Did the man have a family?"

"Yes."

"That's terrible." She paused. "Is there anything I can do?" A few months, maybe even thirty days ago, Gloria wouldn't have asked. When we first met, I think she found the idea of me working quaint in some way. In an ideal world, I wouldn't have needed to, but I blew my money bankrolling my hacker friends when I lived in Hong Kong. Nineteen days in a Chinese prison later, I was back in the States and the object of my parents' ire. They wanted me to get a job helping people; I wanted to work as

136 / TOM FOWLER

little as possible. We soon found common ground: I would work for their foundation and solve cases pro bono. Over time, Gloria took an interest in my work. She had even come with me on some of the more social outings my cases required.

"I doubt it," I said. "I'd suggest you come ski at Wisp, but it's not really the season yet."

Gloria chuckled. "I'm not much of a skier."

"Neither am I."

"You've had some dangerous cases recently," she said. "Is this going to be another one?"

"I hope not," I said, "but I wonder. It seems like the police are watching Rich and me. He thinks I'm paranoid. Maybe I am. Already, a few guys tried to stare us down and dissuade us."

"What happened?"

"They weren't very good at the dissuading part."

"Be careful, C.T."

"Sounds dangerously like concern," I said with a grin I couldn't help.

"I don't want to see anything happen to you," said Gloria. "I . . . enjoy our time together."

"So do I."

"When do you think you'll be back?"

"I don't know. I hope no more than a few days."

"Make sure you get here in one piece," Gloria said in a sultry voice. Even through the phone, it sent a shiver down my spine.

"I'll do my damnedest," I said.

* * *

RICH CAME by about an hour later. This time, I sat on the desk, laptop in its eponymous place, and Rich took the bed. "I heard you on the phone earlier," he said. "Gloria?"

"Yeah."

"When are you gonna marry that girl?"

I snorted. "Rich, come on. I like Gloria, but I'm not sure either of us are the marrying types."

"You two are fooling yourselves," he said with a grin.

"I hope you didn't come over here to give me relationship tips," I said.

"No," he said. "Just wondering if you did any work while you weren't busy talking to your girlfriend."

I was about to point out Gloria wasn't my girlfriend. Rich's smirk changed my mind. Let him have his satisfaction. "I have, in fact. Something Russell said troubled me."

"What was it?"

"When he said Jim was seeing a psychologist and had tried some medication." Rich shrugged. "Psychologists can't prescribe. They're not medical doctors."

"Interesting," said Rich. "Do you know where the prescription came from?"

"I haven't looked yet. His comment got me thinking the organization wasn't so pure. I've been nosing around."

"And?"

"I'm not an accountant," I said. "Thank goodness. But I don't know how they afford their building and all the employees. They show six full-time and eight part-timers. Their current office is more than double the rent at the old one."

"Donations?" Rich said.

"They get some, sure. Not as much as I would expect, and they only make money selling honey and other small things, while ignoring a more lucrative pollination business. It doesn't add up."

"What about Russell himself? He could have money and run the whole thing at a loss."

"Maybe," I said. "I'm going to look into him next. In the meantime, I printed some things for you."

Rich grabbed the small stack of papers. "Let me know what you find about Russell," he said.

"I'm on it. I'll know all the things worth knowing about him soon." I fired up the VPN and anonymizer again. It was time to see what skeletons Pete Russell crammed into the dark corners of his closet.

CHAPTER 6

PETER RUSSELL CAME FROM A LARGE FAMILY. HE WAS THE fourth of eight children. Six of his seven siblings were still alive. Unless any of them hit the lottery, their ages indicated they would still be working. They were. A few minutes of searching found them scattered throughout the east coast and Midwest. All of them had boring jobs that didn't interest me for this case.

Except one.

George Russell was an administrator at the Fairmont Regional Medical Center, named for the city in which it's located in West Virginia. I couldn't count Fairmont among the two cities in West Virginia I'd heard of—Morgantown and Harpers Ferry—so I looked it up. Driving there from Oakland would take about ninety minutes. A regional hospital would have access to all manners of drugs. George could hook up Pete and his shrink with some. I hypothesized this was how Jim Shelton got his medication.

A quick job search told me the salary I could expect to earn as a candidate for hospital administrator jobs. I then poked around until I found where George Russell did his banking and investing. My degree is in computer science, so I'm pretty good at math. Even if I weren't, though, I could have deduced something fishy in George's books. Unless he'd been working for about fifty years—almost quadruple the length of his current career—he couldn't have saved and stashed all the money he did.

I looked deeper. George's paycheck hit his savings every two weeks. He also made small cash deposits once a month, as well as large investments in his brokerage account around the same time. Another savings stash showed irregular cash deposits and ATM withdrawals. If I didn't know better, I'd think George was a drug dealer.

Hospitals received medications all the time. Some were boring, like aspirin and Tylenol, and even though you could buy a bottle of them for three dollars, the hospital would still charge you four bills per pill. Nice racket if you can create it. Other drugs they get are more interesting and far more regulated. Opioid medicines, for instance, required someone to account for them at each step of their journey. Despite this, they ended up stolen and distributed illegally with alarming frequency.

I wondered if the withdrawals from his savings were payments to delivery people or suppliers. *Here's some cash to look the other way while I grab this box.* Then the contents of said box could be sold, generating funds for the deposits I saw. The amount of money meant it would need to be more than an occasional box. I knew some rich people who could have lived nicely on George's money.

Rich needed to know this. It was another path to the investigation. We could drive to West Virginia and nose around. Rich would complain about jurisdiction, but he was already out of his, and I was only licensed to investigate within the state of Maryland, so we needed to confine the out-of-state investigative task force to the two of us. I shut everything down and walked next door to Rich's room.

I wished I possessed more information.

* * *

"I WANT to bring in the FBI," Rich said when I brain-dumped everything to him.

I hadn't expected him to want to run to the feds. There were jurisdiction concerns, and there was punting to the goddamn FBI when it wasn't even fourth down. On top of it all, I didn't want to tell them how I got my information or even what information I gathered on George Russell. "You've certainly proposed a solution," I said.

"You don't agree?"

"Of course not."

"Let me guess," he said. "You don't want to share your info with the feds."

"I don't even want them to know I *have* info," I said. "If it's all the same, I'd prefer to keep my intelligence-gathering methods out of this. They're going to have too many questions."

"I think this is getting bigger than you and me."

"How? So far, we know Land of the Brave looks shady. We know the boss has a brother who might be making money buying and selling pills out of his hospital. This isn't a drug cartel in action here."

Rich crossed his arms under his chest. "You want to risk the investigation because of your shady methods," he said, shaking his head. "Incredible."

"What's the risk to the investigation?" I said. "You and I can do this."

"I think there are more people involved than a charity director and a hospital boss."

"Sure. They have to have a driver or two somewhere, plus the four assholes we sent to the hospital. If those are the best goons they can muster up, I'm not worried."

"This is about Jim!" Rich's face grew red. "I want justice for Jim, justice for his family, justice for—"

"Yourself?"

Rich sighed and glared at me. "I was going to say his kids, but I'm his friend, so yes, for myself, too."

"I don't think we should bring in the feds," I said. "We can do this."

"We have people in Maryland and West Virginia involved," said Rich. "We're talking interstate crime."

"Great. You bring in the feds. When they take over everything, lock you out, and bungle it, don't say I didn't warn you. Even if they don't fuck it up, you're looking at months to get your justice. Hope you have a lot of vacation days." I turned toward the door.

"Where are you going?"

"Back to Baltimore," I said. "You bring in the FBI, I'm out."

"How are you going to get there?" Rich said.

"I'll take an Uber." I grabbed the knob and pulled the door open.

"Wait."

I stopped.

"I still think this is bigger than the two of us."

"Have fun getting stonewalled by the FBI, then," I said.

"If I don't call them, what would your next steps be?"

"I want to look into the brother and his hospital."

"And if we build a case against him?"

"Then we close it," I said, turning back to face Rich. "You came out here to get justice for your friend. If you want to farm it out to someone else, whatever. Up to you, but you're not getting justice then. Someone else is."

"I don't see it the same way," said Rich.

"You and I often see these things differently."

Rich uncrossed and crossed his arms again. He pursed his

lips, rolled his eyes, shook his head. If steam poured out his ears, I would consider my triumph complete. "Thanks to you," he said, "I'm not convinced we can trust the locals."

"Agreed."

"Fine. We'll keep it small for now. If this gets too big for us, though, I'm going to call in some help."

"Not the feds?" I said.

"State Police," Rich said. "I know a guy. He's trustworthy. We can work with him."

"Who decides if the case overwhelms us?"

"I do. My judgment. If you don't like it, go call your fucking Uber."

I grinned. "Really, Rich?"

"What?"

"You don't *call* an Uber. You use the app."

Rich chuckled and dropped his arms. "Go back to your room," he said.

So I did.

* * *

MY FATHER's deep exhalation over the phone made a sibilant hiss in my ear. "I'm not sure this is what we envisioned when we set this up, son," he said.

When I left Hong Kong after thirty-nine months, it was with the strong encouragement of the Chinese government. They arrested my hacker friends and me and threw a bunch of charges at us, but the ones they cared about the most were helping Americans and dissidents hide from the government or leave the country. Most of those things fell on me. My compatriots were into embarrassing the communists, going after their banks, and similar things. I did some of it, too, but even then, my conscience reared its ugly head and compelled me to help people.

After returning to the States, my parents threatened to cut me off from the family fortune unless I got a job helping people. Seeing as I'd burned through most of my money in China, I was forced to consider their position. Before long, I settled on being a private investigator, and got my license thanks to some embellishment of the legitimacy of my work in China. The kicker was I wouldn't charge my clients. My parents hired me into their foundation and would pay me for solving cases. So far, this arrangement chafed me but worked reasonably well. Until this case, apparently.

"What do you mean, Dad?"

"Rich wasn't who we had in mind for your clients."

"I told you the details of the case," I said. "You don't think the family sounds like they need help?"

"I guess so," he said. "It's merely. . . irregular, is all. Clients usually come to you."

"Rich did."

"You know what I mean."

"Do you think it was easy for him, Dad? You know how Rich and I have gotten along—or not—over the years. Since I started this job, he's taken every chance he could to run down the way I do things."

"You never thought his points were perhaps valid?" said my father.

"I'm sure they have some merit," I said, "but Rich and I are very different people. He has trouble with anyone who doesn't do things by the book."

"What are you getting at, son?"

"My point is it took a lot for Rich to approach me for help. He needed to swallow his pride and choke down a bunch of objections about my methods. I could have given him shit for coming to me, but I recognized what it took for him to do it. Maybe you should, too."

Silence was my only reply for a few seconds. Then my father said, "All right. I think you've got a valid point as well. We'll be interested to hear how this one turns out."

"So will I," I said.

"Should your mother start looking for western Maryland newspapers?"

"Dad, I'm not sure the two of you could be seen reading a paper called the *Republican*. What would your rich liberal friends think?"

"I'll let your mother worry about it," he said. We both knew she would. It was probably the thing she did best in the world. OK, maybe tied with sniffing and tsking after I offended her sensibilities. "What are you going to do next?"

"I think we're going to poke around the organization," I said. "They're our best lead right now. Maybe our only lead."

"Good luck, son. You're a long way from Baltimore."

I looked at my motel room. It didn't offer a view of Route 219, but the images had been seared into my head the last couple days. "Don't I know it," I said.

FAIRMONT REGIONAL MEDICAL CENTER RAN A SLICK-looking website. No doubt it had been designed by a well-coiffed chap (or chapette) who sat in the dark and sipped lattes while writing the code. It wasn't built on WordPress or Wix or any other do-it-yourself platform. Whoever created it made a professional, functional, and mostly clean website. The architect even required secure connections over the web.

None of this stopped me from hitting it with a scanner. Services run on ports, many of which are assigned specific numbers, and the scanning program tells me which ones are running. It didn't take long to find the weak link. An older version of File Transfer Protocol was still used for exactly what its name suggests. The problem: it was designed in the infancy of the Internet. No one thought about security then. Thus, no security was ever built into FTP. Everything it transmitted, including login credentials and the contents of files, got sent over the wire in the clear. Unencrypted.

Because FTP is an older protocol, the versions of it installed on web servers are frequently outdated. In other cases, the protocol will accept default login credentials because whoever configured the server never bothered to remove them. The FTP version was current, so I looked up this particular implementation's default credentials. I tried them.

They worked.

Sometimes, it really does prove so easy. While I like to think I'm good at the advanced hacking stuff, there are occasions when simple tactics are the home run hitters. The login I used provided full access to the file system. FTP uses simple commands to list directories and upload and download files. I spent a few minutes nosing around and seeing what directories could house juicy information. My searching turned up a scad of interesting documents, including a listing of privileged accounts. I downloaded them all to my laptop and disconnected all my sessions.

Combing through data was not exciting. I contemplated walking outside and watching some grass grow for a change of pace because of time to kill while Rich went to Jim's funeral. When he mentioned it, I didn't offer to go. He wouldn't want me there. Rich needed his space in a time like this; I understood and respected it. Besides, it gave me the chance to conduct a riveting review of hospital files.

About ninety minutes later, I finished reading all the pilfered material. Nothing jumped out at me as irregular. I even logged back in with an admin account I found on the list, downloaded more documents, and read those. The hospital maintained impeccable logs of all drugs in and out, and they meticulously dotted each I and crossed every T in triplicate when it came to controlled substances. Boxes of Vicodin weren't getting up and walking out the door.

How else could George bring drugs in? I looked for shipments of opioids delivered to the wrong locations, stolen from another facility, or hijacked in transit. The number of results probably shouldn't have surprised me, but it did. A package arriving at the wrong destination could happen. There is no malice in human error. The others, though, involved both malice and muscle. I thought of the four goons who darkened our doorsteps. Give them ski masks and guns, and they could probably abscond with a bunch of stolen drugs.

A box of fentanyl going missing from LA didn't mean much, however. I narrowed my focus. If George Russell sent people to steal drugs, those thefts needed to happen within driving distance of his hospital. You couldn't sneak a bunch of controlled medication on a commercial flight, and using a chartered plane would add both expense and another person who could talk. No, George's crew would stay fairly local. Being a professional detective, I employed the advanced sleuthing tactic of making up a number and setting a search radius of two hundred fifty miles.

Sure enough, I found some. A report of an irregular delivery to Fairmont Regional. A delivery of opioids knocked over outside Pittsburgh three years ago. Another near Charleston, West Virginia, six months after. Yet another near Winchester, Virginia, five months later. I expanded the search radius and found them going back a couple more years, always every five to six months, never more than three in a calendar year. Local cops and the feds were investigating, of course. I read up on the robberies. Different vehicles used every time. Never the same physical descriptions of the crew. Different clothes, masks, and guns each time. No one killed, though a few guards took beatings here and there.

While I read over everything, Rich returned from the funeral. I heard the rumble of the Camaro's V8 in the parking lot, like the low growl of a wild animal. A minute later, he knocked on the door. "It's Rich." I knew already, both from the Camaro and his knock. Rich, despite being a little shorter than me, has larger hands, and the way he bangs on a door is distinct. Kind of like clubbing a tree with a hammer.

I let him in. We chatted about the funeral for a minute before getting down to new business. I told him what I'd discovered about George Russell, his hospital, and the pattern of stolen opioids. "Fuck," Rich said. I found this an adequate summary. "What do you think they're doing with the drugs?"

"Selling them," I said. "My guess is George's random deposits equate to his share of the proceeds."

"Of course they're selling them, but what's the method? How do you move a pile of stolen pills?"

" Not only move them, but do it regularly. They restock a couple times a year."

Rich shook his head. He tried to run a hand through his hair, but his crew cut made the gesture look ridiculous. "I know the manufacturers have tons of pills," he said. "It's a shame . . . they probably didn't even notice the missing stock."

I was about to point out our focus needed to be on distribution when Rich's phone buzzed. He looked it at, frowned, and put it away. "Connie just texted," he said. "Land of the Brave is picking up Jim's last batch of honey tomorrow morning."

Neither of us said anything for a minute. Then the light bulb went on for me. It must have gone on for Rich, too, because his eyes went wide, and his mouth fell open. "The pickups," I said. "They pick up whatever legit products the veterans have, add their drugs, and distribute them through middle men."

Rich's mouth clicked shut. He nodded. "Makes sense. You said the robbery crews seemed to change a lot?"

"Yes."

"I wonder if some of the people giving product to the pickup guy were giving more than honey and vegetables."

I thought about it for a moment. "Rich," I said, "you know what this could mean."

"No," he said. "Jim wouldn't take part in something like this."

"I don't think we can be sure of—"

"I can be sure of it!"

We couldn't get anywhere this way. Rich would get pissed

and tell me to call an Uber again. I had no proof, anyway, so I dropped it. For now. "Fine. But I think you know what we need to do next."

"I do."

"How are your following skills?"

"Good enough to make up for having a big blue Camaro," said Rich.

* * *

EARLY THE NEXT MORNING, Rich and I sat in his car. He parked three houses away from the Sheltons'. We each held the largest coffee Sheetz sold, which was twenty-four ounces. I could have used half again as many. I ate a turkey sausage breakfast burrito of above-average flavor. Rich scarfed down a couple donuts and a bearclaw pastry the size of an actual ursine paw. I couldn't believe he still ate such garbage. Rich is about six and a half years older than me, making him thirty-six. Not yet twenty-nine, I possessed the metabolism to shrug off a morning of ingesting sugary rubbish. Rich was at an age where he could pay for such indulgences. Of course, he had been six feet tall and a solid two hundred pounds for so long, I wondered if he skipped birth and came into the world fully formed.

"How do you think this all went down?" he said after chomping a chunk of the pastry.

I considered making a crack about Rich's breakfast but refrained. Doing pastry puns before eight is not in my wheelhouse. "I think George found out where shipments were going," I said. "He could have access to the information. Then he would tell Pete, who would rustle up a crew."

"I hate this case," Rich said. "Jim Shelton dies, and a bunch of other veterans were probably used as robbers."

"Maybe they got paid in drugs," I said. "Some of them already could have issues."

"It's possible." Rich's nostrils flared. His knuckles were white as he gripped the steering wheel. If we got to arrest Pete and George, they would need some of their own pilfered painkillers after Rich finished with them.

"We'll get them," I said.

"I know . . . and I want to make sure we do it as right as possible."

We differed on methodology. If I found a corner to cut, I would. Technology was a wonderful thing. Rich, by contrast, would quote chapter and verse from the law and the police manual. Our styles didn't mesh. Despite this, we ended up working together in some capacity on most of my cases. I was still surprised Rich wanted me to come with him out here. He knew enough friends on the force to invite someone with a similar level of love for the rulebooks.

Silence ruled the day for the next few minutes. I finished my breakfast burrito, and Rich washed down the last of his pastry with a big swig of coffee. We watched the Shelton house. Nothing. The clock ticked eight. The pickup driver was now officially late. None of the other houses showed any activity. It was a sleepy Saturday morning for everyone except us. I witnessed several leaves shake free of trees in the wind and spiral to the ground. The last of my coffee went down my throat. It was good. I wished they sold a bigger cup.

At about ten after, a cargo van pulled up in front of the Sheltons' house. It was white, no windows after the passenger compartment, and no lettering on the side. Perfectly nondescript. Even if someone saw this vehicle involved in something illicit, there were hundreds like it on the roads at any given time. I wondered if it was stolen. I figured the plates were, or a set would be if the driver or his boss sniffed anything suspicious. A man got out and walked toward the house. His back to us, he looked short and dumpy. If someone stole merchandise from him, he wasn't catching the thief on foot.

The driver knocked on the door. From my angle, I couldn't see anything happening inside. He left the porch a minute later and walked around to the back. I saw Connie Shelton in the backyard. She directed him to the shed, which she unlocked. The driver picked up three boxes. Each was about the size of those paper ream boxes from office supply stores. Connie locked the shed, and the driver carried his haul to the van. Rich and I both slumped down in our seats. He went to the rear of the vehicle, and a moment later, climbed back in behind the wheel. We stayed low while he turned around and drove down the street the way he came.

Rich fired up the Camaro, and it roared to life like a lion denied his breakfast. He eased it onto the roads. We kept the van in our sights. With no rear windows, the driver needed his exterior mirrors to see anything behind him. I figured this would help us follow him, but Rich was the expert here. We got onto Route 219 and took it out of the city onto Route 39. It wound around a lot and became Route 7 after we crossed the West Virginia border. Other twisty-turny roads followed, and I stopped keeping track of the numbers. The Camaro hugged the curves, allowing Rich to keep a reasonable distance behind the van. An old pickup truck got between us at some point.

We soon got onto I-79. Ten miles later, we were back on West Virginia county roads. I expected to hear someone whistle "Dixie" every time we drove past a farmhouse. Eventually, we left Route 19 for Village Way. A large brick building loomed ahead, most likely our destination. The van turned into the delivery entrance. Rich eased the Camaro into a parking lot on the other side of the street, affording us a good view of all the comings and goings. We waited.

Outside Fairmont Regional Medical Center.

* * *

"WHAT DO you think he's doing in there?" I said.

"Probably picking up drugs," said Rich.

"Pretty brazen to distribute them right from the hospital."

"It's also pretty brazen to rob opioid shipments."

This was certainly true. The whole operation was bold. I hated referring to it this way because it sounded like a compliment, and I didn't want to offer praise to the kind of assholes who got people hooked on drugs and murdered veterans. "So if he's adding drugs to those boxes," I said, "we should see where he takes them."

"I plan to," Rich said.

"And then what?"

"We lean on somebody."

"Who?" I said.

"Depends," he said. "Maybe the driver, if he seems like he'll knuckle under. Or maybe whoever he drops the drugs off to."

"He could be making more than one stop."

Rich nodded. "True. This network could be bigger than we thought."

It must have been. I thought the problem lay in Oakland at first. It showed all the signs, but cities across the border in West Virginia were in similar straits. Jobs drying up affected people in both states. Vicodin, oxycodone, and similar pills filled some gaps for people who had holes in the center of them. Eventually, the drugs ruled their lives. Sometimes, they ended their lives. Mostly, they ruined them. This was a nationwide problem. We were seeing it in two communities. We could shut Land of the Brave down, but doing so wouldn't get rid of everyone's pills or addictions. Other suppliers would fill the vacuum. I didn't know how to stop the problem here, and I didn't envy anyone who tried to reverse it on a larger scale.

A few minutes later, we saw the van emerge from the delivery entrance. Rich left the parking lot and pulled out behind him. As we drove, I felt the weight of the .45 holstered at my left side. The chase was on again. I wondered where it would take us.

THE FIRST STOP WAS ABOUT TEN MINUTES AWAY. THE VAN pulled into the parking lot of a small grocery store. Rich drove past and parked at a Chinese restaurant about a hundred yards away. The driver carried one box inside. It was a different guy this time, taller and much slimmer. "New driver," I said. Rich didn't answer. "I guess the boxes still have honey in them."

"Maybe."

"I know they're running a brazen operation, but it would be another level entirely to deliver nothing but drugs to a market."

"I guess," Rich said. He narrowed his eyes and looked around. The grocery store was part of a small strip mall. A third of the businesses were shuttered. Some of their names were still visible as the cleaner portions of the stone front the letters occupied stood out against the grime. I counted five boarded-up windows and doors. You could see more driving down several streets in Baltimore. "Too many people." Rich kept looking around. "His stop doesn't look too busy, but some of the other places are. We can't accost this asshole here."

I nodded. "I guess we'll have to see where he goes next."

"If he takes one box to each stop, he should have two more."

"And the farther he gets from the hospital, maybe the farther he gets from anyone who would help him."

Rich grinned. "There are occasions I like the way you think," he said.

"Try it more often," I said. "You might come to love it."

"No, thanks."

"It doesn't suit you," I said.

"What's that supposed to mean?"

"You are who you are, Rich. You're a guy who knows and respects the law. You've done well for yourself. I'm honestly shocked you're even out of your jurisdiction with your scofflaw cousin."

"I could have brought some cops," Rich said.

"I'm surprised you didn't."

Rich took a deep breath. He did it a lot when he was deep in thought. "You're right; your way of thinking doesn't suit me. It suits you. Another cop would probably think too much like me. Even someone like Paul King." He was another BPD detective. He played faster and looser than Rich, especially in areas of personal grooming, but when it came down to it, King was a cop. Serve and protect. Uphold the law. I came from a different world where rules and statutes often got in the way. The world was flexible, and the law wasn't. People like Rich didn't see this as a problem. People like me bent the law to find solutions.

"If I didn't know better," I said, "I would think you paid me a compliment there."

"Good thing you know better," Rich said with a grin.

The driver walked out of the store, sans box, and got back into his van. He pulled onto the main road. We were close behind him. Rich followed well. He drove a distinctive car, which was a negative, but he always kept a reasonable distance, drove in other lanes, and didn't care if another car came between him and the target.

The dickhead in the van hadn't given any indication he was wise to a tail. Of course, if four more dickheads got out of a crew cab pickup at the next stop, we'd know he spotted us. So far, so good.

"So many overdoses out here," Rich said.

I had done a little reading. Certain parts of West Virginia were especially hard-hit by the opioid crisis. Children as young as twelve overdosed and died. Elderly folks in their eighties met the same fate. People tended to think of drug addiction as some kind of failing of a person's character or moral fiber. The problem there is no twelve-year-old ODs because of character defects. This was a medical problem, and I was encouraged by signs of progress in treating it as such. A documentary about opioids in the area even won an Oscar.

Even with all those factors, it surprised me Rich was wise to the problem. His computer probably had more cobwebs than gigs of RAM. "I'm impressed," I said.

"You're not the only one who can use Google," said Rich.

We settled in behind the van. Thirty minutes and no sign of a stop. We took a road or two I was surprised had ever been paved. Rich hung back father on the less-traveled ones. About fifteen minutes later, we approached a small, nondescript town. The van made a left and then pulled into an alley behind a building serving as a combination clinic and veterinarian. *Get your dog's nails clipped while you wait for your flu shot!* I hoped they were more clever in their advertising.

Rich idled the Camaro on the street. We could barely see the van around the corner of the building. The driver got out, took the remaining two boxes out of the back, and disappeared. "How many clinics you know use honey?" said Rich.

I shrugged. "Could be some holistic quack in there," I said.

"How many of them you think set up shop in small-town West Virginia?"

"Maybe there's a demand for honey on the vet side of the business."

Rich snorted. "I think they're more likely delivering straight drugs here," he said.

"I doubt it," I said. "Keeping them in the boxes with honey is important. What if this shithead gets pulled over and a deputy wants to look in the back. 'See, just boxes of honey.' Lots easier to explain than a box crammed full of pills."

"I guess." Rich pulled forward. "Alley looks empty." It was and ran more than the length of the building, but other than a Dumpster, the white van was the only thing there. "This is his last stop. We'll need to talk to this asshole here." Rich squeezed past the van and parked the Camaro on the other side of the Dumpster. We got out and walked toward the clinic's rear entrance. I stood on one side, and Rich took the other.

We waited.

* * *

MUTED CONVERSATIONS and chuckles made their way through the heavy back door. In my youth, my friends and I would shout at each other under water in a pool. The water, of course, distorted our voices to inarticulate screams. The voices coming from the clinic reminded me of those days. I fidgeted. Patience could not be counted first among my virtues. I looked around the alley. Trash lined the walls, increasing in volume nearer the Dumpster. I also saw two broken hypodermic needles and wondered how much more drug paraphernalia blended in too well with the detritus to be obvious.

Rich stared at the door. His right hand waited to grab his gun; his left curled into a fist. In the quiet of the alley, I could hear his measured breathing. In, out. Even. Between Afghanistan and Baltimore, I wondered how many dangerous scenarios Rich willingly walked into. By now, his slow breathing became automatic in situations like this. I didn't have any routines. I simply wandered into danger and figured I would come out okay on the other side. So far, so good.

The voices inside fell silent. Footsteps replaced them, moving closer. The door arced open, toward me, blocking my view. I couldn't see the driver. I heard him start to say something, but then Rich clamped a hand over his mouth and shoved him into the wall. The door clicked shut. The driver's eyes threatened to bulge from his head as they flittered between Rich and me. "Stay quiet," Rich said through clenched teeth. "You make a lot of noise . . . it won't go well for you. Understand?" The driver nodded. "We want information. Let's start with your name." Rich took his hand away and balled it into a fist. This did not escape the other man's notice.

"Billy," he said in a small voice. Billy might have been in his mid-twenties, but he spent those years doing some hard living. I figured he'd been sampling the delivery product, maybe even taking part of his pay in something like Vicodin. He stood a hair shorter than Rich, but would only weigh 140 pounds if he'd just gone swimming in his clothes. The color of his skin would encourage a mortician to embalm him. His clothes were at least a size too big. When he talked, I could tell he needed to spend about a week in a dentist's chair.

"Billy, I see you're making some deliveries," said Rich.

"Who are you?" Billy said. Rich showed him his badge. "You ain't even in the right state. Shit, man." Confidence brightened Billy's dull eyes. "I ain't gotta talk to you." He pushed off the wall.

Billy hit the wall again right away when Rich punched him in the face. He took the off-the-clock proviso seriously. I never saw him cuff someone around under these circumstances in Baltimore. Billy shook off the cobwebs and grimaced. "What the hell?" he said.

"I told you," said Rich, "we have some questions. You don't get to walk away until we're done."

After more looking between Rich and me, Billy accepted his fate and hung his head. "What do you want to know."

"Everything," I said. "Let's start with collection and delivery."

"OK. We pick up stuff from people who work on the land."

"How often?"

Billy shrugged. "Once a week, usually. Sometimes more often in summer. There's more to pick up then."

Growing seasons were not a mystery to me, but I nodded as if Billy said something profound. It seemed to placate him. Then Rich said, "How many guys make the pickups?"

"Five or six."

"They all look like you?"

"What are you trying to say?"

"I think you know, you skinny prick," Rich said. He crowded Billy, who shrank back into the wall.

"No, no," he said. "Some of them are bigger."

"Like four guys who could play offensive line?" I said.

"Yeah." Billy nodded. "Them, me, sometimes another guy."

"Then what do you do?"

"We take the shit somewhere," Billy said. "Usually the hospital. Sometimes back to base."

"'Base' being Land of the Brave?" Rich said.

"Yeah. Depends where the deliveries are."

"Then you add drugs to whatever you collected," I said.

"We have a guy at each place who does that," Billy said. "They know how to pack everything. If we get stopped, the cops only see honey or vegetables or whatever."

"What if they look closer?" Rich said.

"Then they'd find the pills. Shit ain't invisible. But you ain't gonna see it unless you go looking for it."

"OK, you make deliveries," I said. "Places like this, grocery stores, whatever. Then they sell the pills."

"Yeah," Billy said as if I'd asked him a super obvious questions. And I did, but we needed to confirm the basics.

"Then what happens with the money, asshole? Do you and the no-neck quartet go back and collect it?"

"No. Unless we need to. Then those other four guys go out. Usually, the places just pay. I'm not sure how it works. They don't tell me shit like that."

For good reason, I thought, but I said, "OK, Billy. Maybe a few more questions."

Before I could ask another one, Rich broke in. "How many places do you deliver to?"

"I usually get the same spots," Billy said. "Different days. I guess about ten in all."

"All in West Virginia?" he nodded. "Your collections, too?" Another nod. "You never go to Maryland?" Head shake.

"Wait a minute," I said. "Do any guys in Maryland cross over into West Virginia?"

"Nope. We all stay in our states."

"No interstate commerce." Rich frowned when I spoke those words. "Smart."

"Let's give an award to the criminals," Rich grumbled.

"Am I done?" Billy asked.

"No," Rich and I said at the same time.

I didn't think of anything else we needed him for. Billy was a pickup and delivery guy. He knew exactly what he needed to know to do those jobs. The Russell brothers controlled the information and managed the schedules and routes. They did illegal things, but their drivers never crossed state lines and only made collections when they needed to strong-arm someone. I'm sure a federal lawyer could pin something big on them, but Land of the Brave skirted initial scrutiny. Exactly like their deliveries.

"What else you need?" Billy said. "I told you what I know."

Rich looked at me. I shrugged. "I think we're done," Rich said. Billy started to walk away, but Rich shoved him back into the wall. "Listen, Billy. You're not going to tell anyone about our little chat."

"No?" A spark of defiance lit in Billy's eyes. "Why not?"

"One of my friends died because of the assholes you work for. I have no problem evening the score." Billy stared at Rich, and his expression morphed into one of fear.

"Sure," he said. "You got it. Not a word."

"You'd better be telling the truth." Rich let Billy go. He dashed back to his van like someone fired him out of a sling. With screeching tires, he pulled away.

"Think he's going to dime us out?" I said.

"I doubt it," Rich said. "He looked terrified I was going to kill him."

"If I didn't know you better, I would have thought you'd shoot him on the spot."

"It was tempting." Rich took a deep breath. "Pieces of shit like him got Jim Shelton killed."

"And we'll pin it on them," I said. "All of them. But we'll do it the right way."

"The right way?" Rich said with a smirk. "You?"

"OK," I said, "some allowances need to be made."

CHAPTER 9

WE DROVE AWAY FROM THE CLINIC AFTER I CONVINCED Rich not to kick the front door in and raid the place. He wanted to call the West Virginia police. This was another ledge I talked him off. Short-term satisfaction didn't help us bust Land of the Brave and everyone involved. If the clinic folks got hauled away, the Russell brothers might pack their bags and set up shop in parts unknown. It took a couple minutes, but Rich listened to reason. I wondered what the hell happened to make me the sensible one.

Back at the motel, Rich went to his room, and I returned to mine. He said he wanted to strategize. It worked for me, because I needed to exercise. Too much sitting in the motel, driving around, and eating fast food left me feeling a little sluggish. I changed into a running outfit and pounded the pavement on Route 219. Federal Hill certainly offered more scenic routes, but miles were miles. While I ran, I thought about Billy. Rich definitely scared him, but his four large friends knew where we stayed. He could rat us out, and they could come back, this time with a bunch of guns. I wondered if we should switch to a different place even though we weren't swamped with options.

After four miles, I walked back into my room and took a shower. Once dressed, I knocked on Rich's door to ask if he wanted food. We decided on subs from Sheetz. At this point, Rich and I should have owned stock in the company after our many visits. If being a shareholder got me free coffee, I would take it. I got two subs, a couple bags of chips, some peanuts, and a pair of drinks. I carried it all back to the motel.

As I approached, I noticed the large SUV near our rooms again. "Shit," I muttered as I ducked behind a pickup truck. Rich's door was ajar. My gun was in my room. I was armed with a pocket knife and a bag of food against who knew how many armed goons in the room. Not good. I couldn't wade into those odds.

A minute later, three of the four men we saw before led Rich out of his room, each of them with a pistol trained on him. Two shoved him into the back of the SUV, while the third kicked my door in. A few seconds later, he emerged, shaking his head. He got into the SUV, and it drove off. I scurried into a better hiding spot behind the truck. The SUV made a left onto 219.

I ran back into my room and grabbed my pistol. The one who searched merely looked around; had he opened the nightstand drawer, he would have taken my .45. I stuffed it into the back of my jeans and dashed into Rich's room. His car keys were hidden behind the TV, where he always leaves them. I picked them up, ran out of the room, and fired up the Camaro. Rich likes to practice what he calls "tactical parking," so he backed into his parking spot. This allowed me to mash my foot to the floor and screech out in a trail of smoke.

Without stopping, I made the left onto 219. One car coming from my left slowed, and I fit the Camaro in front of someone coming from the right. The SUV had already turned off the road. I figured they were going the way Rich and I went a couple nights ago, so I made the right turn and got back on the gas. The

Camaro was a big, heavy beast, and visibility in any direction was subpar. But its fantastic American-made V8 knew what to do when I pressed the accelerator. The car surged ahead, and I scanned every cross street for the SUV.

Then I saw it through the trees around a bend ahead. I backed off the throttle and kept the other vehicle in sight without riding up on them. They probably knew Rich's car, and while I had no idea how observant these assholes were, I didn't want them seeing a blue Camaro in the rearview mirror. I kept my distance as we drove on, farther than Rich and I went. Ahead, they made a left turn onto a street full of ramshackle houses. I slowed, approached the intersection, and watched. This was a short street with three houses on each side. None of them looked fit for human residence. The SUV stopped in front of the last one on the left.

I backed up and pulled over. Through the trees lining the street, I saw the three men lead Rich into the house. The door closed, and I saw the X. I eased my way onto the street, parking behind a huge truck in front of the first house on the left. There were only two other non-goon vehicles. They looked as bad as the homes. I wondered if anyone still lived on this street. A couple lights went on inside the last house. I got out of the Camaro and closed the door as gently as I could. The street was quiet enough I could hear my own steps as I approached. I crouched behind a rusted old SUV parked at the edge of the house. The late afternoon sun wouldn't hide me. Everything was silent.

What would Rich do in this situation? Probably call for backup. I didn't have any readily available. The county police were still dodgy to me, and I didn't want to bring them in. The state police were farther away. Anyone else I could call would need a few hours to arrive. I was on my own. A couple months ago, I donned a helmet and bulletproof vest and raided a building with Rich and some other cops. This was a different situation altogether. I had a pistol, no extra ammo, no protection, and no backup. If I went in, I had to do it strategically. If they saw me, Rich could die.

A couple minutes later, two of the men walked out of the house and got in the front seats of their vehicle. I wondered where the other one was. The two in the SUV didn't look in a hurry to leave. I pondered the survivability of making a dash for the door when the other one sprinted out of the building. I sneaked around to the far side of the truck. Once the third asshole got inside, they took off. I could see them laughing. Cold welled in the pit of my stomach as I wondered what they could find so funny.

When I looked back at the house, I saw.

It was on fire.

* * *

FLAMES PEEKED from windows at the back of the house. I could see bright orange through what remained of the glass. Black clouds wafted out, also at the back. They must have started the blaze there. I ran, sucked in a breath, and pushed the front door open. Acrid smoke greeted me, pouring forth and stinging my eyes. I pulled my shirt over my nose and mouth. The kitchen was an inferno, and the flames spread out from there. Much of the first floor was already ablaze. I saw a sea of gray broken up by pockets of brilliant orange. "Rich!" I shouted. No response. I coughed amid the smoke. "Rich!"

"Up here," I heard him say.

I stayed low and moved in the direction of his voice. As I got closer, I could see the outline of a staircase. A couple steps were missing, and what remained looked like it would collapse under a featherweight boxer. If I went bounding up them, I would wind up on the floor. And while I felt sure I could scramble from the house before it became a pile of cinders, Rich may not make it to safety. I couldn't take the chance. "Are you all right?" I said.

"They tied me up," he called.

"I'm coming up." I put a foot on the bottom step. It didn't buckle. One down. A dozen or so to go.

The second stair held my weight, too. The third was missing. I stepped onto the fourth. It squeaked but didn't give. When I pushed off the second and put all my weight on the fourth step, it wobbled. I hopped to the fifth. The sixth and seventh were fine, but the eighth was gone. I did the same thing I'd done to bypass the third. The ninth held. The tenth buckled. When my foot hit the eleventh, the step broke. Wood clawed at my ankle as I clutched the railing, which was barely in better shape than the staircase.

The splintered edges cut my skin. I felt warm blood run into my sock. The railing threatened to pull away from the wall. It took a few seconds, but I extracted my lower leg and made it the rest of the way up. I spared a glance behind me. The all-consuming gray engulfed the lower level. Going back down would not be an option. My chest and throat burned.

I crouched in a hallway in the middle of the second floor. Smoke filtered up here through the vents and the holes in the floor. Heat radiated from the bottom floor. I was already covered in sweat. I coughed a few times. The air was better up here but getting worse as the fire raged below. It wouldn't take much to burn the shambles of this level. Holes were missing from the walls and ceiling. Water damage pockmarked many of the remaining surfaces. I could make out at least two doors looking at me in both directions.

"Where are you?" I said.

"Here." To my right.

I wanted to run along the hall but was concerned the floor would crumble beneath me. Jogging while staying as low as I could would have to suffice. I found Rich in the remains of a bedroom. An old mattress lay in tatters against the wall. The rest of the room looked as bad as the rest of the house and smelled worse. The arsonists left Rich tied to metal chair. He was bound at the wrists and around the ankles. I took out my pocket knife and spent a minute cutting him free.

"Thanks," he said. "How'd you know I was here?"

"I was coming back when they were loading you into the SUV. Let's talk later. This shithole is coming down."

Rich grabbed his gun off the floor in what once was a closet. He put it in the back of his jeans. "Stairs?" he said.

"Total loss," I said. "The first floor is an inferno by now." Sweat threatened to run into my eyes, which already stung. This end of the house was better for now. If we stood here much longer, though, smoke would overcome us. It already flowed from the vent.

Rich looked at the window. The glass had long since broken and fallen away, some of it into the room. He shoved the frame open. "We can get out here." He pointed down. "Look. It must be a carport or a shed." A roof jutted from the rest of the house's first level. We could make the short drop to there and then either climb or jump down.

"You go first," I said. "Your car is waiting outside."

Rich climbed through the window and stood on the ledge, facing away from me. He made the short leap to the roof. I heard a crack and saw a few shingles scatter when he landed, but the carport—or whatever it was—remained intact. Rich moved to the edge, grabbed on, swung his legs over, and dropped to the ground. I saw him look around. "Shit. I think they're back. A gray SUV pulled up. Must want to check out their handiwork."

"They will have seen your car on the way in," I said. "They know I'm here, too."

Rich drew his gun. "Then get down here, and let's deal with

them." He crouched and skulked away toward the other end of the house.

I eased over the windowsill and onto the narrow ledge. It was about three, maybe four feet down to the roof. I jumped and landed atop the carport. It made another crack, louder than the first. Before I could take a step, the roof buckled and caved in, and I went down with it. I'd felt it start to go, and the realization gave me enough time to protect my head in the fall. The rest of me hit the concrete floor of the carport hard. I lay there, surrounded by a few planks and beams. I coughed, and my whole body hurt. If this were a normal fall, I could have sprung back to my feet, even in pain. The fire sapped my strength, though. I wanted to lie on the floor, but I knew I didn't have the luxury. Rich would need help.

While I summoned the energy to stand, the rest of the roof above me groaned. It shimmed, shook, and then fell on me.

I NEVER LOST CONSCIOUSNESS. AS WITH THE FALL, I HAD just enough time to protect my head. The roof battering me doubled the pain I was already in. I might have welcomed the anesthetics of a blow to the noggin, but if the goon squad got past Rich, I'd be easy pickings lying knocked out amid a pile of old wood. If I wanted to be any help to Rich—and myself—I needed to get out of here. The light lumber landing on my arms when I covered my head fell away easily enough.

Next, the three planks lying on my chest. They flew off with a shove which sent a flare of pain blazing down my shoulder. My legs were pinned by a beam across my thighs and a bunch of two-by-fours below my knees. The larger piece of wood did not respond to my first push. I shifted my hips as much as I could, put both arms under the beam, and heaved. It lifted about a foot. My left arm screamed at me. I didn't have the strength or pain tolerance to throw it off. Instead, I turned more and thrust my arms upward. The beam crashed back to the concrete about two inches above my head. I let out a deep breath.

Behind me, the fire raged. A window somewhere in the house popped and sprayed glass into the backyard. I heard voices.

Before I crashed through the carport's roof, Rich left to hunt for the men who brought him here. I needed to help him. They numbered three when they kidnapped him and could have picked up the fourth. I sat up. My left shoulder still hurt something fierce, and the rest of my body was one large dull ache. I reached behind me for my gun.

It wasn't there.

I heard voices again. Harsh, unfamiliar. Definitely not Rich. I looked around for the .45 but didn't see it. It must have fallen out when I took my tumble and got buried by the roof. I rummaged through the detritus. Most of it was brown and darkened by water damage. The color made finding a black gun difficult. If I survived this, maybe I could bling out my arsenal with some nickel grips.

A shot cracked, then wood splintered. I searched faster. Three more blasts came from the direction of the splintering. I heard what sounded like two people grunting and falling over. Digging through a pile, my hand bumped something metal. The gun. I grabbed it, then crouched and looked out from behind a pile of wood in the ruins of the carport. One of the goons ran from my left. Out of the corner of my eye, I saw Rich coming from the right. He stayed close to the house and used the shadows of trees as he moved. The other man didn't see him. By the time he did, Rich was ten feet away, and the shot was easy.

Rich looked at the wreckage and frowned. "You all right?"

"I'll live," I said.

"Stay here. I'm pretty sure they brought a fourth. I'm going to find him." Rich skulked away toward my left. I kept surveying the grounds. No sign of the last guy from the SUV. I also heard no sirens. Even though first responders wouldn't come into the house, between the fire and the shooting, I figured someone would have called the cops. Maybe this street really was empty.

On the far side of the yard past the house, Rich moved away

from the burning structure and deeper into the yard. It was a mess of shrubs and overgrowth, perfect for hiding a goon who didn't mind getting dirty. Then I saw the fourth man stalking Rich with a two-by-four. "Shit," I muttered as I stood and ran. "Behind you!" I yelled, but before Rich could turn, the other guy clubbed him and sent him crashing to the ground. I pushed ahead faster as the assailant bent down to pick up Rich's gun. He grabbed it and stood. "Put it down," I said as I got to within twenty feet.

The gunman looked at me, then the prone Rich, who lay in the grass and groaned. I took a couple steps closer. My pulse thumped in my ears.

"You gonna shoot me?" he said. I recognized him from the fight at the motel, but he had been one of the guys who fought Rich.

"I will if you raise the gun." He held it in front of him, still pointed toward the earth.

"Ever shoot anyone before?" He grinned at me like a predator eying its next meal.

"First time for everything." My heart rate slowed a bit now I wasn't running, but the situation kept it high. I didn't have Rich's practiced calm. I hoped I wouldn't need it. This asshole would put Rich's firearm down, I would pistol-whip him, and it would be over.

"Sure you got it in you?" he said.

"You're close to finding out," I said. I was fifteen feet away and a good enough shot not to miss at this distance.

He looked at Rich, then at me again. "Yeah, I guess you're right." This screamed setup, like the guy who fakes turning away and then throws a punch. I stayed on guard. The goon raised his left hand and started to crouch.

Then the gun flashed up.

I fired once. Twice. A third time.

Three red spots appeared on the man's chest, two on the left side and one on the right. He looked confused. The gun toppled from his hand. He tried to say something, but his mouth didn't work, and a thin stream of blood ran out instead.

Then he fell to his knees and pitched forward.

I dropped my own pistol and stared ahead.

I just killed a man.

* * *

EVERYTHING TRANSPIRED IN SLOW MOTION. Rich sat up and rubbed his head. He peered at the dead goon, then at me. His head pivoted slowly, as if he moved underwater. I kept staring ahead. It was all I could do. Rich looked down and saw the gun. He said something, but I couldn't understand it, like he shouted from behind a waterfall. Rich crouched and shook my shoulders. I blinked for the first time since I dropped the gun.

"Are you all right?" he said, and I understood it this time.

"I . . . I . . . shot him."

"Yeah. Good thing, too. I don't know how the fucker snuck up on me. He would have shot you or me. Or both of us."

"I shot him," I said again.

Rich frowned. "First time, right?" I nodded. He sighed. "Always the worst. Look, you'll get past it. I can help you." He glanced around. "And I will. Wait there." Rich left for a short while. It could have been ten seconds or an hour. Whichever, he came back and stuffed something in his pockets. "Right now, we should go. Who knows if these assholes called for reinforcements?" He collected my .45.

I felt myself nod. What Rich said made sense. We should leave. More goons could be rolling up any minute. I knelt on the ground, unmoving, as if I'd grown roots. My legs didn't want to move. "Come on," Rich said. He hooked me under the arm and lifted me up. I stumbled in the direction of the Camaro. Rich gripped my bicep to steady me as we jogged. He opened the door and shoved me in. I stared forward and fumbled with the seat-belt. The V8's rumble broke my reverie. Rich turned the car around and took off down the street. "We have to change motels," he said as we sped along the road. "Even if we have to stay outside the city, it's worth it." He paused, obviously waiting for me to concur. I couldn't form any words, so I nodded.

Something burned in my gut. I replayed the scene over and over. The man walloped Rich with a plank. I ran toward him. He acted like he was putting the gun down, then tried to raise it. I shot him. Once. Twice. Three times. Red spread across his chest. He lay face-down in the grass. At least his dead eyes didn't stare at me. It may have been too much right now.

The burning traveled up my throat. "Pull over," I managed to say. Rich jerked the wheel and skidded the car to a stop near the treeline. I opened the door, staggered out, and vomited. I puked again and again, until I heaved only air. I closed my eyes and took a few ragged breaths. Rich put a hand on my shoulder. "You did the right thing," he said.

I nodded. On some level, I knew it. "Doesn't feel like it right now," I said in a raw, scratchy voice. Between the fire and throwing up, my throat felt like I gargled with lava.

Rich handed me a couple napkins. I was about to ask where he got them when he said, "You brought a bag of food with you?"

In spite of the situation, I chuckled. "It was in my hand when everything went down." I wiped my mouth. I wished I could have sandblasted it.

"When you're feeling up to it, go ahead and eat." He looked down at the pool of vomit in the grass and handed me a bottle of water. "I think you'll need to."

I drained half of it in one long swig. "Maybe later," I said.

"You better now?"

"Yeah." I stood. A little wobbly, but I made it.

"Let's go, then."

Again in the car, we headed headed toward Route 219. "Let's check out of the motel," Rich said when we were closer. "If it looks like someone is sitting on it, we keep going."

"I want my laptop and gear," I said. Rich glared at me. "It's good stuff. I'm not letting it go just because a couple assholes are outside our doors." We got to 219. "Make a right," I said.

"What? Why?"

"I want to see if anyone is camped out behind our rooms. It'll work better if no one sees your super obvious car drive past the lot."

We snaked our way around the back roads, emerging onto 219 above the hotel. Rich pulled over, and I got out. "Be careful," he said.

"I'll try to leave the shooting to you," I said. I approached the motel from the rear. The rear windows of our rooms faced a grassy lot, then a short fence. I kept low, moving along the fence, but I was the only person out here. A single bound got me over the barrier. Now I hoped I picked the right room. The window in my bathroom wasn't big, but I could fit through it. First, I need it to be unlocked. Of course, it wasn't.

I owned a special keyring full of tools for picking locks, but it was inside. There didn't appear to be a way to open the window from the outside, anyway. So I improvised. I took the gun out of my pants, gripped the slide, and smashed the handle into the glass. I cleared some remaining shards. A few sharp bits remained. I doffed my sweatshirt and draped it over the bottom of the window frame. I lifted myself through the window, grunting in pain as my left shoulder barked at me again.

My feet hit the bathroom floor. I opened the door slowly, my muzzle leading the way. If anyone was in the room, they were the hide and seek world champion. I grabbed my gear and tossed it into my bag. Then I saw my clothes. I liked what I brought. There was space in the bag. I shoved everything in and walked back into the bathroom. No one waited for me outside the window. I craned my neck and looked in both directions. The area was goon-free. I threw the bag onto the grass, climbed out behind it, and dashed back to Rich's car.

* * *

I PERSUADED Rich to pull over. We got off 219 and turned into a parking lot behind a nondescript building. Someone would have to look for us to notice us here. "What are we doing?" he said. I thumbed through a few notes on my phone.

"Finding a place to stay," I said.

"We can find another motel."

"So can the people who tried to kill us."

"You have a better idea?" said Rich.

"We'll see." I found the number and called. Luke Thompson answered on the second ring. "You still want a story?"

"What do you have in mind?" he said.

I gave him a rundown of recent events. "Our concern is they're looking for us. They could have more guys, or they could even have some deputies."

"You want a place to stay." It wasn't a question.

"Plus a place to hide the most obvious car in the county for a day or two," I said. Rich frowned. I covered my phone. "I'm not the one with a bright blue Camaro."

"I think I can help you with those," said Luke.

"Thanks."

"It's not out of the kindness of my heart. I want to fill page one with the story you guys are going to give me."

"I think you'll be able to," I said. "We need a little time to wrap it up, but it could be a career-maker."

"Where are you now?" I told him. "Stay there. I'll come meet you. Then you can follow me. I'll try to keep us off the main roads as much as possible."

I hung up. We waited.

* * *

WE TRAILED Luke's Jeep along the side roads of Oakland. A couple blocks from the *Republican's* office, he led us to a body shop. Rich pulled the Camaro into a vacant bay. We got out. The door closed behind us. "My brother's shop," Luke said when we got into his Jeep Wrangler—Rich up front and me in the back. "He'll keep it in there for a couple days. Shouldn't take you longer than that, right?"

"No," Rich said. "I think we're close to wrapping it up."

"Good." Luke pulled out onto the road. "What else do you need to do?"

"Tie up loose ends," I said. "I need to do some research. There have to be connections here."

"Connections where?"

"Between Land of the Brave, the mayor, maybe the sheriff's office, and whoever provides meatheads for hire."

"I grabbed a couple of their IDs," Rich added. "Doesn't tell us who hired them, but we can still use it."

"I'll see if I can help you with it," Luke said. He steered us down yet another in a series of twisty streets I couldn't distinguish. "I've lived here long enough."

"I do . . . different research than a lot of people," I said.

"Hacking?"

I spoke to his eyes in the rearview. "None of it will be traceable back to you."

"So you're the law and order one," Luke said, inclining his

head at Rich. Then he half-turned to glance at me. "And you're the one who colors outside the lines."

"I'm the better-looking one, too," I said. Rich snorted in the passenger's seat. I saw the top third of his head shaking above the headrest.

"I'll make sure the readers know," said Luke.

"Please do."

Luke owned a small, two-story house with a short driveway leading to a detached garage more like a barn. He parked the Jeep, and we all went into his home. It felt cool, like he hadn't run the heat since spring began six months ago. Ugly green carpeting covered the floors. It went with the beige walls, but it was still hideous. If my house had come with such abominable carpet, I might have burned the whole place to the ground to ensure I was rid of it.

The rest was furnished by and for a bachelor. Luke and I shared similar tastes in furniture if not in quality. The living room consisted of a sofa, recliner, entertainment center with two game consoles, and a large TV mounted on the wall. The dining room held a small square table and four plain chairs. "You can setup here for now," Luke said. He told me his Wi-Fi password. A minute later, my laptop was on his network and connected to the VPN. "You don't take many chances, do you?"

"Not with my technology," I said.

Rich and Luke adjourned to the dining room while I banged away at my research. The people were certain to be connected. The helpful mayor, the nice charity director, guys like Billy, the four goons. I couldn't link them professionally, and in a small town, I couldn't go around and interrogate people. It left Google and other tools. I preferred those to most people anyway.

There are plenty of websites, legitimate and otherwise, dedicated to aggregating information about people. With the right search parameters, you could find a trove of embarrassing information on most people. Humiliation was always nice, but I wanted to see how these people fit together. Ken Dennehy. Pete and George Russell. The two dead assholes whose wallets ended up in Rich's pocket. Even Billy the drug delivery guy. Something other than drugs tied them to each other.

The first domino fell in about a minute. George Russell took his wedding vows thirteen years ago, marrying Dawn Dennehy, sister of Ken. The siblings' older sister Sheila married a man now deceased. Their son William in West Virginia struggled with addiction and often found himself on the wrong side of the law. The dead husband, Edward Leonard, fathered a son from his first marriage. Tyler Leonard's picture looked back at me from one of the dead men's wallets. A family operation, more or less.

This would give Luke his story. He could pull a couple more threads and unravel the whole thing. I did enough of the heavy lifting for him.

Now Rich and I had to bring these people down.

CHAPTER 11

IN THE OTHER ROOM, RICH CALLED SOMEONE HE KNEW IN the Maryland State Police. I heard him make the case for not summoning the feds—the operation was careful about state lines —and it sounded like he won the argument. He hung up and rejoined us in the living room. "State cops will be here in the morning," said Rich. "They're looping in the West Virginia boys, too, for the other side of the border.

"Why so long?" I said.

"They like to work within the law. Gotta take the case to a state's attorney and get a warrant."

"I thought you were off the clock."

"Captain Norton isn't," Rich said.

"I guess you're bunking here," Luke said. "The loft above the garage has a couple beds in it and bathroom."

"Can I borrow some clothes for tomorrow?" Rich asked me.

"I'm not sure my stuff will fit you well," I said. "Besides, you'll look way more fashionable than normal."

Luke offered to get some clothes for Rich in town. While he ran the errand, Rich and I checked out our sleeping quarters. The first thing I noticed was the brown shag carpeting. I hoped Luke didn't choose something so ghastly. With a better layout, the loft would make a functional apartment. It could hold a bedroom, bathroom, living room, and kitchen. As configured, it featured the kitchen and bathroom, and the rest of the place was undefined. Two twin beds sat close to a sofa, which was in the vicinity of an old recliner and ancient TV. With a few weekends of work, Luke could rent this place out.

Speaking of Luke, he came back about an hour later with clothes and food. We ate pizza from Tomanetti's at the dining room table. After our meal, we went over the story. Luke assembled the skeleton of it already, but he was missing a lot of bones and connective tissue. Rich and I provided those for him. He took notes on his laptop, showing off a typing rate my keyboarding instructors from middle school would have envied. "Jesus Christ," he said when we finished. I expected smoke to waft up from his laptop.

"It's a lot to take in," I said.

"They've been pretty brazen about it, too. George Russell using his own bank accounts." Luke frowned and keyed in another note. "I wonder if some of those withdrawals went to law enforcement or federal regulators."

"Maybe." I shrugged. "I figured they were for snatching a box of drugs here and there. Who knows? Maybe you can find out before the police do."

"It'd be safer to let them do it," Rich chimed in.

"Ever the wet blanket," I said.

Rich rolled his eyes. "Nosing around could be dangerous right now. We don't know if Billy blabbed to everyone he knows. They could be wise to us."

"Which is why we're staying here."

"And why you should wait for the police," Rich said to Luke. "Type up your story and send it to your boss the second the cuffs get slapped on. But going off the reservation for a scoop could get you hurt. Or worse."

Luke took Rich's advice better than I would have—and better than I've taken whatever advice he's given me over the years. "All right," he said. "I'll write what I have and send it in. My boss will sit on it until the time is right. Then it'll go out online and in the next morning's edition."

"You have a handgun?" I said.

"It's Garrett County," Luke said. "Everyone has a handgun."

"Fair enough. Might want to bring it with you tomorrow. If Billy ran his mouth, it could get ugly."

"I've never shot anyone before," Luke said.

His words rang in my ears like the three shots I fired. I wished I could still make the same claim.

* * *

THE NEXT MORNING, Luke and I ate breakfast—he ran out to Sheetz—at his dining room table while Rich showered and put on his new clothes. He joined us a few minutes later. Rich's eye for fashion is a couple years behind and hit-and-miss, but he always picked jeans to fit perfectly. The pants he wore today did not. They were carpenter's denims with a bunch of straps to dangle tools from, and they were both too big in the waist and too long in the inseam. Rich's belt did yeoman's work to keep the pants around his midsection, while the legs were rolled into inch-high cuffs. Despite Rich's preemptive scowl, I laughed.

"Want to hang some drywall before we leave?" I said. Rich ignored me, sat at the table, and grabbed a coffee. "Maybe we could saw a bunch of two-by-fours. Is it 'measure twice, cut once'?"

"Yes," Rich said. If a hammer hung from its proper loop, his expression indicated he might have hit me with it.

"Look on the bright side," I said. "If you ever need to infiltrate the guys standing outside Home Depot, you have the perfect disguise."

Luke covered his mouth and chuckled. Rich sighed and looked through the Sheetz bag for breakfast. He pulled out a breakfast sandwich and a donut. We all finished eating, and I wished Luke came back with more coffee. A coffee maker was conspicuous by its absence in his kitchen. "Where is your friend meeting us?" Luke asked Rich.

"Land of the Brave headquarters," he said. "He'll have some state cops with him. At the same time, the West Virginia cops are going to hit the hospital and scoop up George Russell and his people."

"If it's all simultaneous, nobody can tip anyone else off," I said.

"Sometimes, the cops have good ideas, too," said Rich.

"Let's hope it all goes as planned."

After breakfast, we got in Luke's Jeep and drove toward Deep Creek Lake. "Does your state police friend know you're coming dressed like Bob Vila?" I said.

"I'm surprised you know who Bob Vila is," said Rich, ignoring the barb.

"I watch YouTube. Besides, he's part of pop culture."

"I agree," Luke said. "I was way too young for his show, but I know who he is."

"Great," Rich said, "we're all Bob Vila fans."

"Looks like you are most of all," I said.

Rich shook his head, but I saw a brief smirk pass over his face. A few minutes later, we approached Land of the Brave. The parking lot held about the same number of cars it did when Rich and I came before. "Keep going," Rich said. "They're not here yet." It didn't take long for us to encounter the state contingent. A short distance along 219, a convoy of unmarked state police cars rolled past us. Luke turned around while Rich made a phone call.

He told whoever answered we were in the Jeep but declined to mention his inadvertent disguise as a carpenter.

We parked near the police cars. A couple troopers jogged to the rear of the building. Rich introduced me to Captain Casey Norton. He was about my height but broad like Rich with short blond hair and dark green eyes. The hair showed no gray, though a few creases around the eyes made me guess Norton to be about Rich's age. If the police career didn't work out, he could always try out for the Ravens as a linebacker. "Rich told me about you," he said as we shook hands.

"He embellishes a lot," I said. Rich only complimented me to his law enforcement peers after running me down first.

"Your reputation precedes you."

"Is forewarned a good thing?"

"I guess we'll find out," Norton said.

We proceeded inside, bypassing the startled receptionist and heading right to Pete Russell's office. Rich led the way. Russell smiled initially, but his expression soured when he saw the retinue of troopers walking behind Rich. "You're done, you piece of shit," he said.

"What's the meaning of this?" Russell said, standing and banging his desk.

"Peter Russell," Norton said, "you're under arrest for possession of narcotics, distribution of narcotics, theft, conspiracy to distribute narcotics, and conspiracy to commit murder."

"This is outrageous! I run a legitimate charity."

"You killed Jim Shelton," Rich said. He stood nose-to-nose with Russell. "Jim was my friend. I would love it if you'd resist arrest." Rich clenched and unclenched his hands into fists. Norton stared at him and frowned.

"If he starts beating this guy," I said to Norton, "you'll have to pull him off."

"You wouldn't?"

I shook my head. "He's an asshole. He deserves a pummeling."

"We won't let him get pounded."

"Pity," I said.

Russell didn't resist. He put his hands up. Rich stayed in his face until Norton tapped his shoulder. Only then did he relent. Norton and his troopers arrested Russell and led him outside. Rich and I followed with Luke. Back in the Jeep, I said, "I was hoping you'd hit him."

"It was tempting," said Rich. "I'm not sure I could have stopped."

"I wouldn't have pulled you off."

"Really?" Rich said.

"Really."

"I knew I brought you for a reason."

* * *

NORTON and another trooper stayed behind while the rest of the convoy left with Peter Russell. He spent a couple minutes on the phone with a counterpart in West Virginia. We leaned on the Jeep and waited. When he hung up, Norton came down and talked to us. "They got the brother," he said, "plus a few other guys."

"What about the mayor?" I said.

"Being questioned. We don't know what his involvement is."

"And the sheriff?" Rich said.

Norton shrugged. "No evidence that he or his men took part," he said.

"The mayor might have ordered them around," I suggested.

"Then if it happened, it's on the mayor and those deputies."

Norton shook hands with us and departed with his fellow trooper. "You have everything you need for the story?" I said to Luke.

"I think so." He nodded. "There's a version online already. I'll add more details, and updates will go on the site later and out in the paper tomorrow morning."

"Remember us when you're a big-timer."

He smiled. "I like it at the *Republican*. This city and county are more my speed than a place like Baltimore."

"I'll look for your Pulitzer acceptance speech, then," I said.

"I'll start drafting it tomorrow," Luke said. He drove us back to his house, where we picked up our stuff before going to his brother's garage to get Rich's car. From there, we stopped at the motel. The fellow behind the desk wanted to charge us for another night, but a look at Rich's badge and glare changed his mind. We collected Rich's things and pulled onto 219. He drove to the Shelton house. I waited in the car while he talked to Connie at the door. They chatted for a few minutes. Connie's head bowed, and her shoulders shook. Rich hugged her while she cried on his shoulder. After the tears passed, they talked for another minute and embraced again.

Rich got back in the car. "I think they'll be OK," he said.

"Good. What about money?"

"I'm sure they'll sue Russell for wrongful death, if nothing else."

"You know," I said, "I could get back into his bank records. It would only take a few minutes to reallocate some of his money."

"No," Rich said. "The state police are all over this. We can't have an irregularity now."

"OK."

"You understand?"

"Not really," I said, "but I'll go along to get along." I paused. "Did you tell her?"

"Tell her what?"

"Why Jim died."

Rich remained quiet for a few seconds before he said, "I think she already knew he figured something out. They both wanted to believe Land of the Brave was doing good for the right reasons." He sighed. "Jim was always curious and smart. We used to tell him he'd make a good MP."

"Did he take it as a compliment?"

"We didn't really mean it as one," Rich said with a small smile. "We were infantry. Didn't have a lot of use for military cops."

"Yet you basically traded one uniform for another," I pointed out.

"I think Jim could have, too."

"Luke said he's going to mention Jim putting the drug angle together in his piece."

"Good. You convinced him it was worth it?" I inclined my head. "Thanks." Rich pulled out of the neighborhood. A couple minutes later, we turned onto 219 to start the drive back home.

* * *

THE NEXT MORNING, I got the call I expected. "Hi, Mom."

"Coningsby, your father and I read what you and Richard did in Garrett County," she said. Yes, Coningsby is my real first name. It's from family on my mother's side. Why I go by my initials is obvious. The fact my mother insists on not using them is annoying.

"Don't tell me you read a newspaper called the *Republican*," I said. "You'll be a pariah at the rotary club."

"The *Sun* picked up the story, dear. No one at the rotary club will know."

"What a relief."

"I'm not sure I like the idea of Richard recruiting you," my mother said. "I know he did it for his friend's family, so I guess the right people got the help they needed in the end."

"They did," I said.

"And you brought that awful organization down."

"It's a shame. Land of the Brave started out doing good work. I wish they'd simply stuck with it. They could have helped a lot of people."

"Maybe someone will try again," she said. I wondered if my parents' foundation would look for opportunities in Garrett County. It was the kind of thing they would do.

"Maybe they will."

"Your father and I will draft you a paycheck later today. Good work, Coningsby."

"Thanks, Mom," I said.

"Make sure you call Gloria. She's a nice girl."

"I will."

We hung up. A few other calls came in. I ignored them. An article like the one in the Sun always spiked my inquiries in the short term. Most of them could be safely dismissed. I didn't want to take a new case now, anyway. My shoulder and back still hurt from falling through the carport and having the ceiling collapse on me. I would need a few days to recover physically—and following the shooting, maybe longer to recover mentally.

I pushed the memory out of my mind and texted Gloria.

END of Novella #2

Novella #3
Red City Blues

CHAPTER 1

MY SEARCH FOR A PROPER BUSINESS LOCATION CONTINUED. A month ago, a man came into my home office with a gun. While the encounter didn't end well for him, the whole thing made me realize running a private investigator service out of my house was a bad idea. My quest so far proved both unspectacular and sporadic. I worked a couple cases since then, which infringed on the time I might have spent hunting for new digs.

This meant potential clients could still come to my front door unannounced. One stared back at me now. She was a black lady, at least sixty years old and made of bones and sharp angles. I don't think it would have taken a stiff wind to knock her over; a strong breeze whistling between houses could probably whisk this woman from her feet. Her round glasses looked too big for her slender face. Her hair, a mix of gray and black, was pulled neatly into a bun. She wore a plain white shirt and khaki capris. "C.T. Ferguson?" she said.

"Yes, ma'am."

"I might need to hire you."

I invited her inside, and we walked down the hall to my office. I owned an end-unit rowhouse in the Federal Hill area of Baltimore. Whoever lived in it before I did built a study on the first floor and an addition to contain the kitchen. It and my dining room were a little pinched for space, but I found the trade-off worth it. My desk hid two computers beneath it and held three monitors atop. A binary clock on the wall showed my geek cred to anyone who walked in. My prospective client appraised it all before she sat in a guest chair.

She accepted a bottle of water from my mini-fridge. Today was a typical Baltimore summer day with the temperature and humidity both in the nineties. After a long swig, she said, "Like I told you, I might need to hire you."

"Tell me what happened," I said.

"My name is Erma Johnson."

"Nice to meet you."

"Have you followed the local news recently?" I shook my head. "My grandson was shot and killed about ten days ago."

"I'm sorry," I said.

She gave a fractional nod before continuing. "Three days later, my daughter was murdered the same way outside the funeral home at his viewing."

I couldn't find any words. The level of depravity involved rendered me speechless. For her part, Erma Johnson got through the retelling so far without even a crack in her voice. Defiance flashed in her eyes. She was grieving, to be sure, but she also looked mad at the wanton killer of her child and grandson. In her place, I would have felt the same.

"It's been a week," she continued. "The police don't have no leads. I talk to them every day. The fellow on the phone is always nice to me, but he never has anything good to tell me."

"And you're tired of them not making progress," I said.

"I am."

"Tell me as much as you can."

"The cops say my grandson was killed in a gang shooting," she said, shaking her head. "That boy wasn't in no gang."

"How do you know?" I said.

"A grandmother knows these things."

"Miss Johnson," I said, "how old was your grandson?"

"Nineteen."

Way too young to die. "When I was around his age, I'm sure I did things my grandmother didn't know about."

"No," she said. "My boy wasn't in no gang." Now her voice cracked. *Good job, C.T.; make an old lady cry.* "He was a smart kid, got good grades. He was in college."

"What was his name?"

"Dante. Dante Johnson."

I opened a new Notepad file and entered his name. "Why do the police think he was a gangbanger?"

"He was found wearing gang colors," she said. "I don't know which. He and his mother lived in a pretty rough area."

"No other evidence?" I said when she fell silent.

"Nothing they'll tell me. I've said to the cops that my grandson was a good boy. They say, 'yes, ma'am,' and that's it. I call the next day, and there's nothing new."

"What about your daughter?"

"Anisha was a sweet girl," she said. Her eyes softened and grew wistful. "That boy was the light of her life. It ripped her up when he got killed." Her eyes welled. I pushed a box of tissues across the desk, and she snagged one. "I'm sorry."

"Don't be," I said. "My sister died when I was sixteen. I think I kept the Kleenex Corporation profitable by myself for at least a couple weeks."

A smile played briefly on her lips before disappearing. "My daughter was great," she said after wiping her eyes. "She'd just turned forty. Got her degree a few years ago."

"Was Dante her only son?"

Her head bobbed. "My oldest grandchild. His viewing was last week. We had two—one in the afternoon and one in the evening. Before the second one, a bunch of us were standing outside and talking. A car pulled up, and someone shot my daughter. Shot her down like a dog." Erma Johnson dabbed at her eyes. "Right in front of everyone."

"I can't imagine what it was like," I managed to say as I added Anisha's name to my document.

"I don't know who does something like this," she said. "It's monstrous. It's evil."

It was both those things, but was it also part of a gang's play-book? I'd never heard of it before. "Have the police been able to tell you anything?"

"No. I don't even know if they're trying anymore."

They were, but I sympathized with her frustration. "I'll see what I can find."

"You have a good relationship with the police?" she asked.

I almost laughed. My cousin Rich was a Baltimore police detective. He and I got along, which is the best way to describe our relationship. I stayed on good terms with a couple other cops. The rest found me annoying. I figured it was because I solved a bunch of cases they couldn't. Rich even got a couple of commendations by riding my coattails straight to the awards stage. "Good enough," I said.

"So you'll help me?" Erma Johnson said.

"I will."

"God bless you, Mister Ferguson."

I was about to tell her I didn't sneeze, but I simply smiled and said, "I'll take all the help I can get."

* * *

MANY NEWS OUTLETS lamented the gang-related crime in Baltimore. Few of them provided any hard facts. They chronicled the shootings, sure, and wailed and gnashed their teeth at all the right times. Beyond a body count, however, they offered little else. The biggest facts I learned from an hour of research were the names of the two biggest gangs in the city: The West Baltimore Buccaneers and the West Side Pirates. In the business world, two organizations with similar names and purposes were likely to merge. On the streets of my city, they shot at each other and anyone else who happened to get in the way.

As their names suggested, both operated in the western part of the city. Public information didn't tell me much more. I turned to the BPD to fill in the considerable gaps. During my first case, Rich left his computer unguarded for a couple minutes, during which I snagged his IP and physical addresses. Armed with those, I mapped the entirety of the BPD's network and got it to accept my laptop as one of its own computers. This gave me access to their files and resources.

They accumulated a ton of information on gangs. I copied some of the more interesting-looking items to review later. One thing they lacked was any history of what happened to Erma Johnson. Never before in the BPD's files was a young man killed, then his mother shot to death outside the funeral home where he lay. I couldn't fault them for being stumped. Additional research told me an identical crime happened in Oakland, California, eleven years before. Two crimes on opposite coasts more than a decade apart was about as far from a pattern as something could be.

I went back to the local angle. Despite a few smaller street crews battling for chunks of turf, the Bucs and Pirates committed most of the crimes. Erma Johnson gave me her daughter's address. It was smack-dab in the middle of Pirate territory. They wore red. I called up Dante's case file. Photos from the crime scene showed him in a rumpled blue T-shirt and a blue bandanna sitting askew on his head. The Bucs, naturally, wore blue, because gangs aren't original when it comes to color schemes. Erma said he was a smart kid. I believed her. My problem was if he were smart, he would've known better than to wear a shirt and bandanna which may have gotten him shot. If he were a Buc, he wouldn't have been alone. I found no record of anyone else getting shot in the area the same day.

Based on what I'd seen, I believed Erma Johnson: I thought her grandson was a smart kid who was not in a criminal group. Why, then, did he wear clothes advertising his allegiance in the heart of enemy territory? I doubted I would find answers poring over the BPD's scattered info.

I tried a more direct approach.

* * *

AN HOUR LATER, I met Detective Paul King for a late lunch (or early dinner) at The Abbey, recent winner of an award for serving the best burgers in Maryland. I wouldn't quibble. They also boasted of a great beer selection and a convenient Federal Hill location I could walk to in a few minutes. When I entered, King waved from a table against the left wall.

Some people have a youthful or haggard quality working to subtract or add years to their ages. Not King—he was in his mid-thirties and looked it. A mop of disheveled dirty-blond hair sat atop his head. He was about six feet tall, giving me two inches on him, and we both weighed in somewhere in the one-eighties. Depending on our meal choices, we both could tip the scales at a higher number after this.

"Thanks for coming," I said as I slid the chair out and sat.

"How can I say no to The Abbey?"

"No reasonable man could."

A waiter with a hipster goatee and glasses to match asked if we were ready. We were. King built his own burger; I opted for the spicy and excellent Santa Fe. We each chose bottled beers of potent hoppiness and difficult pronunciation. "What do they call this?" he said when the waiter walked away.

"What do you mean?"

"This meal. You have a late breakfast or early lunch, you call it brunch. Every fucking restaurant in the city goes crazy for brunch on the weekends."

"There's no later-in-the-day equivalent," I said. "You can't call it 'dunch.'"

"Or 'linner,'" King added.

"They're both terrible." The waiter returned long enough to drop off our beers. I sipped mine. "This, however, is not terrible," I said.

A few more tables filled up. The bar could claim a few open seats, but much of the small dining room was occupied, at least on the first floor. I only sat on the ground floor of the original Federal Hill location, and only on the second floor of the newer Fells Point spot. Call me old school, but I preferred the original. Being able to get there and back with a short stroll no doubt helped. "It's damn good," said King. He set the bottle down. "You didn't say much about why you wanted to talk."

"Can't it be to soak up your charming personality?"

"No, it can't."

King's personality wasn't as bad as he let on, but it would not be counted first among his virtues. "Your words, not mine," I said. "I need information on local gangs."

My statement made King laugh. His frivolity was interrupted only by the waiter delivering our food. After we had both sampled a few bites of our burgers and fries, he continued. "What makes you think I'm the man to see?"

"I know you've worked in a lot of different units," I said, "including some time on the gang detail."

"You think the bangers talked to me a lot?" he said. "Look at me. I'm as white as fucking Casper the Ghost. They ain't telling me anything."

"You must've made some contacts," I said. "Informants. Something."

"I knew a few guys I could get a little from."

"You still talk to them?" I said.

"I'm in vice now," said King. "I've been upgraded to a different class of lowlife."

"You must have a name for me." I ate some more of my Santa Fe burger. The fresh jalapeños gave it a wonderful heat. I didn't care for food only hot for the sake of it, but I was a fan of honest spice.

"I can give you one. Not sure you'll like it, though."

"Why wouldn't I like it?" I said.

"The guy's a pimp."

I shrugged. "We all gotta eat."

"You're OK with a pimp?" King shot me a quizzical look.

"Better than a drug dealer," I said.

King frowned. "I guess. I'd rather not have to deal with either one, though."

"I think you're in the wrong business."

"Maybe I'll get to Homicide with your cousin one day," King said.

"What's the name?" I asked, steering the conversation away from King's career ambitions.

"Romeo," he said with a straight face.

When he didn't follow it up with anything, I said, "Seriously?"

"Romeo," King confirmed.

"A bit on the nose, isn't it?"

"Christ, you should hear some of the names these assholes come up with. Pimps and bangers love to think they're creative."

"Where can I find this Romeo?"

"Downtown," King said. "His girls used to work the Block plus a street or two over."

I downed a healthy swig of my beer. When I started doing this job almost a year ago, I figured I would sit at my computer and solve problems via my hacking skills. While I still got to be a keyboard warrior some of the time, I spent more hours than I expected hitting the streets, getting into fights, and dealing with characters like a pimp named Romeo. I didn't know how many more beers it would take to make this seem normal, but the number would leave me staggering back home. "Sounds like a fun way to spend an evening," I said.

"It's the Block," King said. "Everybody has fun."

CHAPTER 2

A FEW HOURS LATER, I WENT OUT TO DINNER WITH GLORIA Reading. She and I enjoyed a relationship of fun and convenience—"friends with benefits" as I might have called it in college —though we'd definitely grown closer over the last couple months. Gloria came from a wealthy family like I did, and she didn't need to work a day in her life. Recently, her socialite tendencies got scaled back, and she took a greater interest in my cases. Including this one.

"Gangs?" she said with a delicate frown.

"I'm not convinced the kid was in one," I said.

We ate at Slainte, an Irish pub in Baltimore. When I first met Gloria almost a year ago, she turned her nose up at any restaurant not proudly displaying its Zagat ratings and Michelin Stars in the front window. As she came around in other areas, her willingness to try other types of places increased. One of these times, I would get her to try bangers and mash, but it wouldn't be tonight.

"But he could have been."

"Maybe," I acknowledged. "It seems unlikely, though." I went over my reasons with her.

"It sounds like people in a gang killed him," said Gloria after ruminating on my logic.

"And his mother. It takes a particular kind of barbarism to shoot a woman in front of a funeral home while her son is lying inside."

"This sounds like another dangerous case." Gloria's brows furrowed in concern.

"I do seem be taking a lot of those, don't I?"

"You do," Gloria said. "It concerns me." She reached across the table and grabbed my hand. Before either of us could realize the awkwardness and pull back, our waitress brought dinner. It gave us a convenient excuse to pull apart. The red-headed server set a loaded plate of bangers and mash in front of me and a burger and fries before Gloria. A few months ago, I couldn't fathom her eating a burger, even if she accidentally wandered into a place serving them. I quite liked this newer version of Gloria. She still cut it in half, however, and rarely ate more than fifty percent. But it was progress.

"Aren't your parents worried, too?" Gloria asked once we had both sampled our entrees.

"They are," I said. "We've had a few conversations about it."

"They haven't threatened to cut you off?"

"Not yet." Almost a year ago, I became a rather reluctant employee of my parents' charitable foundation. I took on clients who needed my services but couldn't pay, and my parents cut me a check once I solved each case. They weren't thrilled with the arrangement. Neither was I at first, but I've come to appreciate the work I do over time. My parents still harbored concerns for my safety. I couldn't blame them—I did, too, sometimes. When I decided to do this job, I figured I could remain aloof and use my considerable computer skills to divine the answers. Reality put me on the streets mixing it up with ne'er-do-wells more often than I liked.

"Do they know you've taken this case?"

I smiled and said, "Not yet" again.

Gloria ate another bite of her hamburger. With the amounts she bit off, we would have time for a long conversation. "Are you going to?"

"I'm sure it'll come up at some point," I said. "For now, I'm more concerned about figuring out how to find whoever killed this kid and his mother."

"Of course," she said. "Do you have any idea how to start?"

I shrugged. "The way I usually work. Look some things up, try to make heads or tails of them, ask people questions, hit them when they get mad about it, and see what happens."

Gloria grinned in spite of herself. "That's not much of plan."

"It's usually all I have this early," I admitted.

"What if turns out a gang did it?"

"Then I'll turn it over to the police. They're better equipped for something on a large scale."

"Good." Gloria's chest went out and in with her sigh of relief.

We finished our meal and passed on dessert. My refrigerator contained an abundance of blueberries, so I baked them into a pie. My oven work can be spotty, but my pie game is strong. As I reached for the check, my phone vibrated in my pocket. Earlier, I set an alert to notify me of suspected gang violence in Baltimore. The notification told me another young man had been killed in a shooting being attributed to one of the nefarious organizations.

"Something important?" Gloria said.

"We might need to take a rain check on dessert," I said.

* * *

I MADE Gloria a small sundae for dessert, then busied myself in the office. Paul King told me he used a contact named Romeo. I searched the Baltimore Police Department's records. It didn't take long to find information on Romeo. The moniker proved popular among pimps, but only one owned a file worth mentioning. He was a known procurer of women who managed to avoid arrest and passed that luck onto his girls. He also spent a violent youth in both prominent Baltimore gangs. In homage to his history, all his girls dressed in red and blue. Romeo suddenly became a very interesting fellow.

"I have to run out," I said as I walked into the living room.

Her feet curled under her on my sofa, Gloria polished off her sundae. "You work the strangest hours."

"And I talk to the strangest people. Tonight, I'm going to chat up a pimp."

Gloria blinked a few times. "A pimp?"

"Not my first choice," I said, "but I think he can help."

"Be careful," Gloria said. She stood and gave me a lingering kiss before I left. It was the kind of kiss to weaken my knees and make me want to stay. I left while I still could.

I parked my car in a 24-hour garage just off Baltimore Street. The sights, sounds, and smells of The Block hit me before I stepped onto the pockmarked sidewalk. Tacky neon signs advertised nude girls and strip shows with the unwritten promise of more. Music best left on a porn producer's cutting room floor blared every time a door swung open. Even on the street, I smelled booze, cheap cologne and perfume, and cheaper women.

I saw several of said ladies of the evening walking around trying to look less conspicuous. Their short skirts, ridiculous boots, and push-up tops always gave them away. My keen powers of observation served me well as a private eye: Along with everyone else on the street, I could spot the working girls. I didn't see any pimps until I looked closer; they popped in and out of the clubs or emerged from the shadows next to buildings.

In bygone years, the Block was longer. More recently, it traded overall length for an uptick in quality. Larry Flynt's

Hustler Club brought a higher-class clientele. Sleazier clubs surrounded it, but not as many as before, and not for as many city blocks. The most interesting fact about The Block is it butts against Police Headquarters at its eastern end. It forced more interesting action farther west.

I noticed a few girls dressed in red and blue but didn't see their pimp. The hookers would talk to people and wander off with johns. I never noticed anyone hassling them. Perhaps Romeo gave his girls a little more leash than the traditional late-night proprietor. Regardless, I didn't see him anywhere, so I did the next best thing: I approached one of his girls.

She was white and looked to be in her mid-twenties but was probably younger due to years added by the street. Her blonde hair was natural if a little flat and stringy. Still, she showed a pretty face with delicate cheekbones and stormy gray eyes. I guessed her at five-seven and about a hundred and ten pounds, making her a little skinny for my tastes. She smiled at me as I walked up to her; I noticed she still had all her teeth. No meth, at least.

"Looking for a good time?" she said.

"Actually, I'd just like to talk," I said.

"You a cop?" The smile disappeared so quickly I wondered if it had ever really been there.

"Do I look like a cop?"

She studied me for a few seconds. "You got a cop's eyes."

"Cop eyes don't have depth and sensitivity like mine." This logic failed to persuade her, so I tried a different tack. "Look, I'm a private investigator working a case. I don't care how you make your money. I only need a bit of information, and you're the best person I can get it from right now."

She studied me again before finally nodding. "All right. The pay is the same, though, whether we talk or fuck."

"Ah, romance," I said.

* * *

WE ENDED up at Crazy John's Restaurant and Arcade. Crazy John's had never been the safest place around, but it gave me a good view of the Block and the people who walked up and down it. Sandy—I don't know if it was her real name, but it didn't sound like a faux glamorous hooker name—ordered a basket of chicken wings and fries. I didn't want to eat anything, but to keep up appearances, I got a slice of cheese pizza. We each drank iced tea with our meals. I nibbled my pizza while Sandy tore into her wings as if they were the first things she'd eaten all day.

The meal set me back about sixteen dollars on top of the two bills I paid Sandy for her time. Thankfully, I could afford to live the kind of thrilling life which led me to eat late meals with prostitutes in restaurants growing less safe as the night wore on. When it looked like Sandy slowed her breakneck pace, I started in with the questions. "I hear you work for a fellow named Romeo."

She nodded and washed down a mouthful of food before answering. "Yeah, for a few months now."

"How's he treat you?"

"Really well. He comes around for his money, of course, but he ain't up in our grills all the time, y'know?"

"From what I can tell, he does seem rather *laissez-faire*."

"What the hell does that mean?"

"It doesn't matter," I said. "Tell me about Romeo."

"Why you wanna know?" Her eyes narrowed.

"I don't care how he makes his money, either. I'm working on a case, and I think he might be able to give me some insight into it."

"What kind of case?"

"The kind where three people are dead."

"Jesus," Sandy said, "Romeo ain't no killer."

"He's not a suspect."

"Who is?"

"Right now, nobody. Like I said, I need some insight from your boss."

"Romeo's nice, but there's . . . a dark side to him. Like he's got some stuff in his past, or something."

"Haven't we all?" I said. If only she knew how well-drawn her impression was. "You said he pretty much leaves you alone. Does he ever get violent?"

"Not with any of us," she said.

"What about with the johns?"

"Sometimes they need to know their place."

A few people wandered in and out, but the restaurant never threatened to fill up. No one wanted to remain in Crazy John's for long, me included. "Does he put them in their place," I said, "or does he have someone who handles it for him?"

"He's got a big guy with him most of the time. Calls him Tank."

"Is Tank aptly named?"

Sandy nibbled on fries before answering. She was smart enough to keep her voice as low as she could while we were talking. I tried to find a secluded table, but between the other patrons and the arcade games, there was a decent amount of ambient noise. "He's a big boy," she said. "Probably as tall as Romeo but twice as wide."

Right after Sandy finished talking, I spotted someone outside Club Pussycat across Custom House Avenue from the Hustler Club. The combination of street lights and neon made him easy to recognize. Other than a wispy mustache, he was a dead ringer for Romeo's police file photo. He wore a blue tank top over red leather pants and talked to someone who could have played offensive line for the Ravens. The big guy sported a black T-shirt, a red leather jacket, and blue jeans.

"There they are now," I said.

Sandy ducked. "Oh, God, I hope they don't see me. We ain't supposed to eat with the johns."

"I'm not a john, and I paid you for your time, so his cut is the same." She didn't sit up. I shrugged. "I'm going to go talk to him now. Stay here for a while and avoid him if you think he'll give you any grief."

"All right," she said. "Hey, thanks for dinner." She gave me a sort of uncertain smile, like she sought approval. How had this girl come to be a hooker? She didn't strike me as the sharpest knife in the drawer, but she also wasn't a spoon in a tray of knives. At least Romeo treated her well. I reminded myself I couldn't save everyone, and not everyone wanted to be saved.

"Thanks for the information," I said. I got up from my chair, walked outside, and trotted across the street. Romeo stood in the same spot, but Tank no longer loitered near him. Based on Sandy's description, he should be easy to spot. "You must be Romeo," I said as I approached. Still no sign of Tank.

"Who's asking?" he said. "You a cop?"

"Do I really look like one?"

He stared at me for a few seconds, much like Sandy's appraisal. "A little around the eyes."

I shook my head. "I'm not a cop," I said. "Only a man who needs a little help."

"Shit, man, I got girls for that. Go find one of them."

"I don't need them. I need some insight, and I've heard you're the man who can provide it."

He looked me up and down again. "What if I don't want to give you no insight?"

Before I could answer, I saw something dark speeding toward me. In the fraction of a second before impact, I knew I had no time to mount a defense, so I tried to brace myself as best I could. It felt like a truck hit me across the shoulders, so preparing for impact did nothing. I went airborne and only saved myself from a faceplant by twisting enough to land on my left side. My shoulder and hip slammed into the pavement, taking most of the impact, and I skidded before rolling over a few times. Only a brick wall stopped me when my back smashed into it.

Most of my upper body hurt. The roll into the wall knocked the wind out of me, so I gasped for breath as Romeo and the largest man I'd ever seen approached. Tank. I guessed him to be six-nine and over 350 pounds. The wallop he packed earned him his nickname, but his size belied a surprising amount of stealth and speed; I only saw him coming at the very end. If Tank decided he wanted to stomp on my head until it burst, I doubted I could do much to stop him.

Romeo crouched near me. "A man don't like to be disturbed while he's working," he said quietly.

"Paul King . . . sent me," I managed to say between ragged breaths.

"Shit. *You're* the one he told me about?"

"Not expecting someone so handsome?" Breathing came easier now.

Romeo snorted. "You ain't looking so fine right now."

"This pavement isn't a good color for me." I dragged myself into a seated position. Tank looked down at me, too. He stared ahead, looking menacing—which he was very good at—while Romeo handled the banter.

"King said you needed information."

I nodded and immediately regretted it when my neck throbbed. "Yeah," I said around a wince, "about the gangs in particular."

"All right," Romeo said after a sigh. "Let's the three of us go somewhere and talk."

"You won't need him," I said, jutting my chin toward Tank.

"You think you can stop him from coming with us?"

"Not really," I said.

Tank grinned down at me. It didn't make him any less menacing.

CHAPTER 3

Of course, we went to Crazy John's. I got another iced tea, lamented the lack of Vicodin on the menu, and paid for Romeo and Tank, the latter eating enough for a family of four. Once we were seated and food covered every available inch of the table, I got down to business. "Did you hear about the woman who got shot outside the funeral home?"

"Yeah." Romeo shook his head. "That was fucked up."

"Her son got murdered a few days before. He's suspected of being in a gang. I need insight into them. I heard you spent a few years inside, and they let you walk away. I didn't know they often showed such generosity."

Romeo flashed a brief, rueful smile. "They don't."

"A grandmother came to me after burying her grandson and daughter. I'm trying to help her. You graduated to a more . . . service-oriented industry. I need the knowledge you racked up about your former life."

"Ain't my favorite subject," Romeo said, "but I'll see what I can do."

Across the street, one of Romeo's girls picked up a john. They walked toward the far end of the Block. "Your girls are going to be all alone," I said.

"They be OK," Romeo said.

"You sure you don't want The Mountain here keeping guard over them?"

Romeo smiled. Tank didn't even react, like he hadn't heard me. He studied the other patrons. "My girls look out for each other," Romeo said. "Besides, I make them take a self-defense class when they start."

"Really?"

"Sure. This shit ain't feather boas and Cadillacs. It's a business. Being whores means they gonna get taken advantage of. Me and Tank can't be everywhere. I had to learn to fight when I came up. They should, too." He paused. "So you working the funeral home shooting."

"The grandmother hired me," I said. "She swears her grandson wasn't in a gang."

"What do you think?"

"I don't know yet. All signs at the crime scene indicate he was."

"What do you mean?"

"He was wearing blue in the wrong part of town." I noticed Tank glancing around, rarely letting his eyes sit still on something. He didn't look at me, but I knew he knew I noticed him. I didn't think he missed any details. If indeed the price of freedom is eternal vigilance, Tank paid his share in full.

"Bangers get shot all the time," Romeo said.

"When you were in, you knew whose territory was where, right?"

"Of course."

"If you were to go behind enemy lines by yourself, you wouldn't flaunt your colors, would you?"

"No way, man. That's just asking to get shot."

"You put your finger on my problem with the case," I said. "Dante Johnson was a smart kid."

"Don't mean he was street smart."

"No, but it means he wasn't an idiot. Only an idiot would go alone into the wrong territory in colors."

"You don't think he was a banger, do you?" Tank said.

"I don't know yet," I said. "I think it's possible."

"Maybe," Romeo offered.

"In the meantime, what can you tell me about gangs?"

Romeo and Tank looked at each other and laughed. I frowned, and it amused them. "Did I say something funny?" My question triggered a new round of frivolity.

"Shit, man," Romeo said, "how long you got?"

"As much time as it takes," I said.

"We don't. Me and Tank got a business to run and images to keep up. Talking with a cracker like you don't help either one."

"You silver-tongued devil."

"Why don't you just tell me what kind of insight you want?"

A few more patrons wandered in. Crazy John's wasn't crowded, though, so we maintained our privacy. "Why don't we start with which one you were in."

"Both, sort of," said Romeo. "I tried out for the Bucs. Didn't make it. Then we moved a few blocks away, and I passed my initiation into the Pirates."

"How? Did you have to kill someone?"

"Man, you watch too much TV. You gotta do something, sure, but it's usually just knock over a store or beat up a bum. For me, it was knock around an old biddy always used to yell at us."

This cemented the gangs as bullies for me, and I hated bullies. An unfortunate encounter with one in fifth grade compelled my parents to enroll me in private school and martial arts. In high school, I got in trouble a few times defending other students from the assholes who preyed on them. "Then you were in?" I said.

"No. To celebrate, they brought me back to base and kicked the shit out of me."

I felt myself recoil. "What?"

"Yeah, man. Hollywood don't tell you that. They make it seem like all you gotta do is cap some old man. The reality is you're only in after they finish beating you down." Romeo ate his sandwich as if he engaged in this kind of chit-chat every day. For my part, I felt glad I didn't order any food. This part of the conversation would have made me lose my appetite.

"How far up in the gang would a kid of nineteen be?" I asked.

"Depends on when he started. Could be a new recruit, could be one of the big dogs."

"How high up were you at nineteen?"

Romeo sipped soda while he thought about it. "Third in command," he said. "Ran my own crew. I'd been in the Pirates almost six years by then."

I nodded. "What about retaliations? How fast were they?"

"Someone else dead?" Tank said. He paused eating his regal feast—chicken fried steak, onion rings, an already-consumed order of mozzarella sticks, and gravy fries—long enough to ask a question.

Damn. I hoped to pass my query off as casual curiosity. "Another kid tonight."

"How long since the first one?" Romeo said.

"About a week."

Romeo shook his head. "Awful slow."

"How quickly did you get back at the Bucs in your day?"

"Soon as we could."

"You see why this doesn't add up for me," I said. "It kind of looks like gang violence, so everyone wants to write it as such. I'm not convinced."

He nodded and went back to his sandwich. My feeling was when he finished the sandwich and fries, my time would be up. "The first kid's mom got shot, too?" he said after a moment.

"Yeah. Did you go after family often?"

"No," he said.

"Mothers were off limits," Tank added.

"We might try to recruit your little brother," Romeo offered. "But we wouldn't go shoot your momma."

"How could I find out for sure if these kids were in a gang?"

"Shit. Your best way is to talk to the members."

I smirked. "I'm going to guess they probably don't want to talk to someone like me."

"Ain't no 'probably' about it," Romeo said.

"I'll hope to find another way, then."

Romeo grabbed an unused napkin and wrote on it. "This is my number," he said. "I don't know if you'll need anything else, but if you do, call. We want to help." For his part, Tank offered a fractional bob of his head.

"Thanks." I slipped the napkin into a pocket.

"You know, you ain't bad . . . for a cracker."

"I think I need to update my business cards," I said.

* * *

THE MEDICAL EXAMINER'S office wasn't far, so I stopped there after my chat with Romeo and Tank. The ME shares results and information with the BPD, but they maintain a separate network. I could break into the former if I wanted to, but I always found what I needed via other means. One was waiting for the BPD case file to be updated.

This was the more direct approach.

A few months ago, I discovered a doctor at the ME's office released the body of a murder victim to her killer. In return for not broadcasting the fact, Dr. Gary Hunt agreed to supply me with information when I needed it. He usually worked nights, including this one.

"Oh, Christ," he said when he saw me walk in. "What now?"

"You're awfully salty for a man who didn't get fired and led away in handcuffs," I pointed out.

"Can't I just be unhappy to see you?"

"I don't care as long as you tell me what I need to know."

Dr. Hunt sighed and ran a latex-gloved hand through his thinning brown hair. He stood an inch or two shorter than me and possessed a classic runner's physique. I doubted he would ever invite me to join him in a constitutional, however. "Fine. Give me a few minutes. You can sit anywhere."

I grabbed a chair in the waiting area. It was like the ones in hospitals, only shrunk in square footage by a factor of ten. My seat looked the most comfortable of the six. A solitary and shabby table held the last three issues of *The Baltimore Sun*. I found it an odd choice. Family members waiting to identify a body shared the space with articles about their dead relative. Even the shitty magazine selection at every doctor's office would have been better.

After about ten minutes, I almost got desperate enough to pick up a paper and read it. Dr. Hunt spared me my moment of weakness by returning. "Wanna come to my office?"

"You don't have another body to process?" I said.

He shrugged. "They're dead. The wait won't kill them. Come on."

We walked down the hall and into a small room. If a messy desk were a sign of genius, Dr. Hunt was a savant. Papers, file folders, plastic cups, food wrappers, and assorted other detritus consumed almost the entire surface. His keyboard—its cleanliness was a mystery I would never solve—sat as an oasis amid a desert of disinterest. Any photos a normal person would have on a desk were bumped to the bookshelves. I saw pictures of the doctor and his wife interspersed among books whose organization impressed me. The office made less sense the more I saw.

"What's up?" said Dr. Hunt, snapping me back into the moment.

"A kid killed tonight," I said, calling up the alert on my phone. "Andre Carter."

"Sad. He was young."

"I was hoping to learn more from you than I did from fifteen seconds of Google."

"I don't know a lot yet. He's pretty fresh."

"Let's do some comparisons, then," I said, hoping to draw Hunt out of his reticent shell. "I'm also investigating the deaths of Dante and Anisha Johnson."

Hunt frowned as he started typing. "Those names are familiar."

"Dante was shot. Police are calling it a gang shooting. A few days later, his mother met the same fate outside Dante's funeral home."

"Jesus," Hunt said, expelling a low, slow breath. "Every now and then, I think I've seen everything. Then I wait a few days, and shit like this happens." I found myself in a similar situation. My cases grew more challenging—and the perpetrators more depraved—the longer I worked. When I placated my parents and agreed to do this job, I thought it would be easy. Sit at my computer, hack into something, solve a crime, collect a check. Instead, I got to flex my hacking muscles, but I've also been shot at, forced to shoot a man myself, and gotten into more scrapes than I cared to count. Gloria's concern for me made sense.

Hunt's voice rooted me back in the present. "All right, I have the files up. Keep in mind everything about this Carter kid is preliminary."

"I understand," I said.

"The mother and son were killed by the same gun . . . a three-fifty-seven. Three slugs to the chest each." He squinted. "Any of them probably could have been fatal."

"What about Andre Carter?"

"Three slugs to the chest."

"Caliber?"

"Don't know yet," Hunt said. "Forensics has the bullets."

"How about Dante Johnson, then?" I said. "Other than the three rounds, any signs of injury?"

After a moment of perusing a file, Hunt said, "Nothing recent, no. Looked like he broke his arm when he was a kid, but I didn't see anything else."

"No evidence he'd taken a beating?"

"A bad one?" I nodded. "No. If he did, his attackers were careful enough not to leave him with any signs for later. Why do you ask?"

I recounted my recent schooling on gang initiations. "If this kid were in a gang, he would have been physically inducted."

"Meaning they would have beaten the hell out of him."

"Basically."

Hunt shook his head. "It would leave marks. The body can only take so much pounding before injuries become obvious. I've seen what you're describing before. There are signs, even a few years later, in the bones. This kid didn't have anything like it."

Another check in the *Not in a Gang* column. "I suppose Andre Carter was the same?" I asked.

"I haven't finished my examination yet," said Hunt. "No obvious signs of past injury other than a scar on his leg, though. My guess is he got it ten years ago."

"When he was about eight or nine."

"Kids around those ages hurt themselves in about a million different ways. He could have slipped and fallen on a soda bottle for all any of us know."

His mother should know. I didn't want to descend on her like some vulture reporter, however; I would try and talk to her at her son's viewing. "All right," I said. "Thanks, Doctor. I may come back if I need to run anything else by you."

"Now you value me as a physician?" he said with a brow raised.

"You're an unethical bastard. It doesn't mean I don't respect your medical opinion."

"Aren't you a charmer?"

"I have my moments," I said.

By the time I arrived home, I was ready to fall asleep. One can only take so much of talking to hookers and pimps, eating lousy food, and getting waylaid by men aptly named Tank in a single evening. Even I have my limits. I walked inside and trudged upstairs. Gloria woke up when I entered the bedroom. She rubbed her eyes, sat up, and showed a tired grin. "Late night with the hookers?"

I smiled. "Yes, actually. I don't know if I've ever been propositioned so much in my life."

"What if I proposition you?"

"I'm pretty sure you'll succeed where they failed," I said. I went into the bathroom and got ready for bed, changing into my usual sleeping attire of a T-shirt and gym shorts. When I came out, Gloria still sat on the bed.

"I'm hungry," she said.

We walked downstairs to the kitchen. I wasn't used to making or eating snacks at this hour, so I scanned cabinets and cupboards for appropriate fare. "How about chips and guac?" I said once I completed my survey.

"Sounds good," Gloria said, sitting at the table.

I mashed two avocados, added some fresh salsa—normally, I would chop the vegetables myself, but I made allowances for the late hour—along with salt and a pinch of lime juice. In a few minutes, we could enjoy a bowl of guacamole and a bag of tortilla chips. Gloria dove in. I grazed by comparison. The role reversal was complete.

"What did you find out?" she said after finishing a chip. I watched her dip the next one. Her guacamole-to-chip ratio was too low for my tastes.

"Very large men can be surprisingly stealthy and quick," I said, flexing my neck. I'd be sore for a couple days. "Plus a good bit on the gangs. I don't think the second kid was a banger, either."

"Second kid?" she frowned.

I filled her in on the details. "The ME shares my opinion," I added, "for whatever it's worth."

"What do you mean?"

"The police are probably going to investigate these as gang killings. It's the higher-probability play."

"You can do your own investigation, though," said Gloria.

"I can," I concurred, "and I plan to. I'm just not sure how much help I'll have from the BPD."

"How much help do you usually get?"

I smiled again. "Fair point," I said.

CHAPTER 4

In the morning, I got to work after breakfast and coffee. Normally, I might have gone for a run around Federal Hill Park. Maybe later. My late-night activities in the city would have to be enough excitement for now. Andre Carter, the latest shooting victim, showed no evidence of being a gangbanger. He lived in a rough area known for gunplay, battles over turf, and the like, but I saw no signs he was wrapped up in any of it. Like Dante Johnson, Andre was a good student in a neighborhood where such an achievement was rare. Both finished their freshman years at Morgan State and continued their academic successes. While a gang member going to college and earning good grades was possible, it struck me as improbable.

I contemplated two young men, both of whom lived in bad neighborhoods beset by violence, who got shot in ways normally reserved for red or blue-clad young criminals. Additionally, Anisha Johnson was gunned down outside the funeral home, an act of barbarism no one I talked to heard of happening before. Both Andre and Dante went to Morgan, a historically black college in Baltimore. I wondered how difficult breaking into Morgan's student records would be.

Answer: not very. In my experience, most colleges only used slapdash security to protect their networks. Students' personal information was sometimes sectioned off on the network and harder to access, but the basics proved readily available. Even if Morgan used robust security, I felt confident I could get past it. I learned the science of computers in college and the art of compromising them both at home and in Hong Kong. I taught myself a lot as a teen, then learned a bunch more in China. I might still be there if the government hadn't found us, thrown me in jail for nineteen days, and given me the boot.

I didn't think data like social security numbers—what IT people and hackers called "personally identifiable information"—for either kid would be useful, so I stuck to the more traditional college data. Each pulled a GPA over 3.0 in their first years. Despite differing majors, they took one class in common—African-American Studies 101, taught by a Dr. Maurice Reid. They lived on campus in neighboring dorms and pledged different fraternities. Other than the three days a week one semester they shared a classroom, I couldn't even find any evidence they knew each other. The young men were Facebook friends—and shared other acquaintances on their lists—but barely interacted on the platform. They weren't connected on any other social media.

Two dead college kids. One dead mother. All looked like gang killings, but I harbored doubts as to whether any were. Little in common between the younger victims.

What the hell did I get myself into?

* * *

AFTER A RUN AND SHOWER, I went back to work. I tried to reach Paul King at the station and his cell, but he didn't answer.

Instead, I called Rich. "King mentioned he was working with you on something," he said.

"You didn't try to talk him out of it?" I asked.

"He wouldn't listen, anyway."

"I've learned a lot since I talked to King last. Now I don't think these two kids were in gangs."

Rich laughed in my ear. "Seriously?"

"What?"

"We have two kids shot. Each was wearing rival colors in the wrong part of town. And your brilliant theory is neither one was a banger?"

"It sounds a little flimsy when you put it in those words," I admitted.

"Because it is. If it walks like a duck, quacks like a duck—"

"It could also be a platypus."

"I don't think they quack," Rich said.

"I'll look for your zoology degree next time I visit you."

Exasperation crept into Rich's voice. This happened with some regularity when we talked. "Look. I know you love to be contrary. Sometimes, it pays off. But these are gang killings."

"You working King's detail now?" I said.

"No," said Rich. "I still work homicide, which both shootings were. I've heard tensions are running higher than normal, though. Our gang units are concerned there's going to be a spate of violence."

"If these were turf killings, wouldn't the spate have already started?"

"Everyone thinks these kids were bangers," Rich said after a sigh.

"Groupthink," I countered. "Hasn't the BPD gotten in trouble a couple times for being in lockstep? Maybe a different perspective is what you need."

Rich hung up on me.

Maybe I would peddle my different perspective to someone else.

* * *

MY PHONE VIBRATED on the nightstand. I glanced at the time: two-ten A.M. Caller ID told me it was Paul King. This couldn't be good news. "Hello?" I mumbled.

"Got two gang shootings," he said. "Real ones this time."

I pulled myself into a seated position. "Rich told you my theory?"

"Yeah. You just woke up, so I'll only say it's bullshit and spare you anything worse."

"Where are you?"

"At the scene. Poplar Grove and Riggs. You know it?"

West Baltimore. In the neighborhood Freddie Gray called home, if my geography were right. "Vaguely," I said. "I'm on my way."

"I'll alert the media," King said and hung up.

I threw on the clothes I shrugged out of last night, gargled with some mouthwash, and headed to the west side. I arrived to a gaggle of police cars on Riggs. Their blue and red lights bathed the neighborhood. A local news van joined the melee beside me. I got out of my car, showed my badge and ID to a uniform, and ducked under the yellow tape. King walked up to greet me. "First murder?"

"No," I said, "though I hope I don't have to make these visits regularly." I surveyed the scene. Two dead black men lay partially covered by sheets outside Rehoboth K&K Grocery. A third sat against the brick exterior, a pair of paramedics tending to his legs. Two windows in the corner store got shot out. Behind the grocery lay an alley, and the grass edging it was beset by weeds even in the fall. Rowhouses lined each side of the street past the alley, most in various states of disrepair. "What happened?"

"We don't know the whole story yet," King said. "Guy sitting there says he was taking a walk. The two dead guys ran into each other and drew down. He got caught in the crossfire."

"He going to be OK?"

"Took one in the calf. Ripped up some muscle, but it left without hitting the bone. He'll be fine. Coulda been a lot worse."

I moved closer to the corpses. Blood seeped through their clothes and into the white sheets. It lent the appearance of their chests being blanketed by red coverings. Age was never easy to determine, but I put both around sixteen to eighteen. Regardless, they were way too young to shoot each other to death. "Rich said gang violence is simmering," I mentioned when King stopped beside me.

He nodded. "This might be the first sign it's boiling over."

I let out a slow, deep breath. "A full-fledged war?"

"Maybe," King acknowledged.

"You think you can stop it?"

"After all the shit we've been through and the DOJ smack-down?" He shook his head. "No. Best we can do is clean up the bodies and throw anyone who survives in jail."

I didn't think such a strategy would be very effective, and I doubted whether King did, either.

A gang war. Great.

CHAPTER 5

ANDRE CARTER WAS SURVIVED BY HIS MOTHER, DEBI. AFTER going home from the west-side crime scene and getting a few more hours of sleep, I rang her doorbell at 10:30. She lived maybe a mile from where I stood over two corpses last night. Both were around the age of her late son. None were old enough for their grisly fates. Debi Carter had a small rowhouse crammed in the middle of similar structures. The windows on some were boarded up. All were in need of some level of repair.

When she opened the door only wide enough to peek out at me, I said, "Miss Carter, I'm a private investigator." I showed her my ID. She rolled her eyes. "Erma Johnson hired me."

"Miss Erma?"

"You know her?"

"She's a sweet lady." Her voice was quiet, defeated. I didn't need to ask why.

"She hired me to look into the murders of her grandson and daughter," I said. "It seems the same thing happened to your son. I'm very sorry for your loss."

"Thank you," she said with a small bob of her head. "You want to come in?"

Inside needed as much attention as the exterior. Drab brown carpet covered the floor. The furniture looked like it came from a thrift store, and I doubted they would take it back in its current state. Walls screamed for fresh paint. Someone needed to clean up junk and recent food trash; I figured Debi had more important things on her mind than keeping a clean house. She sat on the sofa. Rather than risk a rickety chair, I took a seat at the other end.

"Thank you for seeing me," I said when we were situated.

Debi smoothed her black skirt. "Some policemen have come by," she told me. "A few reporters, too. I don't want to talk to none of them."

"I understand. I try to avoid both whenever I can."

She offered a token grin out of politeness. "You found anything?"

"The police think Dante and your son were in gangs—"

"My boy wasn't in one of them," she said. For the first time, conviction replaced the defeat in her voice.

"Erma Johnson said the same about her grandson," I told her.

"She's probably right."

"Anyway, the police have their theory. I've done some investigating. I don't think either one was in a gang."

"Of course not."

"The problem is," I said, "it would be easier if they were."

"What do you mean?"

"If they were gangbangers, the violence is understandable. They weren't. So why did they get shot, and why were they dressed like they were Pirates or Bucs when it happened?"

She let out a deep breath, but before she could answer, her phone rang. "It's my pastor," she said. She picked up and asked him to hold on a moment. "I can talk to you later tonight at the viewing. When you leave, you'll see a funeral home on the next street."

"I'll be there."

She told me the times, then went back to her call. I showed myself out.

* * *

PEOPLE FILED into the building as I drove into the parking lot. I saw one marked police car near the entrance and an obvious unmarked one farther back. Considering the funeral home shooting at the genesis of this investigation, I expected a larger BPD presence. I parked the Caprice near the detective's car and got out. On my way toward the funeral home, I patted my side, making sure the 9-millimeter was still holstered under my suit jacket. I tend to prefer a .45, but the bulk of it would interfere with the hang of my jacket. My suits are far too good to be compromised by a bulky gun. We all need to make sacrifices.

A uniformed officer stood at the door, eyeing everyone who walked in. He didn't try to stop anyone, nor did he say anything. He looked at me long enough to conclude I wasn't a serial killer, then his eyes passed to the couple walking in behind me. Another uniform stood in the lobby, and a third was stationed at the door to the viewing room. None of them moved or said a word. They would occasionally smile or incline a head to confirm they weren't statues or wax sculptures.

I nodded to the uniform at the viewing room door as I walked in. He didn't recognize me, though I'd seen him in Rich's precinct a few times. Speaking of my favorite cousin, I saw him talking to a well-dressed man near the casket. The expansive viewing room, at least twenty by forty feet, filled with people. Most of them were probably friends and family of the victim, but I also recognized a few local politicians. I imagined their disappointment at the lack of photo ops; not a single reporter came to the viewing. Selfies with mourners would have to suffice.

I walked to the guestbook and added my name to the many who signed it before I did. Rich finished talking to the man in the sharp suit, so I made my way to him. "Pastor," I said, offering him my hand.

"Good evening," he said, shaking my hand in a powerful grip. He was a dark-skinned black man about my height but a little wider. He looked like he could have played football in college. "Are you a friend of the family?"

"Not really. I'm a private investigator. Dante Johnson's grand-mother hired me."

"That poor family," he said, shaking his head. "To lose two people so young . . . it's really a shame. What did you say your name was?"

"I didn't, but it's C.T. Ferguson."

He frowned in a thoughtful pause. "I think I've heard of you."

"I hope so. I'd hate to think I spent all that time talking to reporters for nothing."

He showed an easy smile. "I'm Pastor Webster, but you can call me Kevin."

"All right, Kevin. Did both the Johnsons and the Carters attend your church?"

"Yes, for years. I've known Dante and Andre since they were in elementary school."

"Did they know each other well?"

"They were acquaintances and friendly, but I don't know if I'd say they were friends."

"Both young men were found dressed in gang colors. Were they—"

"No," he said, cutting me off. "Not a chance."

I nodded. "I'd come to the same conclusion. Do you know anyone who would want us to think both young men were in them?"

Kevin sighed and shook his head. "No, I can't think of anyone.

I know some boys in the gangs, of course. I've talked to them, tried to show them the church is better to belong to." He shook his head again. "Not many of them listen, though. Gangs offer tangible things faster."

"I'd like to talk with Andre's mother tonight."

"I'm not sure it's a good idea."

"Don't worry, Kevin. I know what it's like to bury a loved one before it's time. I'll be delicate."

He bobbed his head—not that I needed his approval—and I walked away. Thoughts of my sister Samantha, dead twelve years now, fluttered into my mind. I took a deep breath and focused on why I came tonight. A crowd of well-wishers surrounded Debi. I stopped at the photo table. Andre Carter had been an active kid, playing baseball and basketball, earning a couple trophies in each sport. I also saw pictures of him in school plays, receiving academic awards, and at his graduation. Andre did a lot and did it well. His profile did not overlap with a gangbanger's. So who wanted to make him look like one, and why?

Rich joined me as I stood at the photo table. He wore a nice suit, but the fit and color may as well have announced he was a cop. I wondered if he wore the same one to work earlier. Rich's clothing regimens can't be disturbed. "What are you doing here?" he said.

"I could ask you the same thing," I said, cementing my status as the man of a million comebacks.

"We want a police presence here, considering what happened last week."

"Aside from the three uniforms, it explains the unmarked but obvious car, and the other plainclothes guy in the room."

"The other one?"

"Standing like a wallflower near the corner." I hitched my head toward a man in his forties across the room, trying to look interested in his cup of water while surveying everyone around him. "Considering his suit looks cheaper than most, I'm guessing he's a cop, too."

Rich looked. "Yeah, he's O'Hearn."

"So you've come around to my theory?" I pressed.

He shrugged. "Merely putting in a little overtime." He paused while someone else took in the table. When the other fellow left, Rich continued. "You know your little theory raises as many questions as it answers."

"I'm still working on those."

"Any luck?"

"I wouldn't be here if I'd been having good luck." I said. "Anything new from the BPD?"

Rich shook his head. "Nothing."

Just then, Debi Carter approached and touched my forearm. "Mr. Ferguson?" she said, "I think I'd like to get some air."

"Very well," I said, giving her the best smile I could summon under the circumstances. She grabbed my forearm, and we walked away.

"I'll send a uniform out with you," Rich said.

* * *

DEBI CARTER and I stepped outside the funeral home. We didn't go anywhere in particular—just a lap around the exterior—but I got the feeling she needed a break from everyone inside. When she talked, her voice took on more energy and life, like a weight lifted from her shoulders.

"You said Miss Erma hired you?" she asked.

"She did."

"And you think my boy's death might be connected to Dante Johnson's?"

"Yes, I do," I said. We walked side-by-side around the perimeter of the facility, making sure to stay far enough away from smokers, well-wishers, and other stragglers outside. The uniform trailed a few steps behind us. He was a young stocky white guy who looked a day overdue for a shave and a month overdue for a haircut. Maybe he took his grooming tips from Paul King.

"Because of the gang colors?"

"Yes. The police are chalking it up to the usual turf wars. I'm not convinced."

"I hope you figure it out. I'd like to see justice—not just for me, but for Miss Erma, too."

"So would I," I said. I hoped I could live up to her expectations; I wasn't exactly off to a roaring start.

Debi Carter stopped at the edge of the grass, so I paused with her. She looked down at the lawn, then back up at me. "Would you mind holding my shoes?" she said.

"Holding your shoes?" I blinked a few times.

"Yes." A smile came over her face, the first real one I'd seen from her. "When I was a girl, we had a big yard, and I loved to run around in the grass barefoot. My mom would tell me my feet were going to turn green." She grinned again, more wistfully this time. "I want to walk in it again. I want to think about my mom and pray."

It all sounded charming in a folksy sort of way, if a little silly. "Sure, I'll hold your shoes," I said. The uniform gave me a funny look as Debi Carter unbuckled her black flats. I shrugged at him. Debi handed me her shoes. She still had pantyhose on, so she wouldn't be barefoot, but it was probably as close as she wanted to get at her son's funeral.

"I'll only be a few minutes," she said. "Thanks for putting up with me."

"Take your time," I said. She had recently lost her son. I never wanted kids, but if one of my parents had recently passed, I would want someone to accommodate my strange requests.

When Samantha died, I didn't do anything like walk around in the grass barefoot. Instead, I sulked a lot, raided my parents' liquor cabinet, got in a couple of fights, and watched my grades spiral downward for the next two months. Even though I eventually recovered, doing something like traipsing in the grass would have been easier for everyone—me especially.

Debi Carter walked a circuitous route, speeding up and slowing down at random as she moved through the funeral home's large front lawn. She settled on a spot a few feet from the sidewalk with her back to me and the uniform. No one walked by, and light traffic normal for the nearby roads passed on all sides. She put her head back and looked up to the sky, then raised her hands as well. After standing in the pose for about ten seconds, she brought her hands together, folded them, and brought them in front of her body.

I watched as Debi bowed her head. She was too far away for me to hear, and I wondered what she said. Years ago, I learned prayers should always begin with thanks. If I were Debi Carter, I would struggle finding something to be thankful for. Maybe it explained why I could never make a regular habit of praying—if I had something to be thankful for, I knew the earthly reason it happened.

Cars drove by sporadically. The lane closest to the sidewalk was turn-only, which veered onto a side street. A blue Chevy Nova straight out of the 1970s moved from the middle lane to the right. It wasn't going very fast. I saw the passenger's window roll down about halfway. A black-sleeved and black-gloved hand held a large revolver out the window. I shouted for Debi to get down, but the sound of three rounds exploding through the quiet evening air drowned my warning. Debi Carter's body rocked with the impact of the slugs. I drew my gun and ran closer. The arm went back into the window as the car lurched forward. I took aim on the Nova as best I could and fired. I hoped to hit a tire, but instead, I put four bullets in the rear of the car, one of them shattering a taillight in an explosion of white and red glass.

The uniform ran from behind me with his pistol out. I strode past him to the body of Debi Carter. She'd been hit three times in the torso. I remembered a similar pattern on both her son and Dante Johnson. The marksmanship made it likely whoever shot also shot them. Debi's chest remained still, which I expected considering the amount of blood spilled out of her and into the grass. I put my gun away and cursed. The uniform joined me again. People would pour out of the funeral home any second now. The young officer looked at the body, his mouth agape. This could get bad quickly.

"Remember your training," I said.

"Right," he said after a second. "I'll secure the crime scene."

Rich ran out of the building, gun in hand. I saw him, and he saw me.

All I could do was shake my head.

* * *

I GAVE my statement to the cops. Rich and Captain Leon Sharpe stood nearby. It all felt very surreal, like someone else dictated what happened, and I watched on a flickering TV. I'd never seen anyone get killed in such cold blood before. I have a lot of pride, but not too much to say I felt shaken.

The detective who took my statement flipped his notebook shut and walked away. He told me his name, but I'd already forgotten it. I stared out into the sea of flashing red and blue lights. The parking lot emptied, the funeral home evacuated. Two kids were dead, and now both of their mothers were, too. What did the families have in common? Was someone targeting them? I needed to see if there was anything there. Leon Sharpe approached me. His expression looked softer than usual, almost sympathetic.

"You all right?" he said. Sharpe stood a good four inches taller than me and outweighed me by at least seventy pounds. He looked like he reported for duty after bench-pressing a car and sacking the quarterback three times. His bald black head never betrayed a hint a single hair ever grew out of it.

I gave a slow nod. "Getting there."

"No tag number on the car?"

"No rear plate." I replayed the scene in my head. The gun hand went back into the window. The car accelerated. I fired at the tires. Four rounds slammed into the rear of the Nova on either side of the absent license plate.

"You sure?"

I rolled my eyes. "Do you really think I'm playing it fast and loose right now after what just happened?"

"You tell me." Sharpe narrowed his eyes and leaned in.

"How about I tell you to fuck off?" I said, then turned and walked away.

"C.T.!" Rich called after me. I heard him jogging to catch up. "He deserved it."

"Maybe. Hell, even I think you're playing it straight now."

"Thanks . . . I think."

"You did fire into the street, though," he said.

"I hit the car."

"With every shot?"

"Yes," I said. "I batted a thousand, for all the good it did. Nobody died, except Debi Carter."

"This time," said Rich. "You can't just shoot at a car speeding off. Sharpe seems willing to look past it, but if you keep telling him to fuck off, he may not be."

"Fine. Next time, I'll tell him to go to hell."

Rich sighed. "Just take it easy, will you?"

"Yeah," I said. "I'll be sure to think about the captain's feelings when I'm trying to figure out who killed four people."

"You think the same person killed them all?"

"There's more than one person involved. Someone drove the Nova while the shooter opened fire."

"True," Rich acknowledged. "Let me know if you come to any conclusions, will you?"

"Don't I always?" I said.

Rich gave me a look. I walked away.

I had a lot of work to do.

TWO DEAD KIDS. TWO DEAD MOTHERS. ON TOP OF IT ALL, gang violence in the city was boiling over.Their war wasn't my problem to solve, but if I could decipher what happened to the two families, maybe I could resolve everything. Until the next time someone wandered onto opposing turf in the wrong colors, at least. In Baltimore, reprieves were temporary.

Gloria called. I sent it to voicemail. I needed to dive into what Dante Johnson and Andre Carter shared in common. If I couldn't find much there, I'd look into their mothers. The two biggest commonalities were their neighborhoods and the college they attended. I'd already done some cursory digging into their records at Morgan. Now, I needed to go deeper. My last intrusion into Morgan's network showed Dante and Andre attended one class together: African-American Studies, taught by Dr. Maurice Reid.

The syllabus looked pretty basic. The course covered from the first slaves in North America through the end of the 1960s, and students who desired Dr. Reid's take on more modern times were told to enroll in the second-semester class. I spent six years in college, took classes from professors who wrote their own textbooks, and dealt with plenty of instructors whose ego filled any empty desks in the room. Dr. Reid topped them all. Each page of the voluminous syllabus featured at least one plug for his expertise, speeches, or books.

If he was so keen on promoting himself, I would oblige him by investigating. Reid earned his Ph.D. from Coppin State—another local historically black college—ten years ago. Since then, he spent a couple years there and the rest at Morgan. Self-promotion came easily to him, and I found a lot of material to comb through. Reid loved making fiery speeches. I watched some highlights on YouTube. He possessed a good delivery, and his anti-gang message was clear and presented with plenty of fire. He also had a book, *African-American Struggles in Modern America*, available on all the major platforms.

I went back to Morgan's network. Basic student information proved easy to access. The schedules and calendars of professors did not present a challenge, either. Tomorrow, Reid scheduled a speech on campus for noon. It promised "tough talk on a post-Freddie Gray Baltimore, including on the blight of gang violence." I didn't know how packed a professor's talk would be on a Saturday, but the Robert and June Ferguson Foundation bought an advance ticket to be on the safe side.

I could hardly wait to hear what the good doctor professed.

* * *

I SHOWED up a few minutes early for the speech and parked in the closest spot I could find. Security guards stood outside the front doors to the lecture hall. The broad-shouldered guard who patted me down looked at my non-detective ID and waved me in. Inside, I saw more security staff roaming the lobby and still more inside the hall itself.

I grabbed a bottled water from a vending machine and

walked into the auditorium. It looked more like a theater except no balcony seats. The stage could hold a play, and the number of seats would guarantee a good gate. I headed to the upper section, filled only halfway. I took a seat near the top and at the end of a row.

A hip-hop song I didn't recognize—it would include most of the recent ones, though I liked my chances in a quiz on the classics—played softly through the audio system. If someone were sitting next to me, we would have been able to have a conversation. I scanned the crowd for anyone dressed like a gangbanger and came up empty. Score one for security..

After a sound check and another couple songs I didn't know, a man in a suit emerged from behind the curtain at eight minutes after the hour. He was a light-skinned black man in a sharp gray suit with a matching vest, white shirt, and black tie. The suit fit him better than a common off-the-rack model. If they gave out programs at this thing, I might have known his identity. "Welcome to Morgan State University," he said. "For those who don't know me, my name is Dr. Benjamin Cameron, Vice-President for Academic Affairs. I hired Doctor Reid, so if you took one of his classes and didn't do well, it's my fault." Dr. Cameron paused for light polite chuckling from the crowd before he continued. "Before we bring Doctor Reid to the stage, the university has invited someone else to say a few words. You may know him as a columnist for *The Sun*. He's written extensively on gang issues, and the problem of violence in African-American culture and inner cities. And he's a graduate of Morgan State University." Dr. Cameron paused for more applause, this round louder. "Please give a nice Bear welcome to Jeremiah Gardner!"

I read some of Gardner's columns over the years. His conservative ideals made him a minority among his city, his fellow columnists, and the black community. Gardner came out from behind the curtain and shook hands with Dr. Cameron. His darker complexion contrasted handsomely with his lighter gray suit and a silver tie bright enough to require batteries. He walked to the microphone to a nice ovation, smiled, and waved to the crowd.

Gardner talked for about fifteen minutes. I sort of paid attention, but I didn't come to see him, so my mind wandered back to the case. Gardner wasn't going to provide much in my pursuit. The parts of his talk I listened to were at least interesting. His opinion on gangs mirrored Reid's, though his resolution lacked Reid's sense of promised apocalypse.

After Gardner left the stage—to less applause than greeted him—Dr. Cameron came back out. The two men did a quick handshake as they passed and Cameron kept walking to the microphone. "I'd like to thank Mr. Gardner for giving us some of his time this afternoon. Now, I'm going to bring out the man you all came to see. He's a professor of African-American studies, a man frequently published in magazines and a recognized expert on inner cities and gang violence. Please give it up for Dr. Maurice Reid."

Reid got the biggest ovation of the day. About a quarter of the people in attendance stood and applauded. He wore a snazzy blue pinstriped suit I would have been proud to claim as one of my own. He paired it with a pristine white shirt and a red tie with thin blue stripes. Reid smiled and gave the crowd a few waves as he walked back and forth on the stage. He took the microphone out of its stand and kept pacing. As a short man, it took him a good number of strides to go from one end to the other. Reid possessed a medium complexion and short black hair graying at the temples.

From his constant motion and easy rhetoric, I got the feeling the professor could win over any crowd. He was assured of a future in politics if he wanted it. For the first part of the speech, I divided my attention between the crowd and him. I wanted to gauge their reactions, especially if it looked like any of them would react violently. No one did. I half heard what the good doctor said, and it sounded much like what I already read.

"My friends," he continued after a few opening remarks to prime his audience, "I teach a lot of people every semester at Morgan State." A few cheers went through the crowd at the mention of the college. "I teach one history class, and three courses specifically on African-American history and culture. You know by now we recently lost two young men who went to this school. They were cubs in a college of Bears. It was my privilege to educate both Andre and Dante on the great history and culture of our people. Anyone who knew them will know they were dedicated students. They asked questions, they were bright, and they were eager to learn." Reid paused. The crowd applauded as he turned away and took a deep breath.

"To lose such fine young men to the plague of gang violence is a terrible shame," Reid went on. "It is a scourge, a blight upon our city. How many more young men . . . old men, women . . . will we have to lose before we decide enough is enough?" Reid's small frame belied the power of his voice. The microphone helped, but his baritone would fill a lecture hall unaided. The crowd sat transfixed. "The gangs don't own Baltimore. They may think they do, but they don't. This is still our city, my friends. It's a city full of good, hardworking people—the kind of people who go to their job every day, raise their children, and go to church. Be sad. Mourn the loss of Andre, of Dante, and of their mothers. Feel it in your hearts . . . but I also want you to steel yourselves. The gangs are getting out of control. It's only a matter of time before their violence consumes them. Maybe then, we can have our city back. Until then, keep strong, my friends, and keep the faith.

"I know what you're thinking—keeping the faith is hard. We tried to keep the faith after Freddie Gray. We tried again when the cops who killed him got off." Murmurs and boos went up.

Reid kept going. "Gangs are taking over our neighborhoods, and we watch it happen. Black, white, young, old doesn't matter. We're enablers. If we don't fight back, that's all we're doing: we're enabling these bastards to come in and take control of our neighborhoods. It's happened for too long here and plenty of other places. And I'm tired of it. I'm tired of it!"

Several people shouted, "Tired!" when Reid punctuated his point. This speech felt like it was shifting to a preacher giving a favorite sermon to the congregation. "People have seen what the gangs can do," Reid said. "They've heard about the random and wanton acts of violence at the Inner Harbor. That's a place filled with tourists and police. If the gangs can wreak havoc there, what stops them from doing it somewhere else?" Reid paused, almost like he expected someone to answer his question. "Nothing. Nothing stops them. Not the threat of arrest, not the fear of the police, and certainly not the fear of the people.

"My friends, it's time to change it all." Applause started in short bursts, but never built because Reid kept talking. "It's time to change it. This country was founded on the principle that we the people can do it. We elected a president—a *black* president—twice based on the principle of 'yes we can.' I'm here today to tell you we the people can take our neighborhoods back from the gangs ruining them." This time, Reid paused for the applause. He allowed himself a smile as he looked over the crowd. Here was a man in his element. "It won't be easy, and it won't happen overnight, but we can do it. Yes, we can. Yes, we can." Reid and the crowd both chanted the refrain for a solid minute.

"I'm not going to give away how to do it now," Reid said once the chant died down. "I'd have to talk until I was hoarse, and you'd have to take a lot of notes." The audience laughed. "But I do have a new book coming out." Another round of applause started. Reid tried to corral it with a few hand waves, but it continued, and he waited for it to end before talking again. "I've been working on the book for a while now. This is a topic not unique to Baltimore, though our problem is closest to my heart. Many cities face problems like ours. In the book, I talk about what the city government can do, and more importantly, what people like you and me can do in our own neighborhoods to take the streets back from those who stole them from us."

More applause went up, and Reid basked in this newest round. I couldn't be surprised at news of another tome hitting the shelves. If any idiot with an Internet fad could get a book deal, someone with the credentials and charisma of Maurice Reid should have publishers fighting over his next manuscript. Good for Reid. His message sounded angry and held potential to cause more violence, but it was a message more people should hear. Turning his speech event into a glorified plug struck me as kind of cheap, though.

I didn't want to hear any more ads for his book. I left the auditorium, got in my car, and drove home.

Doctor Reid just became a lot more interesting.

* * *

FOR A PUBLISHED author with such a natural gift of gab, Maurice Reid's detailed history was lacking. I conducted cursory research on him before. Now, I probed deeper. The problem was Reid's background lacked depth. He could fill a ledger book with things from the last dozen years. Before then, however, he made barely a peep in any context. High school diploma. Bachelor's degree. One credit card. An apartment and a car, the same of both for many years. Only the very basics. Some people lived like this, but I smelled something fishy.

My good friend Joey Trovato is an expert at two things: eating and creating new identities for people. The order of Joey's proficiencies depends on his appetite, but he's been in the ID business much longer than I've worked as a private investigator. I frequently sought his opinion in my cases, and all it cost me was the considerable expense of a meal with an Italian of boundless appetite. I didn't want to bust in on Joey's vacation, however, so I tried to apply maxims he taught me. One of the first was a spotty history past a certain number of years was a likely sign of a fake. Most background checks only went so far. Clearance investigations peaked at ten years. A decade of made-up history was enough to fool most people.

I tried my damnedest not to be most people.

Where was Reid's history beyond the twelve-year mark? I checked the high school he claimed to have graduated from twenty-six years ago. The friendly lady in the office told me they had no record of a Maurice Reid or anyone else with a variety on spelling his last name even attending around the listed time. Another woman at the small southern college Reid supposedly got a degree from from told me the same thing, except with a drawl making me yearn for sweet tea. I could have looked further but didn't see the point. Reid was oh-for-two so far. The swings and misses would only get worse the more I probed.

Instead, I focused on the recent events. Reid legitimately earned his doctorate degree, though now I wondered how closely Coppin scrutinized his undergrad work. Morgan seemed happy with him; they certainly wrote about him and trumpeted his appearances and speeches sufficiently. His students held more mixed opinions. Interestingly enough, both Dante Johnson and Andre Carter left Reid negative reviews on Ratemyprofessor.com. They both mentioned his love for hearing himself talk. Having been to a speech, I could confirm it.

Earlier, I found Reid's talk by checking his university calendar, but I only looked a day ahead. Now I checked the upcoming weeks. Tomorrow, Reid ran a support group for people and families affected by gang violence. The schedule showed it running twice a week. Maybe I would need to alter my opinion of Reid—after all, shameless self-promoters rarely involved themselves in helping people.

I added the support group meeting to my calendar. Might as well check it out in person.

CHAPTER 7

THE SUPPORT GROUP MET IN THE BASEMENT OF A CHURCH I never recalled driving past. Holy Redeemer Church, especially with its very generic name, didn't stand out in any way. It lacked the steeple and spires which lent churches their distinctive look and appeal. This one could have been a retail store in a past life. It was a one-story building with a flat roof, double doors in the front, and large windows designed to show off what was inside. All it needed was the rest of the attractions in a strip mall. I could have used the obligatory Chinese restaurant.

The basement where the meeting took place was an odd fit with the rest of the place. The stairs were narrow and I had to duck as I got closer to the bottom. The ceiling was about three inches over my head. Anyone who stood six-four and wore shoes would be in trouble. The walls needed paint; in some spots, bare drywall showed through. One large room dominated the lower level and a hallway bisected it and led around a corner.

I felt weird walking in, as if I were invading some kind of sacred place. I never felt it when breaking into a house or office or hacking into someplace I didn't belong. Selective morality is a wonderful thing. The people in this group needed to be here—or they thought they did, or someone told them they did. I never attended a support group before. It had been suggested to me after my sister died, but I never went. The shrink my parents insisted I see proved dreadful enough.

As I entered, I saw a table to the right topped with a fresh-smelling pot of coffee, tea bags, and accessories for both along with a box of donuts and a bowl of apples. I thought about taking an apple and making some tea. On the one hand, I already felt out of place. On the other, I needed to look like I belonged. If you're an interloper, looking like you belong can make a lot of difference. Besides, I hadn't eaten in a while.

I heard a couple of voices nearby, but I was the only person in the main room. I walked across the drab tiled floor to the chairs, which were arranged in a semicircle. No chair set apart from the rest. I guess the arrangement aimed to make group members feel Reid was one of them.

Someone else arrived and helped himself to coffee at the refreshment table. He was a tallish thin black man who looked to be in his early fifties. He wore dark blue jeans and a gray sweater. The sweater showed a hole in the left elbow. I sat in a chair far from the center of the semicircle. The latest arrival grabbed a donut to go with his coffee and crossed to the chairs. He walked slowly and didn't look up. I wondered if everyone would look as unhappy as he.

I stood and nosed around the area. An office was situated down the hallway. A sign promised restrooms around the corner, and I encountered a second door to the office there. A few more people wandered in as I walked back to the chairs and sat to wait. I noticed no one looked up or socialized much. Feelings of being an intruder crept upon me again, and I fidgeted in my seat. Reid walked in from the office, a smile on his face. A man I hadn't seen before followed him. He was much taller and broader than Reid and looked like he could win a wrestling match with an alligator.

"How is everyone tonight?" Reid said, smiling and clapping his hands.

The assemblage murmured but didn't put much into their collective response. I stayed quiet in the hopes I wouldn't have to say anything. Stories of AA meetings were full of people who were only comfortable listening. Reid and the other man took their seats; the stranger plopped down next to me, while Dr. Reid sat four chairs away.

"I hope everyone has had a good week," Reid said. "I'm here tonight so we can all share our stories, our pain, and our personal victories." He smiled again, and this time one man and one woman joined him. It was an improvement. "Before we begin, though, it seems introductions are in order. We have someone new with us tonight." He looked at me. "Welcome to the group."

"Thank you," I said.

"What's your name?"

"Trent." I typically gave people my middle name in situations like this. It's less distinct and far less embarrassing than my first name. I have good reason to go by my initials.

"Trent, I'm glad you could come out with us tonight. My name is Dr. Maurice Reid. We're all on a first-name basis here, so you can call me Maurice. The man sitting next to you helps me run this group. His name is Calvin. Going around to your right, we have Jackson, Elizabeth, Chris, Andre, Brent, and Keisha." I got murmured greetings and small smiles from all of them. "Why don't you tell us a little about yourself?"

"I'm twenty-nine," I said. It was probably the last truth I would tell for a while. "I live downtown and work there, too . . . in finance. On nice days, I ride a bike to work."

"All right. We have a rule, Trent. On your first night, you have to share your story. Some groups let you listen indefinitely. I've found hearing other people talk isn't helpful by itself. So how has gang violence affected you?"

My mouth went dry.

* * *

"Trent?" Reid said when I lapsed into silence.

"It's all right," Elizabeth offered in encouragement. "Sharing on your first day is hard. Take your time."

Time was exactly what I needed. I didn't have a story to share here. The closest I got to gang violence was working this case. A dozen eyes stared at me. I debated the wisdom of coming here. Reid would count as a person of interest but what about everyone else? Here I sat surrounded by people with probable cause to hate gang members, led by a man who talked about them with fire and brimstone. Whoever killed my four victims could be in this room. I needed to devise something.

"My sister died when I was sixteen," I blurted out. It was true, though a heart problem caused her death.

"What happened?" Doctor Reid said. He leaned forward and rested his chin on his right hand.

"I was away on a school trip. My sister went to college, got really good grades, was involved in campus clubs. She had an activist streak in her . . . hated war and violence. She and some of her friends were in a club for it, I think." All true so far. Now, however, the lies needed to take over the tale. "One night, they were out downtown, and she got hit by a gangbanger's stray bullet." I paused. I was committed to the story now and needed to keep going. The familiar pain of my sister's death squeezed my chest. The first tears pooled in my eyes.

"That's terrible," Elizabeth said.

I nodded. "Like I said, I was away at the time, so I didn't know what had happened. I got a call telling me my sister died. It wasn't until I turned eighteen when my family told me what really happened."

"You must have felt terrible," Reid said. Wood creaked as Calvin's hands gripped the armrests of his chair.

"Angry, mostly," I said. "My sister was still dead." I felt a few more tears well, and one slid down my right cheek. I wiped at it with my hand. Despite making things up on the fly, I gave these people an amount of truth I hadn't expected to provide. I ended up tapping a real vein of emotion.

"How did you react when you learned the truth?"

I took a deep breath and dabbed at my eyes. "Silence," I said. "I couldn't say anything. I always suspected foul play involved with her death, but to hear about it after the fact was just . . . I don't know, insulting, I guess. I may have been sixteen, but I could have handled the truth."

"Whatever happened to the gangbanger?" Dr. Reid asked.

"I don't know," I said. "I tried looking up news stories to see what I could find, and there's nothing out there. He's as anonymous now as he was before he pulled the trigger." I paused and dabbed at my eyes again. My tight chest needed a breath or two. "I hope he's dead, though."

Dr. Reid gave a subtle nod. Everyone else looked at me, so they didn't notice. I glanced at Calvin. He looked down as soon as I did. He shook his head and inflicted a white-knuckle grip on the arms of the chair. His breaths sounded deeper than mine, and I harbored good reason to be taking deep breaths.

"How do you feel now?" Reid said.

"A little better, I guess," I said. "Getting it out there is bound to help, right?" I wiped at my eyes again. If I thought I would adapt the story of my sister's death for this support group, I would have brought a handkerchief. Or four. Or considered not coming at all.

"That's right, and that's what we're here for."

I nodded. The tears didn't stop. Even thirteen years later, my sister's death felt like a brass-knuckled punch to the ribs.

"If you need the restroom, it's down the hall to the right."

"Probably a good idea." I got up and walked down the corridor and around the corner. The second office door was on my right. I walked past it and into the men's room. I ran cold water and splashed it on my face. After a few slow, deep breaths, the tightness in my chest eased. My brain stopped replaying the night I learned about Samantha's death on a continuous loop of misery. I sloshed more water on my face, then wiped it off with paper towels.

The office. I could probably get a member list from there. The group would expect me to be gone a few minutes.

I rarely needed so much time.

THE OFFICE WAS dark when I walked in. I couldn't turn the light on without alerting everyone to my presence. An ugly L-shaped desk chewed up much of the square footage. I wiggled the mouse, and the computer woke up. The monitor offered some illumination. In addition, it showed me the computer wasn't password-protected. This would be easy, which was always a good thing when limited by time.

Compounding the simplicity was a file on the desktop titled "Member Roster.docx." It always amazes me when people leave valuable files on their desktops. Even a middling hacker could find them elsewhere, but raising the difficulty also makes things take longer. Sometimes, the clock is the biggest factor working against an attacker. Leaving important files in obvious places was a recipe for disaster.

A large HP printer occupied one end of the desk. It looked a few years old, and the dust on it told me Reid didn't use it often. If the printer were noisy, everyone would know I went into the office. Instead, I opened the Word file and snapped a picture of it with my phone. I closed the document, set the computer to sleep again, and walked out via the door I entered.

"How are you, Trent?" Reid asked when I rejoined the group.

"Better now," I said. "Thanks."

"Did this help?"

"I think I got what I needed," I said.

THE SUPPORT GROUP MEETING BROKE UP JUST AFTER THREE o'clock. A few people lingered and talked among themselves. I already felt like an interloper, and I lied in a spot where most people told their darkest truths. Sticking around to make small talk would have been rubbing salt in a nearly-healed wound. Instead, I drove home, changed into athletic attire, and went for a run around Federal Hill Park. Running always invigorated me, and I especially loved doing my laps here. Between the streets of Federal Hill and a stunning view of the Baltimore Harbor, this was the best spot.

I used the few blocks' walk back to my house as a cooldown. It was Saturday afternoon, so I passed people milling about and saw cars navigating the streets. Two doors slammed closed somewhere behind me. I thought I heard footsteps moving with some alacrity in my direction. I held my phone up as a mirror, and it showed me a man about to take my head off with his arm.

If I didn't get the warning, he probably would have knocked me out. As it was, the advance notice allowed me a half-second to duck, and his attempt to clothesline me from behind deflected off the top of my head. It still knocked me off balance—not to mention, hurt—but I wasn't splayed out on the sidewalk. I recovered from my stagger, put a few more steps between me and my assailant, and turned to see he wasn't alone.

Assholes always bring friends. Standing before me were two black men dressed in jeans, nondescript black hoodies, and red bandannas. Pirates. The one who hit me was the bigger of the two, though both were taller, brawnier, and younger. These weren't the goons I was used to squaring off against. I hoped they were untrained. "Recruiting drive?" I said.

"What?" the smaller one said.

"Don't get me wrong. I'm flattered. It's nice to be asked. But I don't think I'm Pirate material."

"We ain't recruiting you," the big one growled. "We just wanna see you bleed."

"I hope you're better fighters than talkers," I said.

They both advanced. Lesser-trained adversaries tend to come one at a time. These two followed a plan. I frowned. The big one smiled like a wolf upon finding an injured sheep. The other one, to my left, was about a step closer to me. His hands were open. The larger man balled his right hand into a fist which looked like it could dent a bank vault. An idea sprang into my head about how they were trying to do this.

Sure enough, the foe on my left tried to grab me. I resisted but only a little. The big one drew his fist back. I reversed the grip the other one held on my arm and pulled him directly into the path of a wallop. His head spun around as far as his neck would allow, and he was out before he hit the concrete.

"Treat all your friends like Bucs?" I said to the larger one remaining on his feet.

He yelled and threw a wild haymaker. Long arms like his take a while to connect on such a blow. I dodged. Another telegraphed punch met the same result. He kept trying them, and I kept stepping to the side or back. He came close to connecting a couple times, but before long, the punches slowed. Even someone in good shape can only go all-out for so long. I still didn't want to put my face in the path of a fist, but my opponent was laboring. I heard his breathing over the blood rushing in my ears.

More wild swings served as the only answer I would get. I let him throw a few more and suck wind even harder before I went on the offensive. I blocked one of his blows, then gave him a hard right cross in the solar plexus to cause serious gasping. I hit him with a few good body shots to bend him over, then planted a kick under his chin, snapping his head back and sending him to the ground.

I turned. The first asshole stirred and pushed himself up to all fours. I kicked him hard in the face, flipping him onto his back and giving him a return trip to dreamland.

While my two foes were out cold, I snapped their pictures. Before I could think of a clever hashtag to gloat about my victory on Instagram, sirens drew closer. It always surprised me when people called the police in Baltimore, and today was no exception.

Officers Brennan and Maine were first on the scene. Maine radioed for an ambulance while Brennan approached me, notepad in hand. "Where's Jennings?" I said, inquiring about his usual partner.

"Vacation," Brennan said. He was a jovial-looking Irishman with blond hair and a strawberry blond goatee. Like me, he probably struggled to grow facial hair beyond it. The curse of Irish blood. "What happened?"

"Two Pirates decided they didn't like me," I said. "I can't imagine why."

"Yeah, I'm sure everyone loves your personality." He jotted a few things.

"Why don't they issue you tablets?"

Brennan snorted. "Shit. No money for one thing. We've had

to do a lot of retraining and buy body cameras after the DOJ kicked our ass. Even if we had the scratch, some asshole would just steal them, anyway."

Before either of us could say anything else, my phone rang. I answered it while Brennan frowned at the interruption. "C.T., you'd better get down here," said Rich.

"What now?" I asked.

"Gang shootings." He gave me the location. "I know you have a theory about all this, but these two are legit. A Buc and a Pirate. Tit for tat."

This reminded me of the call Paul King made a few nights ago. The scene would probably be similar. "I'll be there soon," I said and hung up. "Gotta go, Brennan. Here's my statement: they attacked me. I defended myself well because I always do. The end."

"I might need more," he said. "Where are you going?"

"Gang shooting."

"Shit."

"Yeah," I said.

I PULLED up behind a row of police cars on Poplar Grove Street. I could tell from a few blocks away this would be a bad one. Red and blue lights flashed from down the street. Only as I got closer and the lights grew smaller could I really see the scene. Four patrol cars, two unmarked cars, an ambulance, and the medical examiner's truck sat outside a barrier of yellow tape. So did a bunch of people straining to see what went on.

I got out of the Audi and showed my ID to the uniform who stood guard at the perimeter on this side. He nodded and waved me in, so I ducked under the yellow tape. As the gathered throng of cops, paramedics, and medical examiners parted, I saw three bodies on the ground. Rich only mentioned two. I wondered what happened between his phone call and now. The sheet covering the closest corpse was equal parts white and red. Rich saw me and started talking as he approached. "Another gang shooting," he said. "I heard you saw one the other night, too."

"King tell you?" His head bobbed. "I'm still sticking to my theory on the Johnson and Carter cases."

"Not this one. We got another real gang shootout." He pulled the covering back. A dead black kid of about seventeen lay on the asphalt, his eyes closed. "The victim you're looking at is Dominique Barnes, and his street name in the Bucs is Iceman."

"Do we need to call Maverick and Goose in for questioning?"

Rich rolled his eyes. "This is a legit gang killing, C.T."

"What else went on?" I said. "You mentioned two bodies when you called, but I see three. It's not like you to be off by fifty percent."

"Yeah," Rich said with a wince. "A bystander got hit, too. He was alongside a house at first, so we didn't see him until he staggered out and fell in the street."

"Shit. An innocent caught in the crossfire." The last scene I went to had one, also, though the man there escaped serious injury. This fellow was not so lucky.

"Bound to happen."

I knew it was, but I didn't have to like it, and I couldn't be so matter-of-fact about it. It wouldn't bother me if the gangs wanted to go into an abandoned warehouse, stand in two long lines, and blast away at each other. The problem was it was never so clean and simple. Sometimes innocent people wandered into the path of a bullet meant for some asshole in a bandanna. In other cases, kids got gunned down to attribute the shootings to the gangs, then their mothers met the same fate, for reasons (and by persons) currently unknown.

We walked about fifty feet to the next body. I watched the

crime scene technicians go over every inch of the asphalt. They flittered from one casing to the next to a cigarette butt to anything helping piece together recent events. The team looked like they were drowning in chaos, but their movements were quick and efficient.

"This is John Artis," Rich said as we looked down at the second victim. He looked even younger than the first. "His name in the Pirates is A-Train."

I shook my head, both at the terrible street names and the deaths of two teenagers. "It looks like they got the message," I said.

"You're really still skeptical the gangs killed those two kids and their mothers?"

"I am."

"Why?" Rich said. "Why would someone kill four people and make it look like the Bucs and Pirates did it?"

"To start a gang war," I said.

"To what end?"

"I don't know." I sighed. "I hack into things. Sometimes, I punch people in the face. I don't . . . start street battles."

"You might need a new theory," Rich said.

"Yeah," I said. "I just might."

* * *

BACK HOME, after confirming no more gangbangers lay in wait, I got back to work. The support group meeting didn't tell me much about Dr. Reid. I got the impression he took the group seriously and wanted to help the people who came. He was still a self-important blowhard with a murky past. At least, I could forgive him the self-important part. No one else at the session sparked my interest except Calvin. His white-knuckle chair grips and scowls during my story showed a lot of anger.

Maybe enough anger to kill.

The member list I took a picture of showed him as Calvin Terrell. I hunted around the BPD for information. Four results popped up for the name, and I eliminated the obvious mismatches until only the fellow from last night remained. Calvin's mug shot glared back at me from my monitor. He didn't look any happier in it than he did at the meeting.

The unflattering photo came from the most recent of his four arrests. Four incidents of violence, three of which were against gang members. The first came when Calvin was only seventeen years old. He nearly beat a gangbanger to death. The second time he got popped, also for a violent assault, earned Calvin a ten-year prison sentence. He was out after four. Most recently, two decades after the initial incident, he was a person of interest in the death of Buc lieutenant, Jackson "Steel" Orr. No charges were filed, and the BPD listed the murder as unsolved.

I read the case file. Orr died twenty months ago, not far from the three corpses I saw earlier. He'd been shot.

Three times in the chest.

With a three-fifty-seven.

CHAPTER 9

ERC CONSTRUCTION OWNED A MID-SIZED BUILDING
located amid a large yard in Catonsville, about ten minutes from
Baltimore. The enclosure also held a warehouse, a few smaller
storage sheds, some heavy equipment parked near the main
building, and the usual detritus associated with the industry. The
office manager showed me to Gary Lennox's office and told me he
would be back shortly. I watched her walk away with some interest. She was short, probably just a shade over five feet, but she
filled out her beige blouse and light blue jeans nicely. Her short
brown hair stopped just after the collar of her shirt. She sat again
at her desk and started working. I busied myself with looking
around Gary Lennox's office.

It was small, almost as if someone measured the dimensions
and hung the drywall around the furniture. Between the desk,
chairs, and bookcase, there was barely room to walk. Turning
around would require a year of gymnastic training. Two diplomas
hung on the wall, one a bachelor's in mechanical engineering and
the other an MBA. I wondered how many people who owned
small construction companies could boast of these qualifications.
The MBA was dated from sixteen years ago, likely putting Gary

Lennox around forty. The man walking toward the office confirmed my guess. He was about my height but thirty pounds heavier and with a brawny build to match years of construction work. His black hair showed strands of white at the temples, and his goatee long ago succumbed to its own invasion of gray. Gary Lennox wore faded blue jeans, a tan polo shirt, and a pair of well-worn brown industrial boots.

He closed the door and looked at me. "You're the detective?"

"I am."

"Gary Lennox." He extended his hand.

I shook it. "C.T. Ferguson."

"What's this about?" He sat behind his desk, and I took a seat in one of the uncomfortable guest chairs. Mine were much nicer. On the other hand, I didn't have a bulldozer handy. All in all, probably a wash.

"One of your employees came up during a case I'm working on. I just wanted to find out some more about him."

"Can I see your ID?"

"Sure." I showed him my license and badge. He looked at them, squinted, peered again, and then nodded. "This is a sensitive case, so there is a need for discretion," I said. "Can we keep this chat between us?"

"Sure. What kind of case are you working on?"

"I really can't say."

"Some big corporation has its hooks in you?"

"Not even close."

Gary Lennox frowned. "All right. Whose name came up?"

"Calvin Terrell," I said. "What can you tell me about him?"

"Calvin? He's a good worker. He gets here when he's supposed to, works hard, supervises his crew well. His projects are always finished on time or ahead of schedule, and his workers really like him."

"Any personality conflicts or problems with violence?"

"No company has complete harmony among its employees."

"Anything you can tell me here would be helpful."

"You asked me for discretion," Gary Lennox said. "How far does that go on your side?"

It was a fair question. "I can't say I'll never repeat anything you tell me," I said. "But I will promise only the people who really need to know will learn any of this, and only when they need to know it."

Gary nodded. He must have found my discretion rules acceptable. Most people did. I didn't like the idea of people running their mouths about me, so I tried to minimize doing it to others, especially in the presence of law enforcement. Rich and I disagreed on this, but our opinions varied on a great many things in the policing arena."Calvin would argue with people here and there," Gary said. "Nothing significant. Like I said, every company has it. He got into an altercation with another worker about four years ago, though."

"They got into a fight?" I asked.

"It was headed there, but others broke it up first. They jawed at each other and did some shoving but nothing more."

"What happened after this incident?"

"I transferred the other man to a different crew," Gary said. I wondered if his MBA taught him such tactics.

"Do you know the guy's name?"

He let out a breath and thought. "Tyrone . . . something. Adamson, Tyrone Adamson."

I considered Calvin's BPD file. A bunch of names were in there, but Tyrone Adamson could not be counted among them. Nothing significant must have happened after their little shoving match. "What went down after you transferred the other guy?" I said.

"He quit not long after," Gary said. "Stopped showing up."

Interesting. "I think it's all I need. Thanks for your help."

"Sure," Gary Lennox said. We shook hands again. "I hope Calvin isn't involved in anything bad. I'd hate to lose him."

"Just doing some checking after his name came up."

"I hope that's all it ends up being."

"We'll see," I said.

* * *

I SAT in my Caprice a few houses away from Calvin's. The car was an undefined shade of blue, and I acquired it during a past case where I had to work off the grid. Since then, I took it back to the "automotive reconfiguration engineer" who sold it to me and requested modifications. I figured if I owned an ugly car, I may as well make it a useful one. Bullet-resistant glass replaced the standard Chevy offerings all around, and the body is close to bulletproof. All this work made the car a uniform color, at least, rather than the variations on a cyan theme it sported before. The added weight meant the stock V-8 got replaced by a more eager model. I wouldn't drive it into a nest of machine guns, but some asshole with a pistol would have a hard time hitting me if I sat in it.

Speaking of assholes with guns, Calvin hadn't come out or made a peep. While I waited, I used my phone to do a little more research on him. I made a secure connection to my computer at home, where all my traffic was anonymized and run through a virtual private network at least once. The Nova used in the shooting of Debi Carter didn't have a rear plate. Maryland law required one—and a matching one up front to boot—so driving without it constituted a risk.

Those who gun down women outside funeral homes may be less risk-averse than the average person, however.

It made me wonder if Calvin owned the car. Maybe he stole

it, or someone else did. I checked his vehicle registrations. Like many other people in the country, he owned a Toyota Camry. It was the only car on file for him. Past records didn't turn up a Nova. Calvin's house featured a one-car garage, though, and I saw the Camry parked at the curb.

Either he was a hoarder or the Nova remained hidden behind the garage door. With no activity from the house, I kept digging. Calvin had a brother and sister, but neither owned a car of interest in their lifetimes.

A few minutes later, Calvin emerged from his house. He got in the Camry and drove away. I waited for him to turn off the street plus another minute. Then I got to work. Dusk would provide me some cover from prying eyes. I put on thin black gloves and knocked on the front door. No dogs barked. I didn't see any alarm company signage.

Within a minute, thanks to the lockpicks on my special keyring, I opened the front door. Little natural illumination remained, and I didn't want to risk turning on a light and alerting the neighbors of my presence. Calvin kept a messy home. Even for a bachelor, he was a pig. Ignoring the shopworn living room furniture, plates, bowls, and utensils on the coffee and end tables, I encountered a few pizza boxes piled up in the kitchen. The general odor of the house told me they might not be empty.

Another door beckoned off the dining room, which was the neatest room in the house. Of course, its tidiness stemmed from its apparent total disuse. The layer of dust told me Calvin probably never sat at the table, let alone eaten a meal in here. As an unmarried man, I understood the appeal of eating in front of a nice TV—though Calvin's appeared a bit small by modern standards—but sometimes, everyone needs to eat in the dining room. The door opened into a dark garage. I saw the outline of a car and the bare interior walls.

I flipped the switch on. A blue Nova sat on the concrete. I walked around to the back. No rear plate was attached. Four bullet holes pockmarked the rear end of the car, and one of the taillights was missing.

I TOOK PICTURES OF THE NOVA AND WALKED BACK INTO THE house proper. Calvin didn't seem to be in a hurry to return. I used this time to nose around his sty of a house. Confirming he owned the Nova was great, but I still wanted more. I saved the living room for the end and started in a spare bedroom Calvin turned into an office.

A cheap wooden desk with a mismatched hutch sat against the wall on the right. Completing the trashy look was a collection of printouts and Post-Its stuck all over. I read a few. They sounded like snippets of Dr. Reid's speeches. The attribution on one didn't match, however; it listed Malcolm Reedy as the speaker. I snapped photos of all the various notes. Calvin also left a book by this Reedy on the desk. *The Blight of Gang Violence: A Problem and a Solution*, dated thirteen years ago, sounded very much like something Reid would have penned.

I continued hunting but didn't uncover anything of interest. A .357 would have been a nice find. Either Calvin took it with him, or he kept it well-hidden. I didn't want him to know I'd been here, which limited my searching to more gentle means. After looking out the window to confirm no one was around, I left via the front door and climbed back into my car.

Once seated, I reconnected to my server at home for another secure session. I uploaded the pictures I took, then invoked a script to run optical character recognition and search for the strings of text it found. Results soon appeared. The quotes were a mix, with some attributed to Malcolm Reedy and others to Maurice Reid. There were pairs of very similar sayings, one belonging to each man. Change a few words, plug in a new city, update the president to the current occupant of 1600 Pennsylvania Avenue, and a Malcolm Reedy quote morphed into a Maurice Reid talking point.

I researched the book I saw on Calvin's desk. It took a little digging, but I found an archived photo of Malcolm Reedy from fourteen years ago.

He bore an uncanny resemblance to one Doctor Maurice Reid.

Reedy's records stopped a dozen years ago when he went missing, though never declared dead. As far as I could tell, the Boston police never closed the case; they only stopped trying to solve it after a lengthy time. I got the feeling I could supply an answer for them.

A little more digging convinced me Reedy dropped off the grid and emerged a couple months later as Maurice Reid. The Internet was a Thing then, but the social media explosion wouldn't occur for a few years. People with phones didn't photograph, film, and upload their entire lives. Reedy's reinvention would be a lot harder today—at least without the help of a pro like Joey—but he pulled it off a dozen years ago.

The title of the book piqued my interest. What was the proposed solution? I didn't want to download the entire tome and give a couple dollars to its author. Within a minute, I found a journal article offering a detailed critique, and I pitied the author.

Reedy's solution involved pitting gangs against one another on an ever-increasing scale. The occasional tit-for-tat shooting, he argued, did not rid the city of its problem quickly enough. He went on to posit tricking the gangs into escalation by pinning other murders on them.

Bingo.

More than a decade after Malcolm Reedy wrote those words, Maurice Reid got to put the plan into action with Calvin's help.

I saved all the information on my server and disconnected. Still no sign of Calvin. I didn't need anything else from him or his messy house, however. I drove home.

* * *

AN ALLEY RAN behind my house. Just off it, I recently installed a concrete parking pad. It fit both my cars—I usually moved the Caprice to the street when Gloria visited—and still left enough room in my small backyard for a grill. As usual, cars were parked sporadically on the alley, making navigating it an occasional adventure. I got out of the Caprice and locked the door. Footsteps came from somewhere behind me. I put my hand on my gun and started to turn.

"Don't do it," said a voice. I stopped. Something jabbed into my lower back. "Why don't you gimme the gun? Nice and slow." I took it out of the holster with a two-fingered grip and handed it to my mysterious assailant. He snatched it and stuffed it into the waistband of his jeans. I hoped he would shoot his own dick off but no such luck. "We taking a ride. Let's go."

"In my car?" I said.

"Mine. In the alley." He nudged me with the muzzle, and I walked toward a late 'eighties Mustang GT. It was jet black with the silver 5.0 emblem on the side. Why have a five-liter V8 if you can't tell everyone about it? "You driving." He tossed me the keys.

I got in. Whoever this guy was, he owned a classic Mustang with a five-speed manual. If it weren't for the whole gun thing, I might have liked him.

I hadn't started the car yet. "Where are we going?" I asked. I buckled my seatbelt and looked at my passenger. He was black, maybe twenty or so years old. He wore a blue shirt peeking from under the dark, nondescript hoodie. His face was long though not thin, and it combined with his small eyes for a sinister countenance. He looked a little taller than me when he walked past, and he was built like a basketball player. A baller who happened to have a nine-millimeter pointed at me.

"Head into the city," he said. He sat looking at me, turned about a quarter of the way toward my side. He hadn't buckled his seatbelt. When I started the car, the Mustang beeped to remind us he flouted the safety laws of Maryland. I declined to point it out to him.

I went down Riverside, then picked up Fort Avenue. I took it to Jackson, and then to Key Highway. Past Rash Field and around a sharp curve, Key Highway becomes Light Street, which leads to Harborplace, and from there, any number of roads will take one anywhere in Baltimore. I followed Light to Calvert, then hung a left on Fayette, which was one way headed toward the west side. "You heading west," my passenger said.

"Figured it's where you were taking me," I said. "Or I was taking you. I'm not really sure who's taking whom here."

"Just drive."

"You could at least tell me why you came for me with a gun and have me driving somewhere."

"You a snoop working with the cops."

I wondered how he knew this. My interaction with Calvin happened as Trent the finance guy. Of course, two idiots threatened me recently. Ever since my picture made it into the paper—and online—after my first case, getting identified has been a risk.

"Just because I'm a PI doesn't mean I'm your enemy," I pointed out.

"The police are," he said. "You working with them. That's enough."

"Even though I'm the one who figured out you were being played." We missed the light at Charles Street. When it turned green, I took a right. Years ago, my father taught me the lights in Baltimore were calibrated so a certain speed would make most of them, and different speeds would miss them. Normally, I did my damnedest to cruise through the lights. This time, I decided to drive slower and miss them. Anything to give me more time to devise a way out of this situation.

"What you mean we getting played? And where the hell you driving to?"

"You haven't told me where we're going yet," I said. "Just picking up Franklin." We missed the light at Saratoga Street. "Might as well take a major road."

"Whatever," he muttered. "What's this shit about being played?"

"Those two kids who got killed before their mothers weren't in the gangs."

"Bullshit," my gun-toting passenger said.

"Did you know either of them?" I said.

"No. But I don't know every brother in this gang. Shit, probably a lotta 'em I ain't met."

"Maybe. But *no one* knew these kids. Not in the gangs and not in the police. They were good students at Morgan State. How many of those you have in the Bucs?"

"You saying we all stupid?"

"Just saying being a banger means you probably don't have the time to do well at college." We missed the light at Mulberry, too. So far, my strategy was working. Now I just had to figure out step two of my master plan.

"Don't mean they wasn't in the gang," he said.

"You're right. They weren't." He missed my jab at his double negative, so I added, "Someone wants you to think they were."

"Why?"

"So you'll shoot each other. The easiest way to get rid of Bucs and Pirates is to have you do it yourselves."

"My uncle Calvin says you just trying to stir up shit, man."

There was the connection. Calvin must have doubted my story at the support group. I wondered if he sent the two chuckle-heads who threatened me, too. "Actually, I'm trying to stop the shit from being stirred. The police are finally starting to believe me."

He paused, obviously in thought. I allowed myself a flicker of hope. Then he said, "Just drive."

I shook my head. For a minute, I thought I got through to him for whatever good it might do. "Where are we going?" I said.

"You gonna meet the man."

I presumed he meant the Bucs' leader. "What's he want with me?"

"He wanna know everything you know. Then he wanna cut you. A lot. Probably cut you while he asking you questions."

"Sounds like a charmer." We missed our third straight light. Maybe I'd get lucky and all the assholes we were going to see would be arrested or dead by the time we arrived. "What do they call you?"

"Horse," he said.

"Why?"

"'Cause I'm hung like one." He puffed his chest out when he explained.

"I won't ask you to prove it," I said. I wondered how many times his long face got him compared to a horse as a child.

Horse chortled. What a silver-tongued devil I was: I could charm the pants off comely young women and get gang members to laugh when they pointed guns at me. The words would go nicely on my tombstone, which looked more and more like a looming part of my future. There was no way I could let Horse take me to meet the man. Even if he didn't cut me to ribbons, I knew I wouldn't walk out of the situation alive.

"How much farther is it?" I said as we waited for the light at Paca Street.

"Couple miles," Horse said.

A couple miles. Presuming we kept missing most of the lights —and Horse hadn't said anything about our progress yet—it gave me maybe five or six minutes to devise a way to survive this. Horse kept the gun trained on me, even though he didn't watch me all the time. Still, wrestling it away from him in a confined space, all while trying to keep a thirty-year-old Mustang on the road, struck me as a poor plan. I could try it at a red light, but I noticed he watched me more when we were stopped. Making a move on the road was risky, but I didn't see a better option.

I needed a window of opportunity, but simply because Horse didn't keep an eye on me a hundred percent of the time didn't make him inattentive. As we waited for the light at Carey Street, I put my hands in my lap. Horse noticed. I wanted him to. I did the same thing at the next light, too. If he got used to seeing it, then maybe he would take for granted I was doing it and not pay such close attention.

"You praying?" he said.

"What if I am?" I said.

"Ain't gonna help you none. The man still gonna find out what you know, and he still gonna cut you up."

"Jesus is my shield," I said as seriously as I could.

He snorted. "Shit, man. My momma believe all that shit. Jesus ain't never do nothing for us, y'know? I got a lot farther believing in the Bucs than in Jesus."

We'd hit another red signal in the meantime. Now we sat at

Monroe Street. We came up on it when it was still yellow. I fought the urge to mash the gas, and instead hit the brake and waited. Monroe was a pretty major road. I saw a few cars and a couple trucks go by.

Trucks. An idea took shape.

Monroe Street ran one way southbound from our right to left. A break in traffic happened, meaning the light could change soon. I still needed a way out of this situation before meeting the man. A tractor, sans trailer, sped down Monroe. I looked at Horse. He watched the traffic. The tractor drew closer.

I moved my right hand off my lap and shoved the gun away from me. "What the fuck, man?" Horse said. He pushed against me, but I didn't give. He squeezed the trigger. My ears rang and felt like they would burst as the bullet shattered the windshield. The tractor was close now. If the driver heard the gunshot, he didn't show it. I waited until he was almost into the intersection, then I let the clutch out and stomped on the gas. If I went to the Bucs' base, I was dead. If this collision killed me, at least I chose my own death.

The truck driver realized what was about to happen. I heard his horn. Horse yelled beside me. He kept a strong grip on the gun. The truck driver's eyes widened. The cab cleared as the Mustang plowed into the rear of the tractor.

Metal twisted. Glass shattered. The tractor slid. The rear of the Ford came off the asphalt. Without the benefit of an airbag, my head crashed into the steering wheel. Horse, with no airbag or seatbelt, went out through the windshield, opening a much larger hole than the bullet did.

The Mustang crashed back to the road. My head slammed into the headrest. Everything spun, then stars swam in front of my eyes before the lights went out.

AMMONIA. MY BRAIN PROCESSED THE STRONG SMELL. There was no other awareness, just its scent flooding my nostrils. Air rushed into my nose, my eyes opened, and only then did I become aware of anything else. Horse's Mustang sat on its tires, but if I hadn't known what kind of car it was, I wouldn't have recognized its twisted and battered shell. I lay on the ground, looking up at a slender male EMT. His name tag was blurry, and I had trouble focusing on it, but it looked like it said "Stevenson."

Bits of broken glass lay all around me on the asphalt. I raised my head slowly. Waves of dizziness washed over me. I took a deep breath. Dents and scratches marred the back part of the tractor. I saw a fiftyish man with a bloody face, forearm tattoos, and a tattered baseball cap talking to a police officer. On some level, I remembered what I did: I deliberately gunned the pony car into the intersection and into the rear of a speeding tractor. The possibility of dying in the collision struck me as preferable to the slow, painful, and certain death awaiting me if Horse took me to meet the Bucs' higher-ups.

Horse . . . he exited stage front in the wreck. Stevenson's

mouth moved, but I couldn't make out what he said. I eased my head back down and squinted up at him. "What?" I said.

"You shouldn't pick your head up," he said. "You might have a spinal injury, and movement would only make it worse."

I wiggled my fingers and toes. "I don't have a spinal injury." From somewhere behind me, I heard a brief argument. "How's the other guy?"

"The truck driver is shaken up, but he's not injured. Airbag deployed. He'll be fine."

"I meant the other guy in the car."

Stevenson frowned. "It doesn't look good. He went out the windshield, hit the tractor, then hit the street."

I shouldn't have felt bad, but I did. Then I heard a familiar voice.

"C.T., are you all right?" Rich said.

"Sure," I said. "Just resting here on the street."

"He has a concussion," Stevenson said. "Some cuts and bruises, maybe an internal injury or two. He should go to the hospital."

"Rubbish," I said, "there's a case to wrap up."

"Tell me what happened," said Rich. I told him. "Jesus Christ."

"I couldn't let him take me to the Buc base," I said.

"You couldn't have just run into a telephone pole?"

"I needed something to take him out of the equation." I shrugged. "When I saw the tractor speeding down the road, it seemed like the better option."

"You got lucky."

"Maybe. I need to tell you something, though." I raised my head again. No dizziness. It was progress. I sat up part of the way, propping myself up on my elbows, leading to an instant pain between my eyes.

"I really think you should just lie there," Stevenson said.

"No rest for the wicked," I said.

The headache lingered. I figured it would remain for a while at varying degrees of tolerability. Stevenson was right; I should have stayed on the asphalt. Despite the pain, I sat up. I nearly collapsed back to the street, but I fought the dizziness.

"Go to the hospital," Rich said.

"Later," I said. "Help me up." I stuck out my hand. Rich rolled his eyes and shook his head, but he grabbed my hand pulled me slowly upward. I went to my knees first, then to one knee before standing bent at the waist. Rich let go of my hand. My head swam, and noises sounded distorted and far away. Nausea tugged at my stomach. I put my hands on my knees and slowly straightened. I wish I could say it felt good, but it didn't. I felt miserable, like I would sink back to the street at any second. Rich looked at me with narrowed eyes. He held his hands ready to grab me. I took a few deep breaths, and the sickness lessened.

"Calvin," I said. "Calvin is the key." My brain became foggy. Why did I call him the key? The key to what?

"We can talk more after we get you to the hospital," Rich said.

"They could be ramping up. You've seen the shootings. No time for lying down on the job." I wanted to tell him something else—the name Reedy floated somewhere in the growing haze—but I couldn't retrieve it.

"Let us worry about it. You get some rest. King and I can talk to you later."

"It's important," I insisted. My mouth kept moving, but I couldn't figure out anything I said. I experienced the sensation of falling forward. Something stopped me. I looked around. Rich held me up. Somewhere in the distance, I heard him shout for the paramedics.

* * *

My brain came back to the land of the conscious before my body did. I knew I was lying down. It constituted the whole of my knowledge at this moment. I felt like I slept off a bender in college—foggy, disconnected, and with a headache. My mouth and throat were as dry as a skeleton baking in the desert. Voices coalesced into ones I recognized. My parents were in the room. A few seconds later, I found the self-awareness to open my eyes.

"Robert, he's awake," my mother said.

"I see that. Son, how are you?"

I looked around. I lay in a hospital bed. An IV ran into my arm, and electrodes for a heart monitor were attached to my chest. I didn't have any other tubes or gizmos connected to me. A small flatscreen TV mounted on the wall across the room displayed a commercial on mute. The bedside table had a cup of water atop it. "Thirsty," I said.

My mother handed me the cup of water. I drained it in one gulp. The dryness in my throat passed, and I let out a deep breath. My head still hurt, and I felt as if a layer of gauze stretched over everything. "Coningsby, the doctor says you have a concussion," she said.

"I'm sure I do," I said.

"What happened?"

I told her the story of Horse making me drive at gunpoint, where he wanted to take me, and the horrible things likely to happen there. It took me a few minutes to tell the story because I stopped and restarted a few times. Things got clearer as I went through it. My mother frowned when I finished. "That's terrible . . . having to make a choice like that," she said.

I shrugged. "It's a terrible world sometimes. Any news on the kid who carjacked me?"

"No," my father said. "I haven't asked. I don't really care what happens to him."

"Robert!" My mother's chiding tone hadn't changed since I first heard it as a toddler.

"Just being honest."

My father refilled my cup, and I drank more water. "You guys my first visitors?" I said.

"No," my mother said. "Richard was here a little while ago. I think you talked to him for a few minutes."

"I did?" I searched my memory for any recollection of this conversation and came up empty. Everything since I plowed the Mustang into the tractor was shrouded in fog.

"Yes, dear. He left in quite a hurry."

"I guess I told him something useful, then." My head throbbed, and everything got weird and distant again. "I think I'm going back to sleep."

My father said something, but his voice grew distorted as if he were talking from underwater. Then I didn't hear him at all.

* * *

IT FELT like coming out of a deep sleep: My brain knew I was awake, but my body lodged its disagreement. My limbs felt like they were made of lead. Nary a noise came from the room. As the fog slowly lifted, I opened my eyes. My parents were gone, replaced by Rich and Captain Leon Sharpe. I looked at the bedside table; nurses refilled my water pitcher and cup. I grabbed the table, wheeled it closer, and drained the cup again. "How long have I been out?" I said.

"Almost a day," Rich said.

"Holy shit." Almost a day! How much did I miss lying in this hospital bed? "Did I tell you anything you could use?"

"Yeah, you managed to get it out before you went under again."

"And?" I said when Rich offered nothing else.

"And I put an emergency task force together," Sharpe said. "We got some people from the county and state. By and large, the members of the Pirates and Bucs are sitting in jail cells right now. Three of them died before we could round them up." He frowned. "We got them before the worst of it really started."

"What about Calvin and Reid?"

"No sign of them yet," Rich said.

The slippery bastards got away. "You came here just to deliver this cheery news?"

"And to see how you're doing."

"I'm as well as I can be," I said. "Which you could have learned by yourself."

"You want to know why I'm here," Sharpe said.

"I doubt police captains make many hospital room visits, even for handsome PIs who solve cases for them."

"You caused an accident."

"I prefer to think of it as avoiding torture and death," I said.

"The driver of the truck is probably going to sue you."

"I have insurance." I shook my head. It didn't hurt. Score one for progress. "He would have done the same thing in my spot." I looked at Sharpe for a second. "You would have, too, Leon."

"Probably," he said. "The kid in the car with you is alive. It was dicey for a while, but they think he's going to make it."

On some level, I felt glad to hear this news, but I kept it to myself.

Sharpe took an envelope from under his jacket and tossed it on the table. "Photos from the scene," he said. "My boss wanted me to come down here and chew your ass. I'm not going to. You made the same decision I would have made and he would have made. But he insisted I bring pictures so you could see 'the results of the fool's handiwork,' as he put it."

I poured some more water. The BPD commissioner could

complicate my life if he wanted to. "Is he going to recommend my license be suspended?"

"No," said Sharpe. "I think he was just pissed that a PI managed to learn more about this case than his own cops."

"He'll get over it." I picked up the envelope and opened it. The first picture told the story. Horse lay on the gurney after being extracted from the wreckage of the scene. From the pictures, I figured more of Horse's blood had spilled on the street than remained in his body. I couldn't believe he survived. Cuts from broken glass dotted his face, neck, and torso. The red turned his blue bandanna into a morose shade of purple.

I started to flip to the next photo, then stopped. Blood on the bandanna. It took me a moment to fight through the fog, but I remembered the photos I saw of the Dante Johnson and Andre Carter crime scenes. "Leon, I can prove those first two victims weren't gangbangers," I said.

"That would be nice, but I'm not sure it matters now."

"It matters to their families." I pulled the electrodes off my chest. Immediately, the heart monitor let out a cacophony of beeps and boops. "Rich and I will get Doctor Reid and Calvin. Maybe those two assholes in jail will matter to you." I looked down at the IV in my arm. It wasn't something I could just yank out. Three nurses sprinted into the room as I sat up. "What's going on?" the first one, a pretty Asian girl, said.

"Get this damn thing out of my arm," I said. "I'm going home."

"Sir, you were in a car accident. You have a concussion."

"There's a form I can sign to check out against medical advice, right?"

"C.T., we don't need to do this now," Rich said.

"Yes, we do. So . . . the form?"

"Uh . . . yes," she said, "you can check out against medical advice. I'll have to get the on-duty doctor."

"Good. Have him bring the paperwork for me to sign. But first, please take this goddamn thing out of my arm."

She did. The doctor came in a few minutes later and asked me to reconsider. He said I needed to stay for further observation. I pointed out what "against medical advice" meant and signed the form. Rich protested a couple times, but I think he knew the futility of it; Sharpe didn't even bother. After I collected my clothes, Rich drove me home.

We still needed to round up the instigators.

CHAPTER 12

RICH PARKED AT MY CURB AND FOLLOWED ME TO MY DOOR. Gloria texted as I walked in. She was concerned after not hearing from me for over a day. I smiled at her fretting over me. It was never part of the plan when we began our relationship. Now I wondered where it was headed. I would have to deal with it (and her) later, however. I fired off a quick reply telling her I was OK and busy wrapping up the gang mess.

"Here," Rich said, handing me my .45. "Uniforms found it on Horse. I knew it was yours. Not many HK45s out there."

I liked my Hechler and Koch. It was a little more accurate than the average .45, which made up for me being a good but not great shot. Plus, anyone who took a bullet from it dropped on the spot. I flashed back to helping Rich on an off-the-books case in western Maryland. I shot a goon three times in the chest before he could kill Rich. If I could have gone my whole career without putting the gun's stopping power to the test, I would have done so. Life doesn't always cooperate with our plans, however. If Calvin drew down on me, I'd be ready for him.

"What did you mean about proving those first two kids weren't gangbangers?" Rich said.

"Horse's bandanna," I said, "was soaked with blood."

"Sure."

"The first two kids' weren't. For all the blood they shed, their bandannas were pretty dry. Like someone put it on their heads after the fact."

"Huh." Rich nodded. If I didn't know him better, I might have said he was impressed.

"Tell me where you've looked for Reid and Calvin," I said.

"Everywhere we could think of." Rich ran a hand through his short hair. "Both their houses, where they work, known associates. . . ."

"And you came up empty?"

"Yeah. They're in the wind."

"What about ways out of town?" I asked.

"We're covering those," said Rich. "They can't get on a plane, train, or bus without us knowing about it."

I shrugged. "They can get an Uber, though, and you'll never know."

"You're a wet blanket."

"Wow," I said.

"What?"

"I don't think anyone has been called a wet blanket in about twenty years."

"It's not so old a term," Rich protested.

"Whatever you say, daddy-o."

He rolled his eyes. "You can't be concussed too badly. Your annoying sense of humor is the same as ever."

I grinned and after a moment, so did Rich. "What about the support group?" I said.

"What support group?"

"Sounds like you haven't checked it, then. Reid and Calvin run a session to aid people affected by gang violence. It might be the one good thing they do."

"And you know where these people meet?" Rich said. I nodded. "Let me guess—you crashed one of their meetings." I inclined my head again; Rich moved his on the opposite axis. "You're unbelievable sometimes. People are there because they need help."

"Now who's a wet blanket?" I said. Rich glared at me. "I didn't prevent anyone from getting help. I simply scoped it out and snagged a member roster."

Rich took a deep breath. He probably felt the roster was the bridge too far. Without it, I wouldn't have learned who Calvin was so quickly. While my natural brilliance may have led me there at some point, more casualties could have happened in the interim. "Could you tell me where they meet?"

"Yes," I said.

He waited. "Well? Where?"

"I'll be glad to show you en route." I put my hand up when Rich voiced an objection. "I'm coming along. This is my case, too."

"Fine," Rich said after stewing a few seconds. "I'm calling in Paul King, too."

"The more, the merrier," I said.

OUTSIDE THE CHURCH or store or whatever the hell it had been, Rich and King strapped on Kevlar. King tossed me a vest, and I did the same. "I'm touched," I said.

"Rich would cry if you got shot," he said.

"You know me," Rich said. "I'd weep for days."

While I put the bullet-resistant armor on, I described the general layout of the place for the rest of the raiding party. Doctor Reid and Calvin were likely to be downstairs, as the upper floor didn't offer much in the way of furnishings or cover. Rich and

King checked their weapons. This struck me as an excellent idea, so I followed suit. "Let's go," Rich said.

The outside door was secured with the shabby kind of lock an old store should have, and I got us inside in about a minute. We didn't hear any alarms. Rich and King both drew their guns. Never one to be left out, I unholstered mine, too. They both stalked around the first floor with their heavy-duty flashlights. My LED model looked puny by comparison.

"Clear," Rich said in a quiet voice a moment later.

"They must be downstairs," King said. "You guessed right."

"Don't sound so surprised," I said. We moved to the stairs.

"I'll cover you," Rich said as we stood at the top. King went first, his pistol and flashlight leading the way. I descended next. Toward the bottom of the staircase, my head started to hurt. When I cleared the final step, balance became an issue. Nausea clawed at my insides. I slumped into the wall, grateful for the support. "You sure you're OK?" King whispered.

I nodded. He didn't look convinced. I couldn't blame him—I didn't feel convinced, either. "I just need a minute," I said.

"What's going on?" Rich said as he joined us. He looked at me and frowned. "You really shouldn't be here."

"Bullshit," I said. "I'm proving my championship mettle by playing hurt."

"Let us take the lead," King said. "You got us here." He jerked his head toward the door a couple feet away. "Pick this lock and call it a night."

I pushed off the wall, took a couple uncertain steps, and tried the knob. Locked. I put my gun away, took out my tools, and crouched. Even such a simple action sent my equilibrium askew again. I used a hand to steady myself and took a couple deep breaths until the waves of sickness passed.

"Work from the side as much as you can," King whispered. "If they hear you messing with the lock, they might shoot."

"Worst pep talk ever," I said.

"I don't do pep talks."

"Good thing," I said as I knelt to the side of the door. Working from an angle would slow me, but if it lowered my chances of getting shot, I could take the hit to my pride a sluggish lock-picking time would cause. Rich and King stood behind me, out of the way of any gunfire.

A couple minutes later, I popped the bolt. King materialized on the other side of me as if he had been transported those few feet. I stood. Rich and King both nodded, and Rich opened the door. They both pointed their guns through the opening. The only things to greet us were silence and darkness.

I stood, walked in behind them, and stuck to the wall on the right. At least I didn't feel like I needed it to keep me vertical at the moment. King kept to the left. Rich took the middle of the room.

"Rich, light," King whispered.

"Go ahead," Rich said.

King flipped a switch, and fluorescent brightness flooded the room. "They have to know we're here already," he said.

Quiet voices came from the office, but I couldn't make out anything being said. Rich and King both stared in its direction. We stood about where the semicircle of chairs was setup for the support group. The office door clicked and someone dragged it open about a foot. Two small hands appeared in the doorway. "Don't shoot," Doctor Reid said.

"Come out with your hands up," King said as he moved closer to the door. He kept his gun on Reid the whole time. So did Rich. I didn't like the fact of Reid showing after a conversation. Where was Calvin, and what did he have planned?

"I'm not resisting," Reid said. He stepped out from the office, pulling the door shut behind himself.

King dragged him out into the center of the area. "Maurice

Reid, you are under arrest," he said, replacing his pistol with a pair of handcuffs. He Mirandized Reid as Rich and I looked on.

"I don't like this," I whispered. "Where's Calvin? We know he's a shooter."

"You said the office has a second door, right?" Rich said.

"Yeah, around the corner."

"Keep an eye on it, then." We both moved in. Reid was cuffed and on his knees. King finished reading him his rights. Footsteps came from around the corner.

"You fuckers ain't takin' me alive!" Calvin said.

"Calvin, don't do this," Reid implored. "It's over. We lost. There's no need for anyone to get shot."

"I ain't going back to jail," Calvin hollered from the hidden hallway. King ushered Reid toward the entrance door.

"Calvin Terrell, come out with your hands up," Rich said.

"Fuck you," Calvin said. He came around the corner with a large revolver in his hand. He swung it toward Rich and me. We both fired. Bullets rocked Calvin. His revolver pointed toward the floor. Rich and I watched him, guns still at the ready. Calvin looked at us, then at the gun he held by his side, then pitched forward.

"Calvin!" Reid yelled from outside the main door.

* * *

Rich, King, and I all gave our statements. King drew the short straw and went downtown to fill out more paperwork. Rich and I drove back to my house. "We couldn't do anything else but shoot," Rich said after a few minutes of glorious silence.

I nodded. "I know." I didn't say anything else. Knowing I was forced to shoot Calvin and dealing with it were two different things. He was the second person circumstances impelled me to fire upon. When I got into this job, I envisioned sitting behind my desk and hacking my way to whatever solution the case required. I never thought I would need to shoot anyone.

"How do you feel?"

"Tired," I said. "I may also admit to having some lingering concussion symptoms."

"I mean about the shooting," Rich said.

I thought about it for a moment. "It was easier this time." Again, I lapsed into silence.

"It bothers you."

"Shouldn't it?"

"Probably," Rich said. "You did what had to be done. It was him or us. I'm sure it'll take a few days to sort it all out."

"Did it take you a few days?" I said.

Now Rich fell silent. After a moment, he said, "For me, it was a week into my first tour in Afghanistan. Same thing—it was him or me. I knew I was right. It took me a couple days to process it and come out the other side. I still remember every detail today, though, even down to the blood." He paused. "Especially the blood."

"Did it get easier?"

"You mean as I killed more people?" I bobbed my head. "Yeah, it does. It might sound messed up, but as long as the shootings are legit, you're just coming to terms with everything faster. You're adapting. It's normal."

"I don't know if it's normal," I said, "but I understand. And I guess I'm going to have to deal with it."

"I've been through it. You can always talk to me if you need to."

"Thanks," I said.

We made the rest of the drive in silence. Nothing else needed to be said.

* * *

THE NEXT DAY, I went through the usual conversation with my mother after wrapping up a case. She was proud of what I did but horrified as always about man's inhumanity to man. They would pay me the usual rate for a job well done. I was technically a contract employee of my parents' foundation, and the money for solving cases constituted a salary.

Later, I talked to the press. Reid and Calvin staging the initial shootings to gin up the gangs made for quite a story. I emailed my proof Dante Johnson and Andre Carter weren't gang members to local reporter Jessica Webber. She would have a few details no one else would. Jessica chronicled my first case, though I hadn't seen her much since it ended.

I also talked to Erma Johnson. It was the longest and most worthwhile conversation of the day. Several times, she said, "I told you my grandson wasn't in no gang."

I said, "Yes, ma'am" every time.

END of Novella #3

Dear reader,

Thanks for joining me on these stories. I hope you enjoyed them.

If you didn't start the series from the beginning, that's OK. You can read C.T.'s adventures in any order you happen to find them.

His first case is chronicled in *The Reluctant Detective*. C.T. wants an easy start to his career. Instead, he gets a liar for a client and sees his life threatened several times. You can get the book here.

In the case following the events of *Red City Blues*, C.T. runs headlong into the thin blue line when he doesn't think an accused cop killer committed the crime. You can get *Already Guilty* here.

As always, thanks for reading.
-Tom

THE END

Remember when I asked you if you liked free stories? I have a collection of four C.T. Ferguson short stories I'm giving away. When you join my VIP Readers group, you'll also be the first to know about new releases, promos and giveaways, you'll see cover reveals before the general public, and I give away stuff throughout the year. If this sounds like your cup of tea, please sign up here.

If you enjoyed this book, I hope you'll leave a review. Independent authors like me rely on reviews to help make our books more visible, feed the mighty algorithms, and qualify for promotions. To write a review, go to the book's sales page, scroll down to the review section, select your star rating, and write a few words. You don't need to say a lot; most reviews are only a few sentences. It just takes a minute or two, but it can make a big difference to an author.

The C.T. Ferguson Mystery Series:

- The Reluctant Detective

- The Confessional (novella)
- The Unknown Devil
- Land of the Brave (novella)
- The Workers of Iniquity
- Red City Blues (novella)
- Already Guilty

While this is the suggested reading sequence, the books all stand on their own and can be enjoyed in whatever order you happen upon them.

Connecting with readers is the best part of being a writer. You can reach me via email at tom@tomfowlerwrites.com. I am not a big-timer, and I respond to each email I get.

This book is a work of fiction. Places are either fictitious or used in a fictitious manner. Characters are products of the author's imagination. Any resemblance to actual persons, living or dead, is purely coincidental.

ABOUT THE AUTHOR

Tom Fowler was born and raised in Baltimore and still resides in Maryland. He is the author of the C.T. Ferguson novel and novella series, which are all set in his home city.

At about age seven, polite young Tom wrote a "murder mystery" in which no one died. The story gave him the writing bug, however, and he's been putting pen to paper and fingers to keys ever since.

When not working or writing, Tom enjoys spending time with his family and friends, reading, sports, movies, and writing brief bios in the third person.

Connect:

- [f] facebook.com/tomfowlerwrites
- [o] instagram.com/tomfowlerwrites
- [BB] bookbub.com/authors/tom-fowler-49747e52-66c1-4e43-8224-b5cf41d2a6aa
- [a] amazon.com/author/tomfowler

Made in the USA
Middletown, DE
29 December 2021